GW00858976

To Defend the Earth

William Stroock

Copyright © 2011 William Stroock
All rights reserved.

ISBN: 1461132576
ISBN-13: 9781461132578

Like a lot of people, I've been interested in the idea of an alien invasion of Earth for a long time. I guess the first movie I ever saw about an alien invasion was *War of the Worlds*. I am referring to the 1950s version starring Gene Barry. I must have seen it sometime in 1980 or 1981 at the latest. I was horrified by the apparent helplessness of America's mighty armed forces, the way armored piercing shells bounced off the Martian's force fields, and how even atomic weapons couldn't harm them. I was captivated by the Martian's steady, relentless advance and their eventual destruction of Los Angeles. The movie captured my imagination and has been a favorite of mine ever since.

Independence Day is the successor to *War of the Worlds*, at least for me, and the culmination of forty years of alien invasion movies. The short thirty-second ad that aired during Super Bowl XXX transfixed me. Sneak previews aired during the spring further whetted my appetite. I saw *Independence Day* the first weekend it was out and several times thereafter. Fifteen years later I think it holds up pretty well. Of course it's highly derivative of *War of the Worlds*. The moment the president gave the order to 'nuke the bastards,' I knew they would fail, just like in *War of the Worlds*. I loved how *Independence Day* portrayed events at the highest level. I loved the little details Dean Devlin and Roland Emmerich put in the movie, like the use of Stealth Bombers and F-15 fighter escorts for Air Force One.

A lot of novels have been written about an alien invasion. For my money the absolute best is *Footfall* by Larry Niven and Jerry Pournelle. I first read it in 1993. Anyone who is familiar with this excellent novel will see its influence all over *To Defend the Earth*.

Another inspiration of mine, and I suppose a somewhat unconventional one, is the old Japanese cartoon, *Robotech*. The series, three actually, revolved around a massive alien effort to conquer Earth. There were dozens of sub plots. The battle scenes were well done and unlike other cartoons of the era, I'm looking at you *GI Joe*, actually showed people getting killed. My favorite for 20 years now is the 'Battle Cry' episode. The battle scene in which the aliens (Zentradi) attack a human starship known as the SDF-I is exciting, thrilling, and well conceived; the episode is available on You Tube. Watch it. It will be one of the best sci-fi battle sequences you'll ever see. *Robotech*, which I watched on videotape when I was 17, is one of the reasons I first wanted to write science fiction and made me want to write great battle scenes.

I've wanted to write my own tale of alien invasion for decades. What follows are several short stories I've written over the last six years. Some of these stories are about how people act under duress, about how they look into themselves and change. Some are about their relations with other people and how events affect them. Some are just good old-fashioned battle yarns; if you like battles on land, sea, air, and in space these are for you.

I am indebted to my army of readers who looked over the manuscript. Thanks again, Bill Dodge, Judy Sullivan, Cathy Yuerick and Kirsten Anderson Robbins (!) and also of course, M. Stroock. I'd also like to thank the website ProjectRho.com, where I cribbed a lot of the technical data for the *Battle of Luna*. It's really an invaluable site.

By the way, the first story, *Presidential Briefing*, begins 'Madam President.' I absolutely decline to say whom I had in mind, but the reader should be aware I wrote this story in 2006.

William Stroock
Great Barrington, MA

Chapter 1: Presidential Briefing

21 months till arrival

It wasn't until the year before Arrival that things started to get weird. There wasn't a lot of info out in the open yet, but if you were paying attention, you saw that the government, especially the Pentagon, was doing a lot of strange things.

My family and I were living in San Diego then. Starting the summer before Arrival, there was a constant stream of warships coming into the navy yard to be refitted. You would meet sailors at Chargers games (god I miss the NFL) who talked about how their particular ship wasn't supposed to be due for a refit, yet there they were. A lot of ships got shiny new weapons, missile upgrades and the like. Some were outfitted with lasers. A lot of times ships arrived and left at night. Sailors I talked to said that the big carriers up at Bremerton were worked on day and night.

An old college buddy of mine, an exec at Boeing who was later killed in the war, told me that all of the sudden the company was ordering parts for the old ASAT anti-satellite missiles and assembling them in their plant in Texas. When I asked him how many ASATs they were building, he told me that they were cranking out a dozen a day. Now why would the Pentagon need to build anti-satellite missiles?

Gas prices skyrocketed, and after that the cost of food went way up. Then the price of uranium and other rare Earths began to go up, then sharply up, so much so that new pits were opened in Australia and Canada. Long abandoned mines were reopened too. There was a lot of clueless media speculation as to why; it had to be explained to one news reader that the price was going up because demand was going up. In the New Year, rumors had been flying around for weeks that there was something strange in the sky. A blog post here, a tweet there, an article in some online journal about unaccounted for light—you get the picture. One day my pal over in the astronomy department told me the Feds had shown up and shut down his lab. They seized the big telescope and all the computers and flash drives—everything they had. I called my brother, who was a professor over at UT, and he said the same thing had happened there.

So we figured something pretty extraordinary was happening. It didn't take long before people started putting two and two together. Let's see, strange happenings in the sky, Feds taking over telescopes, hmmmmmmm... Then amateur astronomers continued the reports of a strange object in the sky. I guess you can't go around the country seizing small telescopes. Of course everyone went into the full Spielberg and started talking about Deep Impact. *Eventually there was an official announcement, a big TV address in the oval office. They got their Spielberg films wrong. It wasn't* Deep Impact; *it was* War of the Worlds...

—Excerpt from Before, During and After; Blogging the aliens

In Inaugural Address President Vows to Slash Spending after wars in Mid East, Pakistan

The Wall Street Journal

Deep Defense Cuts on Table: White House Chief of Staff. Congressional critics say new president weak on defense

Roll Call

Prez Sez Nix Nukes

New York Post

(Archivist's note: the president's remarks to the White House Chief of Staff are italicized)

From: Secret Committee for Extraterrestrial Defense
To: POTUS
RE: Extra Terrestrial Defense
Top Secret: Not to leave the Oval Office

Madam President:

The Secret Committee for Extraterrestrial Defense (SCED) would like to congratulate you on your historic victory. *What is this?*

We are an organization answering directly to the offices of the president, the secretary of defense, and the chairmen of the joint chiefs of staff.

After a months-long investigation, NASA and the Kitt Peak Observatory concluded that an unknown stellar object first spotted several years ago is in fact two extraterrestrial vessels bound for Earth. Based on initial estimates made at the time, as well as subsequent calculations, and assuming the vessels maintain course and rate of deceleration, the SCED can tell you with near absolute certainty that the extraterrestrial ships will arrive in Earth's orbit sometime in October of next year. *How could this have been kept secret for so long? Why was I not briefed after I won the nomination?!*

Background

Nine years ago an unknown object was spotted by the Kitt Peak Observatory in Arizona. Astronomers noted that that the object did not alter course or speed and seemed to be on a direct path toward our solar system. After consultation, NASA decided to train the Hubble Space Telescope on the object. *They've known about this for nine years and kept it secret? Question: should we consider announcing?*

Between October 15 and 17 of that year, several hundred photographs were taken by Hubble revealing what the Kitt Peak astronomers, JPL, and NASA already suspected: the unknown object was in fact two alien spacecraft. These conclusions were presented jointly to the president by the heads of both agencies. The president later shared these conclusions with the prime ministers of Great Britain and Canada, as well as the Russian president. *Why not the Chinese? Find out.*

The president ordered the formation of a commission (the forbearer of this committee) to discuss the facts as they were then understood and ascertain to the fullest extent possible the extraterrestrials' intentions. The committee included active and retired military and space program personnel as well as science fiction writers and Hollywood screenwriters. *Find out who was on the commission. Did any of the Hollywood types contribute to my campaign? Which science fiction writers?*

After viewing the Hubble images and analyzing accompanying data, the Committee unanimously concluded the following:

- The vessels are eight miles long, roughly the length of Manhattan.

- The vessels are traveling at .99% the speed of light.

- Subsequent analysis of the vessels' trajectory traced their path back to the star Tau Ceti, 11.6 light years from Earth. Tau Ceti is a Sol-like star, giving off yellow/white light capable of fostering life. Measuring the change in light brought about by an object passing between the Earth and Tau Ceti (transit method), followed by analyzing slight gravitational variations in Tau Ceti (gravitational microlensing), observations by astronomers have revealed the presence of two planets in the Tau Ceti system, one of them .84 AU (astro units) from the star, a distance conducive to Earthlike conditions. It is believed an Earthlike planet in the Tau Ceti system would be especially vulnerable to comet and asteroid strikes due to the star's large asteroid belt and dust cloud. However, the other planet is a massive gas giant nearly twice the size of Jupiter, exerting gravity powerful enough to draw in asteroids and comets in the way Jupiter attracted Shoemaker-Levy in July of 1994.

- Analysis of the interstellar medium through which the extraterrestrials passed revealed the absence of hydrogen in the wake of the vessels. This strongly suggests that the extraterrestrials were using a Boussard ramjet, a fusion drive powered by hydrogen collected from space.

Having determined that extraterrestrials were coming to Earth, the commission engaged in a long debate about their possible intentions. Several scenarios were put forward, many of them borrowed from popular fiction. The extraterrestrials are an invasion force, a diplomatic initiative, or a trade mission. One member of the commission postulated that the extraterrestrials were coming to Earth to recruit soldiers for an intergalactic war. Another argued that they may simply be peaceful colonists. A commission member with a theological background wondered if the extraterrestrials were coming to Earth to convert us to their religion. Following along this line of thinking, the committee wondered if the extraterrestrials weren't simply an anthropological survey sent to Earth to observe primitive cultures. *Yes, why can't they be peaceful? Why does the military have to assume they are hostile?*

The committee could only speculate about the extraterrestrials' intentions until the vessels drew close enough for telescopes to take more detailed photographs of them. The latest photos showed several symmetrical protrusions in the same pattern on both ships, two on the fore and three on the port and starboard facing forward. Both active duty and retired military members of the committee pointed out that the arrangement of these protrusions, assuming they were weapons, gave the ships an excellent forward cone of fire. The commission therefore concluded the protrusions were weapons blisters. *Military types look for military answers. Why can't these have a scientific purpose?*

Subsequent photographs revealed a line of objects arrayed down the flanks of each ship. There are eight objects to a line, for a total of sixteen on each side and thirty-two per ship. These objects are 402 meters long, about one quarter again the size of a Nimitz class aircraft carrier. They narrow from stern to fore, making the objects aerodynamic cylinders. In light of this information, the committee concluded that the objects are detachable vessels that can penetrate the Earth's atmosphere. Given these facts, a forward facing cone of fire and an array of detachable vessels, the committee concluded the vessels are military in nature. *I am lost. What do these numbers mean? Why so hung up on a military explanation? Do they want yet another war to fight? Did the bloodletting in Iraq, Afghanistan and Pakistan not satisfy them?*

Three months later new evidence surfaced that supported many of the commission's previous conclusions. Astronomers at Kitt Peak noticed that the distance between the extraterrestrial ships was gradually increasing as they simultaneously decelerated. At a steady pace over several months, the separation became more pronounced and deliberate. The astronomers calculated that with the new slightly altered course, the extraterrestrials would arrive in simultaneous polar orbit in October of next year. The commission agreed that should the extraterrestrials be hostile, duel polar orbits would allow them to attack each hemisphere and make it difficult for our own forces to counterattack. It is believed that from the North and South Poles, the extraterrestrials could threaten all points of the Earth, and launch their detachable vessels against any target they wish.

After considering everything then known about the approaching vessels, the commission concluded that, with two military vessels taking up simultaneous polar orbit, the extraterrestrials most likely have hostile intentions.

A second informal committee of outsiders, known internally as Team B, none of whom ever met on this matter or knew others were being consulted, was then presented with the committee's findings (Note: because the committee wanted as wide a variety of perspectives as possible, three persons completely unassociated with the military, scientific, or academic communities were consulted. These were the president of a multinational bank, a famous lawyer, and a highly successful National Football League coach). By a final tally of seven to two, Team B agreed with the commission's conclusions. *Thank god they asked someone else. Can we find out which lawyer? Did I ever work with him?*

The commission was thusly dissolved and reformed into the present Secret Committee for Extraterrestrial Defense (SCED).

<u>American and Allied Capabilities</u> *I am skeptical that we can defend against such a civilization advanced enough to travel between the stars. Wouldn't they look at our weapons the way we would look at slings and arrows? This seems farfetched.*

Despite what we must assume to be an enemy whose weaponry is more advanced than our own, about which more will be said below, the SCED believes the United States and our allies are capable of mounting a formidable defense of Earth to an altitude of about one thousand miles. The United States possesses a sophisticated arsenal of weapons with which to contest an extraterrestrial landing. Many of these weapon systems were originally meant for ballistic missile defense and were therefore theoretically obsolete with the end of the Cold War.

The first of these are our Ground-based Midcourse Defense system. As of this writing, the system features twenty Kinetic Energy Interceptor (KEI) rockets based out of Fort Greely Alaska and Vandenberg Air Force base in California. The United States also has a sea-based missile defense system in the form of eighteen Aegis-equipped, guided missile cruisers and destroyers. In the previous decade an Aegis cruiser shot down a malfunctioning satellite.

An older but still useful weapon system is the ASAT, or Anti-Satellite missile. The ASAT is vertically launched from an F-15 at high altitude. For most of the decade the United States had only fifteen ASAT missiles in its arsenal. However, these can be manufactured relatively quickly, as the ASAT is a simple two-stage missile.

Another potent, non-nuclear weapon is the ABL or Airborne Laser. The ABL is a chemical oxygen iodine laser mounted on a Boeing 747. Fired from the aircraft's nose, the laser beam lasts 3-5 seconds, long enough to heat up and catastrophically warp the target, causing its warhead or fuel to explode.

The above-mentioned weapons give the United States the ability to contest the extraterrestrial's control of the exosphere and thermosphere. Defense of the mesosphere will fall to three specific weapons systems. Two of these are land based, the THAAD (Theater High-Altitude Area Defense) and the PAC 3 (Patriot Advance Capability), both operated by the United Sates Army. The United States currently has 85 THAAD launchers and 1,390 missiles. Supplementing the THAAD is the PAC-3. The Patriot already has considerable combat experience in the Gulf War and has since been upgraded. Each mobile launcher, organized into batteries of six, carries sixteen missiles. The army currently has over 1,100 PAC-3 missiles in its arsenal.

Missile batteries may be defended from extraterrestrial counterattack by a THEL or Tactical High Energy Laser. A THEL produces a laser with a range of about six miles. The beam simply heats the target until its warhead or fuel explodes. In tests conducted by the Israelis, THEL lasers have shot down no less than twenty-eight Katyusha rockets. THEL lasers will also be independently deployed around high value targets such as major cities and missile silos. *I am lost. Get someone to summarize these weapons in some kind of closed door meeting.*

Of course, the most powerful weapons at our disposal are those in our nuclear arsenal. There are three primary delivery systems, the old triad of silos, submarines, and bombers. In all the United States possesses an arsenal of over 5,700 active warheads and another 4,600 in reserve. *I will not, under any circumstances, use nuclear weapons. We need to make the military understand this.*

Over a thousand of these warheads are delivered to target by the Minuteman III missile. The Minuteman III is the workhorse of our land-based missile force. Deployed in three wings (Minot AFB, North Dakota, Warren AFB, Wyoming, and Malmstrom AFB, Montana). A Minuteman can carry up to three W87 warheads, each with a yield of 475 kilotons, more than thirty times the power of the Nagasaki blast.

Two thousand warheads are carried aboard the nation's fleet of fourteen Ohio-Class Strategic Submarine Ballistic Missiles subs (SSBM). These warheads are delivered by the Trident III Missile, twenty-four of which are carried aboard an Ohio. An additional four Ohios are outfitted with 154 conventional Tomahawk cruise missiles. Each Trident III missile can carry up to eight W-88 warheads yielding 475 kilotons for a total striking power of 3.8 megatons per missile.

Another two thousand warheads can be delivered via the B-1B Lancer. America's 65 B-1 Bombers are deployed in three squadrons; two active at Dyess AFB ,Texas, Ellsworth AFB, South Dakota and a test squadron at Edwards AFB, California. The B-1B can carry eight AGM-69B Short Range Attack Missiles. Supporting the B-1 are the nation's 21 B-2 Spirit or Stealth Bombers which also carry the AGM-69B.

An additional four hundred warheads are available in the form of gravity bombs deployed at American bases throughout the world, while another hundred are carried aboard sub and surfaced launched Tomahawk missiles. *This is horrifying. We need to talk to this committee now. We need to talk to the military now. Thousands of warheads detonated in and around Earth's atmosphere, are they crazy? Do they know I ran on a platform of environmental protection?*

Extraterrestrial Capabilities

The SCED believes that while the extraterrestrials are more advanced than we are, their weapons capabilities may not be infinitely greater than our own. To state our position another way, SCED does not believe the extraterrestrials possess science fiction wonder weapons such as phasers or anti-matter missiles. If they did, the extraterrestrials would have a far faster way of travel than through normal space at just under relativistic speed. Rather, the SCED believes the extraterrestrials employ lasers, missiles, and bombs similar to our own, though probably more capable, given their ability to travel between solar systems. They also undoubtedly have nuclear technology. Actually, the most potent weapon at the extraterrestrial's disposal may simply be a Kinetic Energy Weapon. For example, this could simply be a small metal or even rock cylinder fired at tremendous speed. Such an impact could have the effect of a nuclear blast without the radioactive aftereffects.

Extraterrestrial Intentions *Which they cannot possibly know*

The SCED assumes the extraterrestrial's battle plan revolves around controlling the sky. Therefore we believe once they take up polar orbits the enemy will deploy their detachable vessels for battle around the globe. This effort will most likely include an attack on our satellite network, perhaps even before they take orbit; this option makes the most sense. If this is the case there is little the United States and our allies can do to stop them. Whatever their battle plan may be, it must be assumed that global communications will be severely hampered leaving us with landlines and undersea cables. *This is all pointless conjecture. If I tried this in court, the judge would laugh at me.*

Communications will be additionally affected by the use of nuclear weapons. Atmospheric detonations will fry computer systems and fuse electrical networks, shrouding the areas underneath the battle zone in darkness. Of course the greatest side effect of using nuclear weapons will be radiation. America's civil defense network is ill equipped to handle the problem. It is therefore strongly suggested that once the existence of the extraterrestrials has been revealed, the public be urged to store food and water, to keep plastic and duct-tape on hand to seal their homes, and to stay inside until the crisis has passed.

To assist in this effort, the SCED recommends the total mobilization of the United States Army and Marines, including reserves and National Guard units and the recall of men and women recently retired. These will not only assist local police departments but be in a position to repel the extraterrestrials' landing. As such, we envision strong deployments of American troops outside possible targets like New York City, Chicago, and Los Angeles. Infrastructure such as the ports of Newark and Long Beach, the Tappan Zee and Bay Bridges, and power plants should also be heavily defended.

Battle Plan *They're serious? Do they really want to fight aliens more advanced than ourselves? Shouldn't we be trying to talk to them?*

The SCED envisions a defense in depth using every weapon at hand. The first line of defense will be our ABM and ASAT missiles. Should the extraterrestrials fight their way through, our next line of defense will be conventionally armed aircraft supported by ground based Patriot and THAAD missiles. These will be defended by THELs, Hawk missile batteries, and even hand held Stinger missiles. B-1 and B-2 bombers can participate in both defensive efforts as can the Airborne Laser. At your discretion, Madam President, nuclear weapons can be deployed to defend all reaches of the atmosphere and even near space.

Assuming the extraterrestrials mean to follow through with their geosynchronous polar orbits, the SCED believes the United States and our allies should mount a vigorous defense of the North and South Poles. A second defense line should be formed in Northern Europe, Canada, and Russia in the Northern Hemisphere, Tierra Del Fuego, Tasmania, and South Africa in the Southern Hemisphere.

Defense of the South Pole should include all weapons at our disposal. As such, the SCED proposes four Ohio-Class SSBMs be deployed around Antarctica. At least two Nimitz-Class aircraft carrier battle groups, one in the South Atlantic, one in the South Pacific should be deployed to the South Pole as well. These surface forces should be supported by land based aircraft, including B-1s, F-15s, and F-22s based in southern Argentina and South Africa, with one squadron of British Tornado bombers and one F-35 fighter squadron in the Falkland Islands. Such a deployment enables American and allied forces to strike the extraterrestrials from all directions with multiple weapons systems.

Defending the North Pole is less problematic and, from the point of view of the United States, more pressing. The SCED hopes the Russians will deploy four of their Oscar-Class SSBMs around the North Pole. A reinforced battle group based on a Kirov-Class missile cruiser and a Kuznetsov-Class aircraft carrier should be deployed to the Barents Sea. Another Nimitz battle group will be deployed in the Bearing Straight. Considerable American and Canadian airpower can be marshaled from bases in Alaska, Canada, and Greenland.

The burden for defending the North Sea falls to Great Britain. They can also be supported by the Royal Norwegian Air Force(two squadrons of F-16s and one squadron of F-35 Joint Strike Fighters). Iceland may be a tempting target for an extraterrestrial landing, and even an alternate point for geosynchronous orbit for one of the main ships. Therefore, the island should be made into a citadel that may draw the extraterrestrials into a desirable battle on our own terms. The SCED also envisions the deployment of one Nimitz carrier group in the straits of Denmark and another off the southeastern coast of Iceland. The old American airbase at Keflavik should be reinforced with a few squadrons of F-22s, THAADs, PAC-III, THELS and at least one Airborne Laser.

Defense of the Mediterranean must fall to the two most high-tech powers in the region: France in the west, and Israel in the east. France (with British help of course) must keep open the Straits of Gibraltar, while Israel must maintain the availability of the Suez Canal (with the help of whatever forces Egypt is able to muster.) The SCED believes the United States should support France and Israel with the deployment of at least one Nimitz-Class carrier battle group.

Significant forces including several squadrons of fighters and the nation's force of B-2 bombers should be kept in reserve for a general counteroffensive aimed at destroying at least one of the extraterrestrial's two main ships. *I am flabbergasted. Why are we not attempting to contact them? Where are the attempts at peaceful settlement? I want a negotiating committee established at once.*

Conclusions

In planning for the threat posed by the technologically superior extraterrestrials, the SCED looked for parallels in Earth's own history. American Indians routinely defeated more technologically advanced enemies; Braddock's wilderness defeat in 1756 and Custer's last stand at Little Big Horn are obvious examples. These may be viewed as guerilla ambushes, but not all such victories are so. In 1879 low-tech Zulu forces decimated a high-tech British army in open battle at Islandhwana. The SCED believes that despite our technological disadvantage, there is no reason why the United States and our allies cannot repel an extraterrestrial invasion. *I had not thought of this.*

Will these be all the weapons needed, or will we need to manufacture more? If so where does the money come from? We must protect domestic programs. Can we shift money around the defense budget or must we borrow the money? I pledged to reduce spending and it would not look good for this administration to start borrowing.

A New Role for Untested Leader
President who planned ambitious domestic agenda now called upon to lead nation through greatest event in history

The Washington Post

(WASHINGTON) Today congressional leaders said they expected quick approval of the president's emergency one-hundred-billion-dollar supplemental defense bill. [snip] Items on the Pentagon's 'wish list' include Mid Course Interceptors, Airborne Lasers, THAAD missiles, and a host of other weapons systems capable of reaching the Earth's upper atmosphere...

The Hill

Chapter 2: **Kim is Ill**

Six weeks till Arrival

The year of Arrival there was a huge construction boom. If you worked a job in construction or utilities, you made a fortune in overtime. I'd drive down the road and run into phone and cable company crews digging huge trenches and laying fiber-optic cable in them. Sometimes I'd see military engineers digging huge holes in the ground for missile silos.

The Feds built a lot of bomb shelters and infirmaries along the interstates. Towns took their own precautions, extra cops on the streets, more firefighters and EMS types, stockpiling of food in schools, public bomb shelters. Heck a lot of people built their own bomb shelters. Contractors got rich building them for private citizens. I didn't have one built. I figured there was no point in a navy town like San Diego, but my brother-in-law, he lived in Santa Fe, had one put in for $4,900.

Most Americans had never seen the kind of military activity leading up to Arrival. There were military convoys on the interstates all the time. I spotted a long line of supply trucks making their way from Las Vegas to Seattle. Another time I pulled over and watched an entire armored brigade, loaded onto trailers, travel north on the interstate. I was politely asked by the state police to get moving. Sometimes the state police would close down sections of highway for the military—they were moving nuclear missiles to and fro.

Well, we were armed to the teeth; why not start a war before the aliens ever got here?

Before, During, and After: Blogging the Aliens

Regime of Kim Jong Il Broadcasts Message to Approaching Alien Ships
Message coded, world governments express concern

The Times of London

Breaking! Washington: White House announces coded message from NoKos contains offer of alliance, military assistance, information. No indication aliens have replied...

Fox News, Special Report

...intercepts leave no question that the regime of Kim Jong Ill is offering to help the aliens and urging them to attack the United States...the National Security Advisor concurs with the Joint Chiefs that if activity continues a military strike on North Korea would be desirable and necessary...Chinese colleagues agree and feel their government would be willing to join international effort so long as they have the lead...

Excerpt from Presidential Daily Briefing, September 14th, Arrival Year

From his command post in Dandong, mere blocks away from the Yalu River, General Sun Liao-pen watched the invasion playing out on half a dozen computer monitors and flat screens. He was big for a Chinese man, with broad shoulders and a square jaw. He had adopted an American-style buzz cut after a tour of the Command and General Staff College in Carlisle. Above his lip was a thin mustache he had grown after studying at Sandhurst. He wore with pride a pair of wings earned with the Israeli Paratrooper Brigade. Even while standing absolutely still and saying nothing, Liao-pen dominated the room.

In the corner, a pair of television sets showed international news broadcasts. People around the world watched in awe as Fox, the BBC, Xinhua, and a dozen other news networks beamed footage of the massive battle to their televisions. Cameras showed Pyongyang's infamous Ryukgong hotel being obliterated by American Tomahawks. Still another camera panned to the presidential palace in time to see it explode in a fireball. A North Korean press agent dutifully reported that the imperialists had destroyed a hospital, an orphanage, a baby milk factory.

Liao-pen ignored these. Instead he watched with pride as computerized maps showed Chinese forces advancing across the Yalu River into North Korea. These weren't the ideological cannon fodder sent into Korea in 1950, but well-trained professional soldiers expected to think and act on the battlefield. They were proving their mettle to the North Koreans and the world. Chinese commandos had already seized the Friendship Bridge connecting the North Korean city of Sinuiju with Dandong. Further east, hundreds of rubber boats carried assault engineers to the North Korean side of the Yalu. Dozens of firefights erupted. On the Chinese side more engineers dropped bailey bridges into the water. Under fire, thousands of brave Chinese soldiers mastered their fear and began assembling the spans.

Fifty-four kilometers up river from Sinuiju, the first bailey bridge was completed in just under an hour. Others were completed soon after.

The chief-of-staff, General Lu, approached Liao- pen. 'General, airborne command wants your permission to launch the second wave.'

'I want an update before I commit to anything.' He studied the computerized battle map before him. It showed the progress of a brigade of the 44th Airborne Division in Pyongyang. The interior ministry was in Chinese hands, as were two bridges across the Nampo River. The Chinese air force was bombing concentrations of North Korean troops east of the city. Intelligence had sent back a photo showing a line of burning enemy tanks on Pyongyang's main avenue.

'General?' the chief pressed.

Liao-pen nodded his approval for the second wave. He spoke into the phone. 'Approved. Send in the next wave.'

Within seconds a second wave of transport aircraft broke their orbit over Manchuria and turned south for Pyongyang.

General Lu punched buttons on his Blackberry; Liao-pen had never seen him without it. An aid called him away.

Liao-pen watched the battle's progress on the digital flat screen map. To the southwest, blue arrows indicated that American aircraft had destroyed the Sea Barrage at the entrance of the Nampo. As tons of steel and concrete smoldered in the water, dozens of assault craft entered the river and landed the lead platoons of the 3rd Marine Expeditionary Force on either bank.

The chief interrupted him again. 'General, the defense minister for you.'

Liao-pen sighed. 'Very well.'

He walked across the bunker and picked up the phone. 'Liao-pen.'

'General, this is the defense minister. The premier wants your report. You are on speaker phone.'

'Minister, we are across the Yalu in force and consolidating our bridgeheads. Our forces in Pyongyang are expanding their hold on the city.'

'Casualties?'

'I have not asked commanders to send me casualty reports.'

'And why not?'

'Sir, because we are not the Americans.'

There was a moment of annoyed silence. Then, 'The premier wants to know if you are aware of reports circulating through the western media.'

'Please tell the premier that I have not had time to monitor western media outlets. About what is he concerned?'

'They are reporting rumors of emaciated and starved civilians.'

'I have received no such reports yet, sir.' He replied. 'Is there anything else?'

'Yes, how would you judge the attack?'

'So far, Minister, I am pleased.'

'Thank you, General.'

They are worried, Liao-pen thought. *Politicians. Next they'll want me to lead a memorial service for every soldier killed in the line of duty.*

The battle developed further. In the second hour of the war, RPG and anti-tank-missile-armed infantry groups on the Friendship Bridge broke up a hasty counterattack by armored elements of the North Korean VIII Corps. Six hours into their massive assault, Chinese field commanders reported that the lead brigades of two infantry and two mechanized divisions were across the Yalu and fighting to consolidate their bridgeheads. The already battered and shell-shocked North Korean troops, desperately fighting in isolated and ever shrinking pockets, could not hear the drone of engines high above, the second wave of transport aircraft carrying crack Chinese paratroopers south to Pyongyang. As planned Liao-pen ordered two reserve infantry divisions to begin crossing the Yalu. Once across these divisions were to advance along two axes toward Pyongyang, one near the coast, and one further inland. The 4th Armored Division would come up behind these two divisions for an eventual dash to Pyongyang.

Liao-pen had been concerned that Kim would lob Scud Missiles into China. He didn't. Instead he launched them at Japan. None got through, however, as the Japanese Navy's Aegis destroyers shot them out of the sky. Several dozen North Korean jets also tried to fly across the Sea of Japan, but these were engaged and destroyed by the Japanese air force. By noon the Americans reported that a brigade of the 82nd Airborne Division had secured Yongbyon but could find no weapons of mass destruction. *Again?* Liao-pen said to himself. Most importantly as far as he was concerned, the coastal column had pushed more than thirty kilometers inside North Korea and was reporting that resistance was slackening dramatically. The inland column was about halfway to Pyongyang.

General Lu looked worried. He handed Liao-pen the defense ministry phone. He took the receiver and spoke, 'Liao-pen.'

'Have you seen what the American press is reporting, General?' asked the defense minister.

'With all due respect, sir, I have more important things to do than to monitor the media.' *Now this. What could possibly be this important?*

'Bodies, General, first dozens, now hundreds of bodies are floating down the Nampo River through American lines.'

'Bodies?'

'Civilian bodies, General. Horribly emaciated. Most seem to have committed suicide.'

Liao-pen saw the TV screen switch from an anchorman to a field reporter. *I'm going to see what is happening before I address this.* 'Excuse me, Minister, I am needed elsewhere. I will get back to you as soon as I have more information.'

'Do so, General Liao-pen.'

He walked over to the TV. An American TV reporter decked out in body armor and American-style helmet stood on the south bank of the Nampo. On the north bank an American M-I tank burned. The woman, pretty, Liao-pen had to admit, looked pale and haunted. He listened. 'Only a few at first, Brett, but the bodies kept coming and coming. I lost track at one thousand seven hundred and twenty-two.'

'My god who is doing this, Reena?' the anchor asked.

The reporter held up a hand. 'Hold on, Brett, more bodies are coming down,' she spoke to the cameraman. 'Steve, get a shot of the river, not too close, but let the public see what is going on here.'

Human lumps drifted down the river, sometimes singly, sometimes in groups.

'Reena, why aren't the Marines...picking up the bodies?'

'Brett, I'm told that there are fears that the bodies may be booby-trapped. These have already been encountered here in Nampo and also at Yongbyon.'

'Have the Chinese encountered anything like this?' asked the anchor.

Liao-pen turned to General Lu. 'Find out right away. And if our forces haven't encountered this yet, make sure the commanders on the ground know to be mindful of booby-trapped bodies. And find me a commander on the scene. I need information.'

'Yes, General.'

After a few more minutes there was audible screaming off camera. The camera panned to a spot on the river where a squad of Marines was gathered. They were in complete shock. One of them rolled on the ground in the fetal position, another was screaming, 'He shot himself, he saw what the bastards are doing and shot himself!' The Marine pointed to one of his comrades who was lying face down in the dirt, a pistol in his hand. Liao-pen saw another Marine on both knees crossing himself over and over again. Several more Marines ran across the camera. The reporter grabbed one by the arm, stopped him, and said, 'Excuse me, Sergeant, what's happening?'

The man's face twisted in rage. 'Are you blind, you stupid bitch? Look!' he pointed to the river. The camera panned down river, this time it showed hundreds of small human lumps floating toward the American lines.

'Oh my god, they're children. They're the bodies of children...I, I don't know if you can see, Brett, but hundreds of dead children must be floating this way.'

The horror unfolded before the world. Liao-pen could see that the staff inside the bunker were transfixed in shock. He turned to his staff and said, 'Whatever the North Koreans are doing, we still have to do our duty! Everyone get back to work!' The staff scrambled, 'I want updates on the drive for Pyongyang, now! I want to know what our paratroopers are doing there! How many members of the North Korean leadership have we captured?'

Liao-pen waited for the info and did his best to ignore the TV. The Western media had switched to covering almost exclusively the North Korean suicides. He looked to the TV tuned to Xinhua. To his disappointment, he found that they were concentrating on the suicides as well. He turned from the TV and watched the operational map. He followed the advance down both the coastal and inland routes. General Lu interrupted him. Beside him was a dust-covered officer.

'General. This is Colonel Li. His regiment opened up the gap in the North Korean lines along the coast.'

The colonel wore combat fatigues and a combat helmet and looked tired. He saluted.

Liao-pen returned the salute. 'First of all, I congratulate you and your men on the job you have done.'

Colonel Li looked pale and shocked. 'Thank you, General. My men are good soldiers.'

'What can you tell me? What is happening?'

'General, my regiment advanced into a North Korean town ten kilometers south of the border. After clearing it of a company of North Korean troops my men found atrocities similar to what has been shown on world media...I don't...I'm not sure...'

'Colonel, I want to know what your regiment has encountered.'

The colonel stiffened. 'Starving people, dead people. People who had been starved to death,' he paused.

'Go on.'

'Forgive me, General...Many of the bodies had been rigged with explosives. One of my squads found a crying little boy in a house full of dead people. After being picked up by a medical detachment, the boy detonated a bomb he had hidden in his clothes. I lost most of my medical company. One of my infantry companies was rushed by several teenagers armed with suicide bombs. From there it only got worse. They had armed little girls with spears...'

Liao-pen held up his hands. 'I see, Colonel.'

'Will there be anything else, General? If not then I'd like to see to my men. They've been through much.'

'Of course. Thank you, Colonel. Is there anything your men need?'

'I do not know what could help my men right now, General.'

'Very well.'

The two officers exchanged salutes.

Liao-pen busied himself with reports from the front. Operations were going well, with the inland column pushing toward Pyongyang. Fighting was bloody, but the Chinese superiority in manpower and training was beginning to tell. He was looking at casualty reports when Lu interrupted him and said, 'General, you need to see this.' The chief of staff urgently pointed to one of the TV monitors. This one was tuned to CNN. The camera showed a hill in the distance. At the base of the hill were numerous explosions, artillery shells bursting, Liao-pen realized. The British reporter was aghast, '...shells into the valley. Thousands of people in white robes, apparently singing songs about the Dear Leader,' he said.

'And the North Koreans are shelling them?' asked the perfectly nonplussed BBC anchor.

'...Yes.'

'The defense minister for you, General,' said General Lu. He held out a phone.

Liao-pen took the phone, 'Liao-pen here.'

'General, you should know that the western media is reporting that thousands of white-robed North Koreans are marching into the DMZ and singing songs about the dear leader and praising the approach of the aliens while their own artillery bombards them.'

A weary Liao-pen said, 'I am watching now, Minister. These reports no longer surprise me. My commanders are reporting suicide bombers and worse.'

'I want your men to put a stop to it.'

Liao-pen came close to betraying actual emotion and sighed. 'Minister, we are dealing with it. We are defeating the enemy.'

'General Liao-pen, the premier orders that you take concrete steps to stop these suicides and suicide attacks.'

'With all due respect, Minister, what does the premier expect me to do?'

'Your men should secure the towns and villages. The air force should be targeting whoever is carrying out these heinous acts.'

'Just how am I supposed to do that, Minister?'

'You are to abandon the drive on Pyongyang and fan your army across the peninsula.'

'Abandon the drive on Pyongyang?'

'Is there a problem, General?'

'Minister, I have one brigade engaged there, and I've ordered another to go in.'

'Call them back, and if you can't, I will find someone who can.'

Before Liao-pen could answer, the defense minister hung up the phone.

He walked over to the digital battle map. It showed a pair of blue lines starting at the Yalu and running south toward Pyongyang, the twin armored thrusts of the inland and coastal columns. There was an icon in Pyongyang proper, the airborne brigade, and a second, blinking airborne icon, meaning the second brigade was now jumping into Pyongyang. He punched a button below the screen, conjuring up hundreds of little orange circles, each representing an encounter with North Korean forces. Dozens of these were clustered on the Yalu, of course, and a string ran along the advance of each armored thrust.

Heavy concentrations of orange circles appeared again, usually ten to twenty kilometers south of the Yalu. Even as Liao-pen watched new orange circles appeared. He punched another button bringing up North Korea's road network. According to the plan, one armored thrust was to enter Pyongyang from the north, while the other would use a North Korean highway to circle around and enter from the east. To placate the minister he was going to have to change the plan.

I have no choice, he thought.

'Send orders to the 46th Infantry Division. Tell them to branch east.'

'Yes, General.'

'And order the 4th Armored Division to advance down the inland route.'

'Yes, General.'

The 46th Infantry Division will carry out the minister's order. Liao-pen thought. *4th Armored Division will take up the drive on Pyongyang.*

Over the course of the next few hours Liao-pen's plan unfolded. Though there were several small firefights, the 46th Infantry Division advanced on the town of Taopjong with relative ease, and its advance elements were on the river overlooking the town by nightfall. To the north, though, North Korean resistance took an unexpected turn. After crossing the Yalu and advancing down the inland route, the lead brigade encountered stiff resistance. It began about twenty kilometers south of the Yalu, where North Korean militia engaged the brigade's lead battalion with mortars and RPGs. After this brief encounter the column was hit again and again by truck-borne suicide squads. The first attack was made by three North Korean trucks, with the first two advancing in tandem and laying down cover fire for the third, which sped into the column and detonated a massive bomb, destroying two APCs and a tank. The attack was repeated several times over the next few hours, bringing the brigade to a virtual halt.

The situation on the coastal route was similar. The 46th Infantry Division was on the banks of the Nampo River by nightfall and was preparing to move on the town of Choojire, about ten miles southwest of Pyongyang. To the north, a follow-on brigade was hit by dozens of suicide squads, who attacked again and again, inflicting heavy casualties on the lead battalion, forcing the brigade commander to halt about forty kilometers inside North Korea and bring up reinforcements. Curiously, in the central and eastern parts of the country there had been little North Korean resistance after Chinese forces broke through the Yalu River line.

Now why would that be? Liao-pen asked himself. There was definitely a pattern. Liao-pen called General Lu over.

'Look at the map, General. Tell me if you see the same thing. The North Koreans fought tenaciously on the Yalu River line. Since our forces pierced that line, they have let them advance deep inside North Korea. In the last few hours resistance has stiffened significantly in the west. Why?'

Lu thought for a moment 'General, it seems clear that they allowed our armored spearheads to get sucked into an ambush. That ambush, this spate of suicide attacks, is now being unleashed.'

'Did our troops encounter these suicide attacks on the Yalu? Get me the intelligence officer.'

The chief intelligence officer came to the map readout. He carried a clipboard in his hand with dozens of pieces of paper affixed to it.

'Colonel, are there any reports of enemy suicide attacks on the Yalu line?'

'No, General,' he started flipping through his papers, 'The earliest report of a suicide attack I received occurred twelve kilometers south of the Yalu. They came in waves along the entire front.'

'And after a time the attacks ceased, no?'

'Uhhhhh,' he flipped through more papers. 'They did not cease entirely, but there was definitely a slacking off as our columns advanced.'

'Followed by this second surge.'

'Yes.'

'Why would the North Koreans want our units pinned along the Nampo River? Why not simply try to stop us on the Yalu, why...?' Liao-pen stopped as the reason occurred to him. 'I want information from your American counterpart now. Find out if they have found any WMDs, anything at all.'

'Yes, General.'

'Quickly.'

'Yes, sir.'

He examined the digital battle map for a few more moments and briefly considered pulling his columns back but quickly decided against doing so. Instead, 'Contact both the inland and coastal columns. Order them to advance and punch through the enemy's defenses, regardless of losses.'

'Yes, sir. Are follow-on reinforcements to rush to the battle area?'

'No, tell them to halt and consolidate. I don't want them anywhere near the front.'

He called his air liaison over to the map. 'The brigade groups are to have whatever air support they need when they need it.'

'Yes, sir.'

The intelligence officer returned. 'My colleague in the American headquarters says there is no evidence of any WMDs.'

Liao-pen cursed under his breath.

'What do you suspect, General?' asked Lu.

'We have been lead into a trap.'

'You believe the North Koreans are going to target the lead brigade groups with nuclear bombs?'

'Yes.'

'With all due respect, shouldn't we fall back, General?'

'No, the lead brigades will advance out of the ambush; it's the only chance we have.'

'General, what about—' but Lu wasn't able to finish the sentence.

There was a flash on one of the televisions. The screen went white and fuzzy, and when the picture cleared, the screen was dominated by a mushroom cloud. Liao-pen realized in horror that it was the TV tuned to Xinhua, and the image it showed had been of Pyongyang. Two brigades of paratroopers had just been incinerated. Moments later the chief of staff said, 'General, the 46th Infantry Division HQ just went off air, so has the 4th Armored Division.'

Another television screen flashed white, this one an American network which had been covering the action at Yongbyon. When the picture cleared, a second nuclear explosion was evident in the distance; a bomb had been detonated at Taopjong.

'General,' said Lu, 'we need to get you out of—'

Before the chief of staff could finish, everyone in the headquarters was slammed to the floor by a massive blast. The entire bunker shook with tremendous force, shattering television monitors and computer screens. Sparks flew through the air. There were shouts and screaming. There was a loud *thump* sound as a crossbeam fell to floor; this was followed by a horrific scream. The bunker went dark for a few moments until the backup generators kicked in.

Liao-pen picked himself off the floor and staggered forward until he was able to slump against a desk. He stood there for a few moments and then made his way to the door. He opened the inner door and saw that at the end of the corridor the blast had knocked the outer door off all but the lowest hinge. Liao-pen walked down the corridor, hand against the wall for balance, and kicked the door off its last hinge. Outside he saw several overturned tanks. The Friendship Bridge had collapsed into the Yalu, and beyond that he could see a mushroom cloud where the town had been.

'It must not have been a very big bomb,' said Lu, startling Liao-pen, who had not realized he was there.

'It was big enough.'

He watched as dozens of soldiers staggered sightlessly down the street. Here and there an uninjured soldier tried to help a comrade. A pair of ambulances turned a corner and stopped. Medics got out.

'We should get you away from here, General, or at least inside. The radiation.'

'It does not matter. I expected to die in this, or the upcoming conflict.' He coughed as he took in dust and soot from the blast. 'Do you know what this means?' He coughed again. 'The aliens will see this. They will know we have nuclear weapons. They will know our capabilities.' Liao-pen shook his head. 'Damn...'

Washington: American and Chinese officials continue to point fingers at one another over the botched invasion of North Korea [snip] Privately Chinese officials blame American forces for failing to secure Kim's WMDs and American intelligence for missing key information pointing to the North Korean plan. This information includes [snip]...still officials in Washington and Beijing insist that the North Korean disaster would not alter joint defense plans, should they be necessary...

The Washington Post

Aliens most definitely saw nuclear blasts

The Daily

President fails first test of crisis

Lead editorial, National Review

Chapter 3: **Lieutenant Wales, the King**

Arrival + three days

Prez Sez: Nukes Not Nixed

The New York Post

Washington: Under direct orders from the president, American forces on land, sea and air launched a massive counterattack against the alien invaders. [snip] Meanwhile, Pentagon officials expressed puzzlement at the posture of British forces, which as of this writing had not...

The Washington Post

Com-Ice: My forces are about to take a pounding here in Iceland. What the hell is the RAF doing? Why aren't we getting any help?
CINC-RAF: I'm sorry, General, but the Prime Minister has ordered our forces to stand down.
Com-Ice: Stand down? [expletive deleted].

Excerpt from phone transcript between commander, US Forces, Iceland to Commander-in-Chief, Royal Air Force.

So you don't think a couple of spaceships full of aliens can occupy Earth? Remember, during the height of the British Raj, no more than 100,000 soldiers and bureaucrats ruled India. The aliens will just need cooperative leaders, or leaders unwilling to fight them.

Before, During and After: Blogging the Aliens

The darkened streets of London were filled with people either milling about aimlessly or running around with great and untoward purpose. For his part, Roy Johns slumped forward onto his cab's steering wheel. He was drunk, having long since emptied a bottle of Tullamore Dew and thrown it out the driver's side window onto Villiers Street at Embankment Station. *Why not?* Roy had asked himself as the aliens, the American president had said they were called Jai, pummeled Great Britain.

Roy was shaken from his drunken snooze by someone opening his cab's passenger door and sitting down beside him. He looked over to the passenger seat and saw a very tall, rather imposing man. The rear door opened, and three other persons got in.

'What are you doing?' Roy groggily asked.

'Number Ten Downing Street, please,' the man in the passenger seat said politely but firmly.

'Huh?'

'I said, Number Ten Downing Street.'

'Downing Street! Are you a nutter? You want to go over there when the aliens are blasting every military target on the whole island. Why last night I saw them wipe out a whole column of tanks over on—'

The man reached out and grabbed Roy by the back of his collar. 'Take us there. Now.'

Roy turned to the other passengers, 'Hey, are you gonna let your mate do that to me? I never...'

Roy stopped talking when he got a look at the men in the back seat. Since he did not follow politics, Roy didn't recognize the secretary of state for defence or the chancellor of the exchequer. But he knew the bloke in the ragged army uniform sitting between them alright. It was the younger prince.

Roy held up his hands, 'Alright, mate...uhhh...Your Highness...Downing Street it is.'

Instinctively, Roy reached for his radio to call in the fare, but the bodyguard grabbed his hand and said, 'Don't.'

Roy nodded.

They proceeded down Villiers Street and took a right onto Victoria Embankment along the Thames. The streets of London had given over to mob rule. Most of the storefronts were smashed, their merchandise strewn along the sidewalk. Roy drove past several crowds of young men dancing in the streets and shouting 'Allah Akbar!' A cleric out of Finsbury Park said the Jai were in fact the 12th Imam sent by Allah to install the World Caliphate. There had already been several homicide bombings, one ironically enough aimed at a throng of peace activists at the American Embassy protesting that country's massive national effort against the invaders.

As the cab neared Downing Street, Roy weaved through several abandoned police barricades. There were overturned vehicles as well. Not until Derby Gate were the barricades manned. Here police in riot gear and heavily armed members of the Cold Stream Guards stood watch. The bodyguard need only to flash his ID at the sentries to get them through.

When Roy pulled up in front of Downing Street, the prince leaned forward and said, 'How much fare?'

'You're kidding, right, sir?'

The bodyguard patted Roy's shoulder. 'Good man.' Then he reached for the keys and yanked them out of the ignition. 'You stay here.'

The man got out of the cab. Roy saw him a flash a badge at one of the Bobbies standing at the entrance and motioned for him to come forward to the cab. 'Make sure he stays here.'

Unlike Bobbies in peace time, this one wore body armor and carried an automatic weapon. He stood right beside the door and said to Roy, 'Stay put, chap.'

Roy nodded, reached into his windbreaker, and took out a cigarette and asked the Bobby, 'Got a light, mate?'

The four passengers got out of the cab and walked over to the gate. A quartet of police officers guarded the entrance.

'Your Majesty?' one asked.

'Yes, Sergeant. We are here to see the prime minister,' the prince stated.

'Yes, Your Majesty,' then he remembered he was speaking to a man in military uniform who must be addressed properly. "Uhh, Lieutenant Wales.' the flabbergasted sergeant said. He turned around, 'Open the gate!'

The prince and the ministers walked through. Before following, the bodyguard said, 'You are of course aware of the destruction of Balmoral.'

'Yes.'

'Absolutely no word of Wales' presence gets out. Is that understood?'

'Yes.'

The quartet was let into the gate onto Downing Street. They walked past more soldiers and heavily armed Bobbies and a pair of armored personal carriers. Un-ceremoniously they were let into Number Ten.

They went directly to the Cabinet Room. Lieutenant Wales walked to the head of the table, pulled out a chair, and sat down. In contrast to the ornate surroundings around him, his uniform was dusty, torn at the arm where a piece of shrapnel had grazed him, and smelled of cordite. His boots were caked with mud. On his belt, Wales wore a loaded side arm. He tossed his battered helmet onto the table, not caring that the Kevlar ruined the sheer finish, and ran his hand through his brownish-red hair. The prince slumped, as if he were pushed down by the burden he never thought he'd have to bear.

The prime minister came in. He looked disheveled, his blazer long since discarded, shirt sleeves rolled up, tie loosened. He gave a slight bow.

'Your Majesty, please excuse my appearance. We did not expect you here.'

'No, I don't expect you did,' Lieutenant Wales replied.

'I was on the phone with the UN secretary general.'

'I see.'

'I was hoping he might be able to open a dialogue with the aliens.'

'My father already tried that,' said Wales. 'The delegation you appointed him to lead was vaporized in the first minutes of the war.'

'I was most sorry for your loss, Your Majesty.'

'They knew exactly where most of the important Royal residences were,' said the secretary of state for defence.

The PM replied, 'I believed that by telling the Jai about ourselves, by being completely open, the aliens would see we are no threat to them.'

'You told them how to decapitate the Royal Family,' said the prince. 'They have since destroyed Edinburgh, Glasgow, Belfast, York…' Lieutenant Wales said. 'And still our forces remain idle.'

'I can't help but think that if we could just talk to them, the Jai would stop their attacks. Your Majesty, surely a race capable of space travel is enlightened. Besides, would people who could cross the stars not possess extraordinary weapons?'

'They do, Prime Minister. I and my men saw those weapons first hand when they landed on Lindesfarne Island. One of their whistle bombs reduced the monastery there to rubble. I saw a laser fired from one of their armored vehicles slice a Challenger tank in half. But my men still fought. We killed many of their soldiers and destroyed one of their armored vehicles as it traversed the causeway to the mainland. If I was allowed air support, I might have been able to stop the Jai.'

The PM said nothing.

'That's when these ministers requested I come to Downing Street.'

'What is it you want, Your Majesty?'

'Order the Royal Air Force and Navy to fight back.'

The PM shook his head, 'I do not think that emulating the Americans in this case is prudent.'

The defense secretary spoke again. 'The Americans have done significant damage to the Jai over the Atlantic, Prime Minister. They even brought down one of those large carrier ships that were bombarding Scotland.'

'By using nuclear weapons, Mr. Secretary. I cannot abide such action. In fact, I fear that our close association with the Americans during the late war is one of the reasons why the Jai are attacking us so vociferously.'

'Neither China nor Russia supported America,' said Lieutenant Wales, 'and they too have been attacked.'

'Still-'

'There's no making the man see reason, is there, Mr. Secretary?' Lieutenant Wales said without taking his eyes off the prime minister.

'No, Your Majesty, I'm afraid there isn't.'

'Very well then.' Lieutenant Wales stood up. 'Prime Minister, I dismiss you from office. Your government is herby dissolved.'

'You can't do that! You're not even—'

'King?' Lieutenant Wales interrupted. 'My grandmother, father, brother and sister-in-law are all dead. I am the ruling monarch.'

'But I won the last election.'

'Your party won the election, and as such, my grandmother asked you to form a new government, which I have just dissolved.'

'This is a coup!'

'This is a constitutional monarchy of which I am the head. Now get out. I have to choose a new prime minister.'

The bodyguard stepped forward and offered to help the ex-prime minster from the room. He needed none. The bodyguard said, 'There is a cab waiting for you outside. It will take you wherever you would like to go, sir.' He reached into his coat pocket. 'Here are the keys.'

The bodyguard quickly led the ex-prime minster out of Number Ten Downing Street to the gate. From there, a trio of soldiers walked him to the cab.

When the former prime minister got in, Roy turned around and said. 'Hey, you're the PM! My wife loves you! Wait till she hears. Where to, Prime Minister?'

'Ex-prime minister,' was his reply.

Back in the Cabinet Room, the king turned to the chancellor of the exchequer and said, 'Mr. Chancellor, I would like you to head the new government.'

The man stood up and bowed. 'It would be my pleasure, Your Majesty. For now, the cabinet's current makeup will suffice I should think, and I will hold onto my portfolio until such time as a replacement can be found. I'm thinking a certain MP from the Midlands will do.'

The king nodded.

'Until then what orders, Your Majesty?'

'Defend the realm.'

'Yes, Your Majesty... Mr. Secretary, what is the disposition of our forces?'

'All four of our ballistic missile submarines are at sea. The *Prince of Wales* and *Queen Elizabeth* are cruising off the Orkneys and have full air contingents, and we have two fighter squadrons at Stornoway. We should contact the Norwegians. I have a friend in their defence ministry. Perhaps they can join in our counterattack...'

The new prime minister looked over at the monarch, but he was asleep. The secretary of state for defence was about to wake the king, but the PM stopped him.

'The king has done all he can.'

LONG LIVE THE KING!
King Harold fires weakling PM, orders UK counterattack
First Royal firing since 1834

London: Amid political turmoil not seen in Great Britain in decades if not centuries, British forces launched a massive counterattack... [snip] 'The attack included all elements of our armed forces: land, sea, and air. I am pleased to say to the British people that their military is living up to expectations,' said the new prime minister...[snip] aircraft from bases in northern England, along with squadrons from the Prince of Wales *and* Queen Elizabeth *attacked the Jai ship then hovering off the coast of Scotland...[snip] Though British forces incurred significant losses, the combined RAF/RN effort forced the Jai ship to reenter orbit.*

The Telegraph

Chapter 4: **The Waiting Below**

Arrival + 3 weeks

The Russians, of course, have been reluctant to provide western governments or media outlets with information. Nevertheless, our intelligence services can paint a fairly accurate picture of events there.

The Russians have thrown everything they have at the Jai, up to and including their new RS-24 ICBMs. Consequently the Jai have concentrated their attacks on Russia military infrastructure. Norwegian intelligence suspects that St. Petersburg and Murmansk have been destroyed. We know that Russia air and naval bases on the Kola Peninsula have been destroyed and much of the vaunted Northern Fleet sent to the bottom of the Barents Sea. It is unclear if the Russians have employed their Oscar Class SSBNs. It is the opinion of the NSC that these potent platforms remain under the Arctic ice.

British MI-6 has an intelligence source (note this is the only description they are willing to provide) who claims that the Oscar Class submarines are being saved for some kind of doomsday scenario. This is in stark contrast to the USN's decision, backed by you, to make full use of our own Ohio Class SSBNs. Of course several Los Angeles-Class attack subs have been set aside...

Presidential Daily Briefing, Week Four

Wartime Commander-in-Chief?: is the president up to the job?

Lead editorial, Commentary Magazine

Dear Julie:

Three weeks now. We cruise, we wait, we wonder. We hear noise on the surface, explosions, splashes, what not. Something is happening up there, but we don't know what. And we can't find out either. I've been running a lot of drills; each day we work on something new. So far we're holding together. The officers and crew all know our orders and are prepared to carry them out.

The men have been holding up ok, but I don't know how much longer that's going to last. I can only imagine how they feel. Actually I don't have to imagine because I know. I'm torn up inside. Not just because of what's happening, but because of the way you and I left things...

Commander Boeteler put his pen down and considered what to write next. After a few minutes he reminded himself that the letters he had been writing to his estranged wife could not possibly be mailed and would just go in his desk.

He lay his head in his hands and drifted off to sleep.

Boeteler was awakened by the beep of his phone. He picked it up, 'Boeteler.'

'This is the XO. Propellers, Commander, lot's of 'em, running fast, twenty-five knots plus.'

'I'll be right there, Mr. Sanchez.'

Boeteler left his quarters and walked forward to the sonar room. 'Any ID?'

Smith, the sonar tech, shook his head. 'Nothing certain, but something big, at least a Tico. I'd be surprised if there wasn't a carrier too.'

'Alright.'

Smith listened for a while, then, 'Explosions, Commander...something hitting the water like debris.....wait...a big splash...now another and another...wow!'

'What?' asked the captain.

'A big explosion,' replied Smith

'Nuclear?' Sanchez asked.

'Possibly.'

'There's another blast.'

They waited for a few more moments, then, 'Sounds of a hull breaking, twisting...now something big just crashed into the sea.'

'Crashed?' Boeteler asked.

'Like a plane, but bigger.'

'Seven forty-seven?' Sanchez asked.

'It was big whatever it was,' said Smith.

'No reason for a seven forty-seven to be in a battle area,' Boeteler said.

'One of those Airborne Lasers?' asked Lt. Geary, the communications officer.

'More hull pops...there, another crash, now a lot of little splashes, not like propellers though...something else.' Smith held out the headphone to Boeteler. 'You want to listen, Commander?'

Boeteler took the headphones and held them to his ears and listened for several seconds before handing them back.

'How far away do you think, Smith?'

'Twenty-five, thirty nautical miles north, northwest at least.'

'We're headed right for the action,' said Sanchez.

Boeteler rubbed his chin. 'Alright. All stop.'

'All stop,' Sanchez ordered.

'We stay here until the fighting's finished.'

The weapons officer spoke, 'Then we have a look?'

'Absolutely not, Mr. Dalton,' Boeteler replied.

'Sir.'

They listened for over an hour as the fighting raged on the surface.

'Propellers drifting off, north, northeast,' Smith reported.

'Orders?' asked Sanchez.

'We wait.'

After Boeteler was satisfied the battle above was over he ordered the boat due west at five knots. He returned to his bunk to try to get some sleep.

Of course word of the contacts spread throughout the boat. After much speculation, the crew decided that the aliens had concluded an alliance with China and Russia and had attacked the United States, which explained the nuclear detonations above (it was assumed the aliens were so advanced they didn't need nukes). The boat's daily bible study class shifted focus from Salvation to Armageddon.

Since the beginning of the cruise Boeteler had held special Sunday dinners with his officers. The Sunday spread was better than the weekly fare, and afterwards they drank scotch and smoked cigars. But on this Sunday the mood around the wardroom was bleak, with the officers discussing possible scenarios to describe the battle that they had heard.

'It sounds like the United States Navy has taken a beating,' said Dalton.

There were nods and grunts.

Lt. Geary held up his hand. 'Well maybe not.'

'What do you mean, maybe not?'

'Let me restate. I think it's clear we took it on the chin, but we could certainly have inflicted some pain on the aliens.'

'No way to know.' Sanchez said.

'Well let's think...' Geary said. 'How long did we pick up the sounds. How long did they last?'

'A good while,' said Sanchez.

'So there was definitely a fight.'

The officers nodded.

'And it took a while?' asked Geary.

There was more nodding.

'What difference does that make?' Dalton asked.

'Maybe we gave as good as we got.'

'You don't know that,' said Dalton.

'You're right, I don't. But there were lots of small splashing sounds, right? And assuming our ships were getting sunk, and I bet we probably lost some, they went down one at a time. The aliens had to concentrate on them, pool their fire.'

'And we still lost,' said Dalton.

'Yes, but it cost them too.'

Boeteler finally spoke up. 'He's got a point, Mr. Dalton.'

'Maybe it's not even aliens, maybe we're at war with China,' Sanchez said.

'Sorry, sir,' began Geary, 'but if we're at war with China, and we're fighting off of the west coast, we're in big trouble, aren't we?'

'Ok,' Sanchez said, 'But which is worse, losing a war to aliens or losing a war to China?'

Furious debate ensued.

After dinner Boeteler spent a few hours on the bridge before retiring to his quarters. He undressed to his skivvies and lay down on his bunk. Boeteler closed his eyes but could feel no sleep coming on. He picked up a framed photo of his family, Julie and their three girls—seventeen, fifteen, and twelve—all standing on the front porch of their home outside of Tacoma. Looking at them, how all three of the girls were just younger versions of their blonde-haired, blue-eyed mother, Boeteler felt his heart breaking. He put the frame down and closed his eyes again. Sleep still wasn't coming, so he got out of his bunk and took the orders out of his safe. *Is there anything*, he thought, *that possibly allows me to get in the fight?* Even though he memorized them long ago, he read his orders once more.

To: Commander, USS Olympia
From: The Secretary of Defense via COMSUBPAC
RE: Operation Masada

Pursuant to Presidential Executive Order 1010 *USS Olympia* will, two weeks before Arrival, sail from its berth at Bremerton and proceed south, taking up a position off of Southern California. *USS Olympia* will remain submerged for the next twelve weeks. During this time *USS Olympia* will not surface for any reason whatsoever, regardless of circumstance. Nor will she have any contact with the outside world.

Exactly ten weeks after Arrival *USS Olympia* will, as circumstances warrant, surface and await orders. If no such orders are received *USS Olympia* will launch a nuclear strike on Southern California. Targets will include Los Angeles and San Diego. Additionally two Tomahawk Missiles each will be targeted on the northern and southern suburbs of these cities. You are free to use your remaining six Tomahawk Missiles on targets of opportunity...

Dear Julie:

Five sour weeks. Everyone is antsy, but morale is as good as can be expected. Some of my officers are war-gaming an alien attack. The crew is running a video game tournament on the boat's Xbox. They invited me to participate in the Guitar Hero tournament, just like the girls always wanted...

Boeteler savored the taste of his Sunday Arturo Fuente Gran Reserva as he made his way to the galley. He wanted to talk to the cook about varying the crew's meals, but when he got to the galley Boeteler heard a man sobbing. He looked into the galley to see one of the cooks sitting next to the stove, Indian style, hands in face.

'Rashid?' Boeteler asked.

Rashid looked up from his hands and stood up. 'Commander.' He managed.

'What's wrong?'

With those two words Rashid broke into tears again. 'Los Angeles,' he managed.

'LA? What about it?'

'That's where I'm from, Commander.'

'So?'

'The news, I heard it was destroyed.'

Boeteler felt a combination of annoyance and rage building up within him until finally he said, 'Attention!'

Rashid snapped out of his stupor and stood ramrod straight.

'What news? There has been no news.'

'No news, Commander?'

'This boat received absolutely no information whatsoever about the status of Los Angeles. Is that understood?'

'But the sounds we picked up—'

'Mean absolutely nothing.'

Rashid sniffled. 'Aye, aye, Commander.'

'You are a sailor in the United States Navy, Rashid. Start acting like it, goddamn it.'

'Aye, aye.'

'Get back to work.'

Boeteler turned his back on Rashid and walked away. After stopping by the engine room and talking with the sailors there to see how they were doing, Boeteler went to his quarters. He sat at his small desk and picked up Plutarch's *Lives*—it was on the boat's book club list. He had started reading Plutarch the previous week, but on this night he just couldn't get into it. Boeteler sighed, put it down, and instead picked up his bible. He read several Psalms.

In truth Boeteler couldn't blame Rashid for thinking LA had been annihilated. The night before *Olympia* had picked up the sound of several massive explosions coming from the coast. A huge shock wave rippled over the water above the boat. At the time *Olympia* was 104 miles north, northwest of Los Angeles. It didn't take long for everyone in the crew to assume that the aliens had annihilated LA. Boeteler was inclined to think that they had nuked the great docks at Long Beach. Whatever the target, nukes had been used. They had detected a massive radiation spike not long after the initial explosions. On Boeteler's orders *Olympia* had spent several days on station off the coast, more or less idle. After that Boeteler ordered the boat due west at five knots. Now they were three hundred miles due west of Catalina Island, cruising at three knots in a simple ten by ten box pattern.

After the incident with Rashid, Boeteler had dozed on his bunk for a while, he wasn't sure how long, when his phone beeped. Boeteler picked up the receiver.

'Commander.'

Dalton was on the other end, 'This is the Weapons Officer. Commander, something just appeared in the water.'

'What do you mean?'

'I think you better come up here.'

'On my way.'

When he got to the control room Boeteler noticed that it stank of BO. He looked at the bridge crew and saw men unshaven, clothes wrinkled, and shirttails out. Dalton had allowed his hair to grow longer than regulations permitted.

'OK, Lieutenant. What do you mean something is in the water?'

'Seventeen nautical miles northeast of our position something big landed in the water.'

'Big?'

'Really big. Huge splash.'

'And sunk?'

'No, Commander, it's sitting on the surface and emitting electronic signals.'

'Can we read the signals?'

'Negative.'

Boeteler ran a hand over his face. 'Alright, all stop. What's our current depth?'

'Seven hundred and fifty feet, Commander.'

'Keep us steady, Lieutenant.'

'Aye aye.' A few seconds later, Dalton said, 'Commander, you know what this has to be.'

'You think it's an alien ship?'

'What else could it be?'

'Don't know.'

'Commander, we have a full complement of torpedoes.'

'I know...'

'It probably doesn't know we're here.'

'I know...'

'Right now, six MK forty-eights-'

'Enough!' Boeteler said through bared teeth.

Dalton looked visibly chastened. Boeteler hoped no one heard the exchange.

'Alright, Lt. Dalton. Come up with a firing solution. Give me a plan of attack.' *That should keep him out of my hair.*

'Yes, Commander.'

They waited for several minutes. Finally, Smith said, 'Sounds of explosions, Commander, right near the contact...and more explosions.'

'Ours, theirs?'

'No way to tell, but they're coming from the contact...lots of splashes, small ones.'

'Debris?'

'I bet, yes, sir, Commander...holy cow! Explosion, big one, massive blast, lots of waves, big ones too...we're going to get rocked...'

A few seconds later *Olympia* was hit by a shock wave. The boat swooned.

'That has to be a nuke,' said Dalton.

Radiation levels spiked.

'Probably a tactical,' said Dalton.

Boeteler nodded. 'Contact still there?'

'Aye, aye...more splashes too. Stuff hitting the water...whoa! Here comes another.'

A few seconds later *Olympia* swooned with the force of another shock wave.

'Contact?' Boeteler asked.

'Still there, not moving.'

'Alright, get us out of here. Course one eight zero give me twenty knots.'

'Twenty knots?' Sanchez asked, 'That will make a lot of noise.'

'Yes, but there's a battle up above; that will cover us up.'

'Commander,' Dalton began. 'There's a fight, we're in perfect position, and I have a firing solution.'

This time Boeteler spoke so the bridge crew could hear him. 'Mr. Dalton, you will shut up right now and carry out my orders.'

'Aye, aye.' Dalton was visibly angry. He added, 'Then why did you ask for the solution?'

'To get you out of my hair.'

They sailed south at twenty knots and got well clear of the battle area. When *Olympia* was a hundred miles further south, opposite the Mexican coast, Boeteler ordered speed reduced to five knots and a course of zero zero zero. Dalton still seethed.

On his nightly inspection of *Olympia*, Boeteler took a pad with him to jot down notes about each section, the crew's outward appearance, and bits of chatter he picked up. Half the crew was angry they didn't get into the fight, the other half, depressed. He saw out of the corner of his eye one or two crewmen shooting him angry glances.

The next day Boeteler was called to the infirmary by the boat's doctor, a recent med school graduate named Rao. Lying there in the bunks were two sailors, both of whom, to Boeteler's eye, looked like they were near death. They were pale and emaciated. One slept fitfully while the other lay face down in his bunk quietly weeping into a pillow.

'Commander,' Rao said. 'There's nothing physically wrong with these men.'

'Then why are they here?' Boeteler asked.

'They're sick as dogs, yes. Curtis here,' he pointed to the weeping man, 'is convinced the world is ending. He came here a few hours ago. He said he'd been vomiting all night.' He pointed to the other sailor, 'Jefferson says he has no appetite and in his words—hurts all over.'

'What have you done for them?'

'I'm about to give them sedatives, make them sleep for a while...' Rao waited a few moments. 'It's psychological. Whatever is wrong is in their heads. I'm not a psychiatrist; I can't fix that.'

'Can't you give them Prozac or something?'

'We don't have Prozac, Commander.'

'Then what do you suggest?'

'I don't know. But I have to tell you, I think you'll see more of this.'

'Alright, doctor. Do what you can.'

Rao held his gaze for a few moments as if to say, *I was going to do that.* He said nothing.

Dear Julie:

Six weeks. Halfway. We're trying to feel like we've reached a milestone, but we don't. This just means we've waited six weeks, and we'll wait six weeks more. The crew is starting to make mistakes, stupid stuff really, mistakes they would never make under normal conditions. The Chief of the Boat's been kicking the hell out of 'em.

On the seventh Sunday morning of the cruise, Sanchez came to Boeteler with a piece of paper in his hand. 'The officers and I want you to see this, Commander.'

Boeteler took the paper and read it:

We, the officers of the *USS Olympia*, request the Commander consider breaking radio silence and inquire as to the current situation.

It was signed by every officer onboard.

'You too, Sanchez?'

'Yes, sir.'

'OK.' Boeteler folded the paper and put it in his pocket. 'That is all.'

'Aye, aye.'

The officers clearly hoped to talk things over at dinner. That night Boeteler walked into the ward room as he did every Sunday night. The officers stood, and he invited them all to be seated. He looked around the wardroom and saw hopeful and eager expressions. His eyes settled on that night's dinner, roast turkey, gravy, and candied yams.

Boeteler grabbed the turkey platter and heaved it over. Then he swept the bowl of candied yams off the table. The bowl clanged onto the deck and spun in the terrible, awkward silence.

He reached into his pocket and took out the letter. 'All of you will shut the fuck up about this right now,' Boeteler said through gritted teeth. 'While you officers have been writing this bitchy little letter to me, the crew has been going to pieces. You remember that you are naval officers and fix this situation now. I will do you a favor and forget about this when it comes time to write my report.' With that he left the wardroom.

It was at that moment that Boeteler realized he had lost the officers.

The next day no officer would look Boeteler in the eye. Neither would any of the crew. Sonar picked up some distant sounds, more splashes and explosions, but nothing like they'd heard the day before. That night after his tour of *Olympia*, Boeteler asked the Chief of the Boat to see him in his quarters. When the chief entered, Boeteler looked him over. The man was clean-shaven and healthy looking. His shirt and pants were pressed and immaculate.

'At ease, Chief Fallon.' he said.

'Commander.'

Boeteler motioned for him to sit in the desk chair while he sat on his bunk.

'Tell me about the crew, Chief.'

'The crew, Commander? They're not good. Terrible.'

'That's what I thought.'

'I figured you did, Commander.'

'What do they want?'

'Easy. Find out what's happening.'

'We can't do that.'

'I know, Commander. And I understand. But I think *you* need to understand that a lot of the crew thinks the world is ending. A lot of 'em think their families are dead. They're wondering why an attack boat loaded out with torpedoes and nuclear tipped Tomahawk and Harpoon missiles is hiding. Some are figuring if we're all gonna' die anyway we might as well get into the fight. Hell, a lot of 'em figure we can help win the fight.'

'I think I understand.'

'Men are going to get desperate, Commander, you need to get that.'

'I do.'

'I figured you would, Commander.'

'Anything else?'

'No, sir.'

'Dismissed. Thank you, Chief.'

Fallon saluted.

Boeteler lay down on his bunk, thinking about his conversation with the Chief. *Men are going to get desperate* he heard him say over and over again.

Dear Julie:

Eight weeks. Things aren't going well. The crew is starting to fall apart, and there doesn't seem to be anything I can do about it. Half of them can't sleep. You can imagine how well they do their jobs after being up for a couple of days. Others don't want to leave their bunks. When the shifts change, I've had to go down to the crew quarters and personally roust men from the sack. Some of them aren't eating. One man has lost thirty pounds on this cruise, and Dr. Rao is worried about him. Actually, I've taken off several pounds myself, like you wanted.

I've been thinking about our last conversation and what you said...

When Boeteler convened the next Sunday dinner, the officers talked amongst themselves, mostly avoided Boeteler's glance, and answered his questions as briefly and vaguely as possible. Boeteler wasn't in the mood for whisky and cigars and excused himself after putting them on the table.

A few hours after retiring he was woken by the OOD, Dalton this time, who informed him that sonar was hearing more explosions. Boeteler spent half the night on the bridge listening to the sounds above. The sounds were trailing generally in *Olympia's* direction, so Boeteler ordered the boat down to a thousand feet and sailed due west. There was more of the same noise the next day, a quick battle in the morning, a few explosions but nothing more, and a longer battle in the afternoon. For an hour they listened to the sound of explosions, splashes, and twisting steel. The highlight was a massive splashing sound so impressive that Smith invited Boeteler to listen in on his headphones.

'What do you make of that, Smith? Something landing?'

'No way, Commander, that was an impact, a big one. If you ask me, we just shot down a big alien ship. No way to tell, I suppose.'

'I guess not.'

They heard only silence after that.

Over the next several days, *Olympia* received no more contacts, heard no more noise. Just silence, as if a great battle had been fought and lost. As the boat cruised north radiation levels spiked, declined, and then spiked again, staying at dangerous levels for several hours.

'What's our position?' Boeteler asked.

'Two hundred thirty-four miles north, northeast of Catalina Island,' Sanchez said.

'What do you make of these levels?'

'It's like were taking a bath in radiation, Commander.'

Boeteler nodded. There was nothing for him to say.

He toured the boat that night. The crew was depressed. Some men seemed suicidal. A few that he spoke to had puffy cheeks and red eyes; they had been sobbing. Boeteler tried talking to a few sailors but doubted he did any good. They didn't want inspirational talks.

As Boeteler headed for his bunk, he walked past Sanchez's quarters, and heard him shouting.

'This is stupid, Dalton!'

'You in or out?'

'Out.'

'Are you going to sell me out?'

'What do you take me for?' Sanchez asked. 'Get out.'

Boeteler walked around the corner before the door opened.

He called Fallon to his quarters that night.

'How's the crew doing, Chief?'

'Terrible, sir.'

'Officers aren't doing well either.'

'I noticed.'

'I think I might need a sidearm.'

'Seems like a smart idea to me, Commander.'

'Can you quietly have one delivered to my cabin?'

'Aye, aye.' Fallon opened the door, stopped and looked over his shoulder. 'If it's all the same to you Commander, I'll be keeping one handy myself.'

'Appreciate it.'

Boeteler sat in the wardroom that night for dinner with the rest of the officers, trying to pretend he hadn't heard Sanchez and Dalton. Geary tried to strike up a conversation about his latest war gaming efforts but no one seemed interested. Boeteler ate a little bit and then excused himself. From then on he took his meals in his quarters.

Dear Julie:

Nine weeks in. I keep trying to think that we have only three weeks left to go, but it doesn't feel like that. It feels like nine grueling weeks. I am losing the men of this boat. Actually, I'm not losing the officers and crew; I've lost them. The crew seems to blame me for what's happening above, and the officers hate me for not breaking orders. Every time there's a knock on my door or I'm summoned to the bridge, I have to wonder if it's the first step to a mutiny…

Boeteler sat groggily in his bed, trying to digest what Sanchez just told him.

'Suicide?'

'Yes, Commander.'

'Two men?'

'Yes.'

'Alright, give me a minute. I'll meet you down in the galley.'

'Aye, aye, sir.'

Boeteler hauled himself out of his bunk. He rubbed his eyes and pulled on his pants and went down to the galley. Sanchez waited there, as did the chief and Dr. Rao. Two bodies lay on the deck, covered by blankets. A pool of blood had spread beneath them.

'So how did they do it?' Boeteler asked.

'Simple, Commander. They slit their wrists.'

'Why?'

Rao and Sanchez exchanged glances saying, *He has to ask?*

'Here's what we think happened,' Sanchez began. 'O'Neill and Foster here were good friends. And they entered some sort of suicide pact.'

'Was it a gay thing?'

Sanchez looked at Fallon, 'Chief?'

The chief shook his head. 'No way, sir. They were just pals. I did see them consoling each other a lot, but they weren't homos.'

'Alright, Doctor. Get them out of here. Get them cleaned up. I'll make an announcement to the crew.'

'Yes, sir.'

Boeteler went to the bridge and got on the PA. 'This is the Commander. It is my regret to tell you that Seamen O'Neill and Foster have,' he paused, 'died. There will be a memorial service later today. That is all.'

Boeteler headed for the hatch, but was stopped by Dalton, who had gotten out of his bunk and come up to the bridge in his boxers and a T-shirt. He stood in front of the hatch, blocking Boeteler. 'Are you happy now, Commander?' he asked. His fists were clenched.

'Get out of my way, Lieutenant, or I'll kick your ass.'

Boeteler stepped forward, Dalton got out of the way. There was shouting on the bridge, Boeteler tried not to listen, but knew important decisions were being made.

The funeral service was conducted by one of the bible study guys. When the sailor finished his brief sermon he stepped back and said, 'Commander, we would like you to say a few words, a prayer.'

Boeteler stepped forward. 'Bow your heads, please. Lord, we do not know what made these two men take their lives. We hope that you take them in your loving embrace now. They were good sailors and good men, and we will miss them. We pray you keep our friends and family in safety and peace. Amen.'

The officers and crew murmured 'amen.' Boeteler looked around; many of them had tears in their eyes. Men shook hands and hugged. Boeteler saw Geary look at Dalton and nod. He seemed to step forward, but then back. Dalton gritted his teeth and mouthed, 'Do it,' but Geary shook his head. Boeteler could see Geary mouth the words 'Not now.' Dalton shook with rage and then stormed out of the room.

Dear Julie:

They tried it. Or I should say they tried to try it. But they chickened out. I got lucky. Next time I won't be. I don't know how it will happen or when. But when it does, I'm not handing the boat over. Not to Dalton, not to anyone.

I hope they deliver this letter to you. I hope you and the girls are there to receive it. I want you to know that despite everything I've done, I love you. In these last moments I'm thinking about you, and the good times we had. We did have good times, I keep reminding myself. Not enough, though, and that's my fault. I spent too much time worrying about my career, and too much time being unfaithful to you. I wish now that I hadn't. Easy to say now, I know. But we still have the girls, and whatever happens to us if I come back, I hope we can still be good parents for them. I'll do my best...

Boeteler was woken up by commotion outside his door. There was shouting and tussling in the passageway. He got up and took his pistol out of the holster; he was already in uniform. He'd been sleeping in it for several days now. He opened the door and saw a group of sailors at the end of the passageway. Dalton led them. Chief Fallon stood in front of them, blocking their way. A sailor lay at his feet, and above him on the bulkhead was a bloody patch where the chief had smashed his head.

'Out of the way, Chief!' Dalton shouted.

'No.'

A sailor stepped forward. He had a monkey wrench in his hand, but Fallon dropped him with a devastating right hook to the jaw. The crowed surged forward. The chief braced himself but was brought down by the mass of men. He was all flailing arms and legs. One man flew back as the chief landed a punch on his face. Then fists flew for several seconds until the chief stopped moving. His body was limp and his face a bloody pulp.

Boeteler stepped into the passageway. The rush stopped.

'What the hell are you doing?' he asked Dalton.

'We're taking the boat.'

Boeteler pointed his pistol at Dalton.

'What do you think you're going to do with that?' Dalton asked.

'You think I'm giving you the boat? You think I won't fight?'

'You can't shoot us all.'

'No, but I can shoot you, Dalton.'

Dalton said nothing as Boeteler leveled the pistol at his face.

'Go ahead, mutiny. You won't be around to skipper the boat, though.'

Dalton laughed and pointed behind Boeteler. There stood Sanchez, pistol on his hip.

'Wipe that smile off your face, Dalton,' Sanchez said. He drew his pistol and pointed it at Dalton.

'What are you doing?' Dalton asked.

'Stopping this.'

'You can't.'

'I am.' Sanchez looked behind him, 'C'mon out.'

Geary came out, he too had a pistol.

'Sorry, Dalton,' he said. 'This isn't right.'

'But we can get in the fight, we can find out what's happening.'

'We'll find out in a few weeks anyway, Dalton,' said Sanchez. 'Is this how you want it to end? As a mutineer?'

On the floor the chief moaned.

Boeteler stepped back inside his cabin and picked up the phone. 'Dr. Rao, commander's cabin.' He stepped back into the passageway. 'Help him up!' he shouted.

Two sailors helped the chief from the floor and propped him against the bulkhead.

'We win, Commander?' he asked.

'I'm still skipper of this boat.'

'Ahhh.'

'Alright, everyone back to your stations. You too, Dalton.'

'Me?'

'I need my weapons officer. In a few weeks we may have to fire our Tomahawks. Our orders don't say anything about our Harpoon Missiles, though. We'll find some aliens to launch them at.'

'Yes, Commander.'

Two weeks later *Olympia* came to periscope depth ten miles off the coast at the entrance to Santa Monica Bay.

Boeteler said, 'Up periscope, let's have a look.'

He stepped up to the periscope and pointed it at LA. His heart sank. The city smoldered. A great dark cloud hung above the ruins. Several ships were sunk near shore. There was a large ship poking out of the water near the beach that he didn't recognize. It was cylindrical.

'That must be an alien ship,' Boeteler said.

'What do you see, Commander?' Dalton asked.

'Nothing good.'

Someone on the bridge began to weep.

'Settle down,' Dalton said.

'Communications, anything yet?' Boeteler asked.

'Nothing yet, Commander,' Geary replied.

'Alright.'

'Nothing, Commander?' Sanchez asked. 'See anything?'

'No signs of life from here. Could be behind the mountains, I suppose. Have a look.'

Sanchez went to the other periscope. Shaking his head he said, 'Looks like we lost the battle of Los Angeles.' Then, 'Sail up the coast, see if there's anything?'

'Seems like a good bet. Might as well.' He turned to Dalton. 'There doesn't seem to be anything left in Los Angeles to destroy, Lt. Dalton.'

'Aye, aye, sir.'

'Looks like we'll have to find some aliens.'

'Throw the active sonar on?' Sanchez asked.

'Not yet I—'

'Commander!' came the shout from the communications shack 'Emergency Action Message!'

The printer churned, and after a few seconds spat out a piece of paper. Geary took the paper and walked it over to Boeteler. It read:

TO: USS OLYMPIA
FROM: COMSUBPAC
NEW ORDERS. REPEAT NEW ORDERS
Proceed to Bremerton for rest and refit. Standby for...

American West Coast, especially Southern California, all but annihilated in alien onslaught
Russia Today

I admit it, I didn't think she could do it. But from everything I saw, the president did an outstanding job during those first weeks of the war, especially after our defeat at the Battle of the West Coast. No one complained about her management of our military, and after we lost, she rallied the nation and made us believe that we could fight on. Not bad for a junior senator and former Midwestern mayor whose career before running for office was in environmental law.
Before, During, and After: Blogging the Aliens

Throughout the crisis, the president's leadership has been remarkable. Every day she takes to the radio, and when possible, the television, to reassure and rally nation. Some days she can be found touring a shelter in Ohio, or visiting the crew of a THAAD battery, or simply stopping in a local restaurant for a bite to eat. She is always on the move. One night, a speech from the Oval Office, the next, a radio address from a secured undisclosed location. The day after that, a very public appearance in....
The Washington Post

Chapter 5: Citadel

Arrival + 4 days

President Grows in Office Opposition Senators Say
   Washington: The Senate Majority Leader was blunt, 'I did not think she was up to the job. I was wrong. The president has grown into the position of Commander-in-Chief, in fact, I would say that of recent presidents. . . .

The Washington Examiner

A Reluctant Warrior, President Winning Accolades for Handling of Conflict
The Washington Post

The Battle of the Atlantic is now beginning. Iceland is the critical point. The aliens cannot cut Atlantic communications without neutralizing Iceland. They may decide the best way to achieve this is a physical landing and occupation of the island.

Analysis from Strafor

I watched General Lutch hang up the phone.

Much has been written about this moment, none of it true. Had Lutch been a growling, cigar-chomping caricature of a general sent straight from central casting, I suppose a barrage of curses would have followed. Ok, he did say 'Well goddamn' to the British general on the other end of the line, but Lutch wasn't angry, at least not outwardly.

General Ureth, the Marine commander, was there, and he asked, 'What's wrong, General?'

Lutch calmly adjusted his glasses and said, 'The British have stood down.'

'They what?'

'They're out of the fight.'

It was general Ureth who spat fire and stomped around the headquarters in a rage, not Lutch.

So there we were, or there was Lutch, all hell breaking loose across the globe, two Jai carrier ships bearing down on his Icelandic command, a key ally suddenly bowing out of the fight, and all he says is, 'Well, we'll have to deploy some forces east.'

In the lead up to Arrival, Iceland had been turned into a citadel. Stationed there were two squadrons of F-15s, two squadrons of F-22s, two squadrons of F-16s (Air National Guard), and a squadron of A-10 Warthogs. On the ground were several battalions of Hawk, Patriot, and Patriot-3 missile batteries. There were also two batteries of THAAD missile launchers. Scattered throughout the island and concentrated at key points were THEL lasers and an American version of the Israeli Iron Dome anti-missile system. Garrisoning the island was the entire 2nd Marine Expeditionary Force. At sea were two surface action groups, each centered on a Ticonderoga-Class Guided Missile Cruiser. While Iceland's right flank was now wide open the left flank still held. Stationed at Greenland was one squadron of Canadian F-18Cs and one of Danish F-16s (it was their territory after all).

On a hunch, I got Roger, that scrawny, self loathing misanthrope of a human- and my editor, to send me to Iceland. I spent my middle years reading techno thrillers on flights to journalistic hot spots like Beirut and Managua, so I appreciated the importance of Iceland to transatlantic communications. I figured if the aliens did mean war, they'd have to hit Iceland; that way North America and Europe would be cut off from one another.

I was right.

So Ureth cursed and stomped for a while until he ran out of steam and said, 'I better get to my HQ.'

'I think so.' Lutch nodded.

Lutch ordered a Patriot battery that had been held in reserve to redeploy for the east coast and scrambled some F-22s to cover. Then he waited.

I realized that the story wasn't happening in the HQ anymore, and asked my PAO, a public affairs guy detailed to babysit us, if we could head out and find some action. I say 'us' because Roger sent a cameraman with me. The PAO was a young officer, a nice southern kid who said he wanted to get into TV journalism after the army, use the GI to get a degree in communications.

'What the hell for?' I had asked him. 'I'm a college dropout, and I produce news videos all the time.'

He gave a big spiel about Keith Olberman or some such. Like I said, nice kid. I only hope he doesn't get suckered into J-School.

Anyhow, my PAO guy, Scott, took me out of the HQ to his Humvee. Waiting there for us was my cameraman, or I should say, camera girl. Denny, Denise was her real name but she always called herself Denny, something about not wanting people to think she was a trashy Jersey Girl. She sat behind the Humvee with her gear spread out before her. Laying there were two bags, two digital cameras, a tripod, and assorted lenses, which she was meticulously cleaning. Denny took her work seriously. She first got the editor's attention with a You-Tube video that went viral. You see, she figured she could get her college administration to ban reruns of the Sopranos because it was anti-Italian, or something. Denny even got them to hold hearings before she revealed the prank, for which she was thrown out of school. She wasn't a conservative activist so to speak, she wasn't the kind to read Hayek or anything. Denny was just a prankster. She liked tattoos, tights, boots, halter-tops, and black leather jackets. Denny turned a lot of heads on Iceland. Hell, she turned my head. Behind her back I referred to her as my 'camera hottie.'

As Scott and I approached, Denny looked up from her gear. I clapped my hands and said, 'Let's mount up!'

Denny sprung to her feet and packed up her cameras and assorted equipment. We all got in the Humvee. Scott drove.

'Where're we goin?' Denny asked from the back seat.

'Scott?' I asked.

'My orders are to take you wherever you want.'

'What about those hills east of Reykjavik? We'll get a good view of things, should keep us clear of the fighting.'

'Alright.'

So we drove out from Keflavik east along the highway. We passed a lot of SAM batteries and just outside of the city, a Marine mechanized battalion, all hunkered down with their vehicles under camo netting. By the time we drove past Reykjavik air raid sirens were blaring. We kept heading east until we got to Pingvallavatn Lake, a large body of water about twenty miles inland. We set up on a small hill nearby. Behind us was a range of mountains, to our front facing north was the lake and a grassy, mossy plain bracketed by a river in the far distance. We knew there were some Patriot batteries behind us, and we could see military vehicles moving to our north. So we thought there would be plenty of action for us to film and report on.

Denny got her equipment set up. As the sun was going down I asked Scott, 'Any reason why we can't start a fire? It's going to be cold.'

Scott shrugged. 'I don't see why not.'

Denny and me gathered scrub brush and sticks and got a small fire going. She made hot chocolate. I warmed my hands. After a while she said, 'Well this is boring. Maybe we picked the wrong place, Scott?'

Scott shrugged. 'I'm a PAO not a general. I take you where you want to go. You want to go someplace else, I'll take you there.'

I was too old to ask something like what I asked, but I did anyway. 'Can you get on the radio, find out what's happening, see if we can get close to the action?'

'I can try.'

'Hey look at that!' Denny shouted.

The northern sky flashed yellow, and in the distance we could see flashes on the ground and then rocket trails. These were followed by more flashes and distant booming sounds. Denny trained her camera on the northern sky. A minute later we heard jet engines in the distance. Then we saw a quartet of jets flying low about five miles to our west; they were moving fast and were practically level with us. These were followed by another quartet of jets and then another.

I grabbed a mic and as Denny recorded, did a quick report about what was going on around us. We gave it a quick edit on the IPad and dashed it off to the office.

A few minutes later my cell phone rang, it was Roger.

'What the fuck was that!' he screamed. 'All hell is breaking lose over here and you send me a report about distant explosions!'

'Uhhhhh,' replied I.

'Get up there and get the story god damn it!'

He hung up.

'What'd the boss say?' Denny asked.

I flashed my trademark sarcastic smile, 'Says great work. Keep it up.'

Scott walked back to the Humvee and started working his Blackberry.

For my part I walked over to Denny's impromptu campfire, 'Having fun yet?' I asked.

Denny looked up at me and smiled in the firelight. With the distant explosions Denny's tune had changed. 'This is great!' she said.

'Just wait till we get up close to some fighting,' I replied. 'That'll be great alright.'

I don't think Denny got the irony I was trying to convey. 'Sure will be.'

I blame myself.

While Denny enthusiastically taped every flash of light and explosion she saw, I sat in the passenger seat and dozed. At dawn I got out of the Humvee. I saw Denny and Scott both sitting at the campfire.

I walked over to them.

'Glad to see you awake, sir,' Scott said.

'Knock off the 'sir' shit, will you?'

'Sorry, can't stop thinking of you that way.'

'What the hell for?'

'You're the same age as my dad.'

I hung my head in shame.

'Geezer,' Denny helpfully added.

'Any news?'

'My guy over at HQ says the Jai just hung out a hundred miles off the coast and flung missiles at the island.'

'Meaning?'

'Meaning we were just being probed.'

'Heh, heh… probed,' Denny laughed.

'What are we, in junior high?'

'Would you like that, perv?' She laughed again.

Scott's pocket beeped. He reached inside and took out his Blackberry. After looking at the number he held up a finger as if to say 'one minute' and walked away from the fire. He talked for a few minutes, turned to me and said, 'Great news! I have a friend with one of the PAC-3s. Says we can hang out with his battery so long as we stay out of the way.'

'How'd you pull that off?' I asked.

'Had to promise a few favors, including some camera time from you all.'

'Doable.'

'He said come on over anytime.'

We got in the Humvee and drove north.

Denny sat in the back watching last night's footage.

'Why don't you sleep while you can?' I asked.

'Can't sleep, must edit,' she said robotically.

I turned to Scott, 'Any news?'

'Hold on,' he said. He took out his Blackberry. 'Hey, Carl? This is Scott. Yeah…me too. Anyhow, can you get a news summary together and shoot it over to my Blackberry…of course I mean now…ok ok…yeah I can do that.… alright, bye.' He put the phone back in his pocket. 'I'll have a write up for you shortly.'

We drove on for a few more minutes. Scott's Blackberry beeped. He picked it up off the seat and said, 'Ah here it is.'

He handed me the Blackberry.

'Scott, if I may ask, why are you busting your hump for us?'

He shrugged yet again. 'It's my job.'

I called out the bullshit I was seeing, 'Bullshit.'

'Bullshit?'

'I've dealt with PAOs in half a dozen other countries; none of 'em ever did more than the bare minimum, so what gives?'

Meekly he said, 'I'm hoping down the road you might be able to help me out with a network job.'

I laughed.

'What's so funny?'

'You know, Scott, I'm not exactly welcome in most network newsrooms. I call up my old boss in Chicago, he'd hang up on me. My last gig for WFIE they had security escort me out. I can still hear the manager shouting at me to stay the hell away from the interns.'

In the back Denny clapped her hands and laughed. 'That's why he has to work for our little internet outfit! Ha!'

'Shut up, you.'

We continued north for about half an hour, passing several convoys along the way. We topped a ridge before which opened a great plain. Running along the ridge were half a dozen PAC-3 launchers. When Scott stopped the Humvee, I turned around only to see that Denny had fallen asleep.

'Wake up!' I shouted.

They had quite an impressive setup there on top of that ridge. There were half a dozen truck driven trailers, each carrying four missile canisters with four missiles per canister. They were concealed under thick, gray/green camo netting. There were several command trucks and trailers, a radio antenna, and a radar array. A large truck mounted crane was in the process of removing spent canisters from one launcher. A truck with missile reloads waited nearby. Several hundred soldiers were present. Some worked on the trucks, others milled about. Scott beeped and flashed his lights. A soldier came out of one of the trailers and waved.

Scott talked with the soldier and then came back to the Humvee. 'He says to park over by the command trailer and stay out of the way. We can interview whoever we like so long as we don't send out any info about the battalion's pos.'

'Sure thing.'

After interviewing Scott's contact, Denny, and I walked around. She was popular with the crewman; they talked to her until an officer or noncom told them to stop.

'Guess we got plenty of man on the missile battery interviews huh?' she laughed at her own joke. Scott laughed too, though nervously. I noticed that Scott stuck by her side the whole time.

After an hour or so we had a decent story. Denny and I put it together, did some quick taping of me talking, and sent it in to Roger. Basically this missile battalion sat tight throughout most of the night's battle and only got to fire when a Jai ship came in toward Keflavik. The crewmen thought it was something smaller than the big bastards we've heard rumors about over the poles. Then they fired a half dozen Patriots. No one thought they had hit anything. There were some large explosions in the sky, but that was from the Jai shooting the missiles down.

'You see any of our guys getting hit?' I asked a specialist we were interviewing.

'Yeah,' he replied. 'Saw a huge explosion about fifteen miles east, where Battery C had been stationed.' He shook his head. 'I don't think they made it.'

We got a lot of footage like that, edited it together, and sent it off to Roger. My phone rang a few minutes later.

'What the fuck is this?' Roger demanded.

'You don't like it?'

'You ain't doin' some post-tornado interview for some hick Kentucky TV station. Get out there, get up front, and get me some goddamn riveting footage. Comprende?'

'Yeah.' I said. 'So you're not going to use it?'

'Oh it will go up,' he said. 'I hyped the whole man on Iceland angle for two weeks, so what your sending me has to go up on the site.'

'Thanks.'

'You're just lucky,' he said. 'Now get to work.'

After that I tried to get an interview with the battery commander, but he was way too busy. We decided to leave. Denny and I talked it over and decided to go into Reykjavik. We had a couple of rooms there, and both me and Denny could use a change of clothes. On the way in, there was some sort of Jai attack, so we pulled over and hid out in a drainage ditch for more than an hour. We didn't see anything except some air force jets flying low. When the all clear came over the airwaves Scott called the HQ to find out what had happened.

'They thought the Jai were making a big move on Iceland; turns out they were sending one of those ships against Scandinavia,' he said.

When we got into town, the streets were deserted except for the military, so it only took us a few minutes to get to our hotel. After showering and changing, we took to the streets. A battalion of Marines was garrisoning the town, and road blocks were at all the major intersections. The Iceland Crisis Response Unit, a small peace keeping outfit that had been expanded to include several hundred men and the local police, were on the beat too. The locals weren't talking, and the Marines we approached gave us that 'keep moving or I'll blow your head off' look I used to see in places like Somalia and Croatia.

So we went to our hotel's bar.

The bartender was surprised to see us but seemed grateful for the company. I ordered a gin and tonic. Denny ordered a shot of whisky, downed it, and then asked for another, which she also downed.

'Where did you learn to drink like that?' I asked as I took a dainty, girly-man sip of gin and tonic.

'When I was in high school, I dated a lot of older men.'

'What about you?' I asked Scott. 'You drinkin?'

'I'm on duty.'

Denny punched him in the arm. 'Aw c'mon Scotty, have a round on us.'

Scott visibly blushed but declined. Instead he ordered a coke.

The TV there was on the BBC, which showed lots of pictures of things on fire, like cities and what not, and maps indicating where the conflagrations were. A professorial looking commentator seemed indignant that the Limeys were still out of the fight.

After a while Scott's Blackberry rang. 'Yeah,' he said. 'OK….ok….right…. thanks.' He hung up. 'My contact at HQ says something's brewing.'

'Like what?' I asked.

'Says he's not sure, but we definitely want to be in a place to see it.'

'Well let's get out of here then and get going,' Denny hopped off her stool.

I got my wallet out of my pocket and took out the company credit card Roger reluctantly authorized for me.

'Can we get the tab?' I asked. 'Oh, and can you convert it to soda and burgers?'

The bartender said he couldn't.

Screw it, I thought and handed him the card.

'So where to?' Scott asked.

I remembered the verbal tongue lashing Roger had given me about getting up front. A smarter, more idealistic man would have listened. Not me.

'Why don't we just head up to the roof?'

Denny was incredulous.

'With all this going on you want to—'

'Steady, kid,' I interrupted. 'If they hit Keflavik, we'll have a great view. If they hit something to the north, we'll have a great view. Either way, you'll get some good footage.'

She thought about it and nodded. 'OK.'

'Besides,' said I, 'we can set up some chairs, get nice and comfy, maybe some cocktails.'

'Lush.'

So we set up shop on the roof of our hotel.

Here's what we saw. There were a lot of flashes on the ground; to our front and on both the right and left, great bursts of light followed by rocket contrails into the sky. During the previous launches we would see a quick burst of rockets and then nothing else. But not now. This time the army was really pouring on the fire, and missile after missile streaked upward. The launches were inevitably followed by explosions on the ground as the Jai found each launch site and destroyed it. There were sonic booms above as air force jets joined the fight. Lots of jets were knocked out of the sky. This went on for more than an hour. Eventually there was a great fireball in the sky, an explosion, then a ground shattering crash to the north. I of course did my full Edward R. Murrow. Denny videotaped me reporting on the battle above with plenty of 'Look over there!' and 'Oh my gosh!' and 'What was that?'

When we sent it in, Roger was marginally more satisfied with the effort.

In the morning Scott got the lowdown on what had happened. 'One of those big Jai carrier ships came down into the atmosphere with the intent of bombarding the island.'

'Intent?' I asked, 'It did.'

'Let me finish.'

Scott briefed us.

General Lutch threw just about everything he had at the ship, and a great battle developed as the ship hovered just off the northwest coast. Patriots, THAADS, jets, Midcourse Interceptors, you name it got into the fight. The Danes and Canadians out of Greenland even got into the act. Well, someone got lucky and inflicted a catastrophic hit on the carrier ship and it crashed about fifty miles up the coast from Reykjavik.

'Now, don't say I never did anything for you,' Scott said. 'But I have clearance to take you over there right now.'

Denny screamed and threw her arms and legs around Scott. 'You are so awesome!' she shouted.

Scott blushed.

Denny packed up her gear. In a minute we were on the road.

It took more than an hour to get to the crash site. The road was strewn with military wreckage, a Humvee here, an APC there, MP roadblocks, and once we were nearly driven into a ditch by a convoy of trucks making their way south. We passed a lot of smoldering equipment on the side of the road and sometimes large craters. We had pulled over next to a crater to take some photos and talked to a couple of tired looking soldiers. They pointed to the debris field around us and said this was where their missile battery had been. The Jai had hit it with those same annoying whistle bombs we'd heard all night, obliterating the battery and killing everyone in the unit except them. They did a quick interview on camera before we got on our way.

When we got near the coast we were stopped by the MPs. Scott explained who we were. They escorted us in. You could tell something big was going on because there were plenty of helicopters in the air and jets overhead, I counted at least three pairs of F-16s. On the ground there were lots of Marines—including tanks. We topped a small rise and there in the surf was a Jai carrier ship. It lay on its side. There were great black marks down its hull. At least ten feet of the bow had been blasted off. Smoke rose from the ship in several places.

Denny hopped out of the Humvee and took pictures.

The MPs kept an eye on us.

'It crashed down beach,' Scott said, he pointed north to a big pile of sand that had been turned up, 'and rolled a few hundred over to where it is now.'

'Controlled landing?'

'I guess.'

'Hey who are those guys?' Denny asked.

We looked down the beach, maybe a quarter of mile, to where dozens of people were sitting. A half dozen ambulances were parked nearby. They were surrounded by armed Marines.

'Holy shit!' she said. 'I think those are aliens!'

She got a pair of binoculars out of her sack and trained them down the beach. 'Aliens! Aliens do you believe it?'

'Wow,' I said as I took the binoculars form her.

They looked more or less human, though it was hard to tell at that distance. They had two arms and two legs anyway; their heads looked more elongated than a human's. All seemed to be wearing uniforms, some green, most were blue. Separated from the main group a row of aliens lay dead on the ground.

'Got to get down there!' Denny shouted.

'She's right,' I said.

'Gee, I don't know,' said Scott.

I could see him wavering, and I tried a bit of manipulation.

'Any journalist worth a damn is going to get down there and try to talk to those aliens. Now, do you want to be a TV journalist or not? This is where we find out what you're made of.'

Unfair of me to pull that on the young kid, I know, but hey, I had a job to do.

Scott went over and talked to the MPs. They were commanded by a woman lieutenant.

'Are you out of your freaking mind?' she asked.

I went over there to lend a hand.

'C'mon, Lieutenant,' I said to the MP. 'Don't you want to be famous?'

'Famous?'

'Yeah you take us over to the aliens, and you can give us the tour, on camera.'

The MP rubbed her chin, 'Hmmmmm...' she seemed intrigued.

Never fails, I thought.

'Alright, I can't get you in on my own. But I can talk to my CO.'

'You sure you can get him to let us over there?'

She flashed a toothy grin. 'He's an old guy and has no idea how to deal with strong women.'

'And cute,' I said.

'I'll be right back,' she replied.

Denny punched me in the arm. 'Knock it off,' she said.

'Can't blame a guy for trying.'

And then the sky exploded. Denny and I were thrown to the ground by the force of a shockwave. The next thing I remember is some kind of strange streaking sound. I looked up to see a Jai ship, about the size of a 747, hovering over the beach and spitting fire. I saw a Humvee explode, followed by a pair of Bradley Fighting Vehicles. A burst of fire from the Jai ship knocked a dozen engineers off the crashed carrier. Another burst blew up a couple of Blackhawk helicopters that had landed on the beach. There was a second screeching sound and then a third. I saw two more of those Jai ships. One landed on the beach near where the captured aliens were. To their credit, the Marines didn't run; they just got down on the deck and returned fire, not that their rifles did much good against the ship. I looked over and saw the MP lieutenant lying in a heap on the sand. Her head was gone.

Being young and fearless, Denny crawled over to the sand dune and trained her camera on the unfolding battle. Since I was middle aged and terrified, I curled up into ball until she shouted. 'Get up here you pussy!' Well, even a journalist like me wasn't going to let his manhood get questioned by an over-talented college girl. I managed to uncurl myself and crawl up beside her.

A small battle had erupted before us. Rifle and machinegun fire came from many quarters. Marines seemed to be coming from everywhere, running past us to the sound of the guns. A pair of Marines set up a 50-caliber machinegun not ten yards from where Denny and I were hunkered down. A moment later artillery shells impacted on the beach. Then a platoon of Bradleys drove up to the dune and opened up with 20mm cannons and missiles on the three Jai ships. I saw one missile explode right on top of the Jai bomber hovering over the crashed carrier ship. By this time, despite the hail of fire, the second Jai bomber landed on the beach. Soldiers got out of the belly of the bomber and returned the Marine's fire. The whole dune to our right seemed to explode in a blizzard of sand. I buried my head in my hands, but Denny kept filming and got great footage of the Jai from the downed carrier getting on board the bomber. The ship slowly lifted off the beach and headed into the sky. The other two bombers continued to return fire until the first had escaped. By then rockets and SAMs had come into play. The bomber over the beach shot down the first two incoming missiles but a third and then a fourth got through its defenses. Its port wing was blown right off. The bomber crash-landed onto the beach. Seeing the fate of its wingman the last bomber, the one over the carrier ship, gained altitude, fired its afterburners and escaped the fight.

There was one last explosion, this one so fierce it picked me up and threw me back several yards. I landed with a thud. When I finally got my breath back I knelt and frantically looked around for Denny. She had crawled back over to the top of the dune and was filming the chaos on the beach. I crawled over and saw that the wreck of the carrier ship had been blown in half, each was now burning out of control.

'You get all that?' I asked

'What do you take me for?' She lowered her camera and packed it in the bag.

'We got to get this back to Roger,' I said, 'Even that sorry, unappeasable son of a bitch will have to like this.'

'Just think of the headline,' she said. 'Military Lets Captured Aliens Escape.'

'Hey, where's Scott?'

From a clump of tall grass a few yards away we saw a hand go up. 'Over here,' Scott whimpered.

Denny and I ran over to him. We found Scott lying on his back. Blood poured out of his nose and from his lower lip.

'Oh, you poor thing!' Denny shouted. She knelt down beside Scott and hugged him. I don't know if he noticed, but I saw the kid smile. *Good man*, I thought.

After patching up Scott, we got some more footage of burning tanks and APCs, smoldering air frames, a lot of dead Marines, ambulances, and frantic medical teams. Denny recorded me doing a quick report with the smoldering carrier ship in the background before we headed back to the Humvee. She edited the footage and got it ready to go on our way back to Keflavik.

My phone rang ten minutes later. As soon as I picked up the phone I heard Roger's pleasant voice. 'Why the hell couldn't you get footage of the ship crashing!' he shouted. 'I got tape of Jai ships exploding over the North Pole, crashing on Long Island. Some enterprising kid in South Africa sent me a tape of Jai vehicles in Cape Town. Why can't you ever be where you need to be when news happens?'

'Gee thanks, Roger,' I said over his berating. 'You're right, that was dangerous work by me and this twenty-year-old girl you sent with me to Iceland. I'll pass your thanks along.' Roger was still yelling as I hung up the phone.

'Well it's not every day you get a compliment like that from the boss,' I said to Denny and Scott.

'Really?' Denny asked.

'Oh sure,' said I. Denny believed every word. I wondered how it was that she wasn't living in a trailer someplace with a toddler on her hip, lighting up a Marlboro Light 100. 'So now what?' I asked.

'Why don't we hang at the general's HQ?' Denny asked. 'See if we can get a story.'

'Good idea, kiddo,' I said.

'Don't call me kiddo.'

'Can you get us back in, Scott?'

He reached for his Blackberry. 'Let me make a call.'

Scott got up, chatted on his Blackberry for a few minutes, made another call, and talked more. When he was done with the second call he turned to us and said. 'OK, you can get in, but no cameras and—'

I cut him off, 'Stay out of the way?'

'Yep.'

'No cameras?' asked an incredulous Denny.

Scott looked disappointed. 'Sorry.'

'But we can report on what we see, right?' I asked.

'So long as I look it over first.'

'Sounds fair.' I stood up. 'OK, let's head over there.'

As we rolled up to the command bunker, we saw several missile contrails streaking into the sky. We heard several sonic booms as air force jets raced north. Just as we stepped into the bunker there was a series of large, loud explosions to the northwest.

In contrast to what was happening outside, inside the bunker everything was calm. Technicians sat at their computers. A few aids walked back and forth between the banks of terminals. General Lutch stood before a large flat screen. He sipped a cup of tea as a pair of red dots made their way down the island's northwestern coast.

He sipped his tea and said, 'Keep the fire coming.' A blue triangle off the coast flashed. A second later a sinking ship icon appeared next to it. 'Damn,' said Lutch.

'What does that mean?' I asked Scott.

'Means one of the S-A-Gs just lost a ship.'

'S-A-Gs?' Denny asked.

'Surface Action Groups.'

We weren't supposed to bring any recording devices into the bunker, but I still had my cell phone on me. As things got tense I hit the record button. I'm not sure who Lutch was on the phone with, but it was someone high up for sure. There was a lot of military talk but basically two Jai ships, one of those big carriers and what turned out to be a transport, were making their way along the coast.

Here's the money quote, 'Tell the national command authority that I need my nukes released...that's right...this is a formal request...Hold on? I need to fire now... OK....OK....No I haven't asked the Icelanders...I don't have time for this...alright.'

He hung up the phone and issued orders. 'Alright, weapons free. Nuke those incoming ships.'

Getting right to the heart of the matter as far as I was concerned, I asked Scott, 'Any danger to us?'

'I dunno.'

We heard air raid sirens.

What exactly they fired I didn't know at the time. I later learned that one of the cruisers in the surface action group fired off a trio of nuclear tipped cruise missiles. The nukes nabbed a pair of smaller ships, those bombers that were about to cause so much trouble for the Marines, but the carrier ship and the landing ship, survived. The nukes scared them off, though, and the Jai withdrew into space.

A few hours later they came back. This time a barrage of missiles preceded them. These took out suspected missile sites and troop concentrations. The missile attack was followed up by Jai bombers. A great air battle erupted over the island. Denny went outside and shot some footage but all she was able to get was contrails and some distant explosions. She did capture some footage of a parachute, one of ours. General Lutch kept throwing aircraft in the fight, with heavy casualties resulting, but it wasn't enough, and the Jai were able to seize control of the air.

With air superiority achieved a pair of Jai carriers escorted a landing ship into the atmosphere. Lutch had one last surprise for them though. While the invasion force was still in the upper atmosphere, he committed a squadron of ASAT armed F-15 Eagles. None of the missiles got through, but they did complicate the Jai descent, forcing them to pause while they dealt with the Eagles. This last ditch effort was joined by a battalion of THAAD missiles, and finally, the battery of Mid-Course Interceptors that had been deployed to the island. They scored a couple of hits on one of the carriers, but that was all. The Jai landed at Stadur, a village at the head of a deep fjord on the northern coast about eighty miles from Reykjavik. One carrier stayed behind with the assault ship.

A Marine battalion was stationed nearby and within minutes a recon team was on sight and beaming footage back to Lutch. Denny and I saw it projected on the big flat screen. Two ships lay at anchor in the fjord. They were massive. Actually the landing ship was even larger than the carrier. A pair of great doors were open. A causeway had been erected to the shore, across it moved vehicles, one by one. The camera man zoomed in on one vehicle; it was some sort of tank. On the shore were soldiers, alien soldiers carrying rifles and clad in body armor. You could clearly see Jai giving orders and directing squads to different points on the shore.

'Looks like an invasion,' said Lutch.

'We could try nuking the site,' said one of his aids.

'Na, they've no doubt thought of that. We'd just be wasting our nukes. We'll hold tight for now.' He adjusted his glasses. 'Get me General Ureth.'

Lutch consulted with General Ureth. Here's what he said, 'Yes, by all means, fight them. Use your discretion as far as committing forces, but I want you to keep a couple of battalions in reserve in case we need them….OK….their target? Impossible to say for sure but they are most likely driving on Keflavik…. OK good, and, General, good luck…'

Denny elbowed me. 'You know where we have to get.'

'Yeah, I know.'

'So let's go.'

'Scott,' I asked, 'can you get us embedded with one of these Marine outfits.'

He nodded. 'Shouldn't be a problem.'

Denny tugged my arm like a six year old. 'C'mon.'

'Just wait Denny. First we have to get a report ready about the landing, then we head out.'

'OK.'

We recorded a quick report and sent it off to Roger.

Denny, Scott and I hooked up with the 1st Battalion, 8th Marines. Together with the three other battalions of the 8th Marines the 1st was deployed right in front of the Jai advance and told to slow it down so other battalions could hit it in the flank. Later, I was able to talk to one of General Ureth's aids who debriefed me on the battle. Basically Ureth had deployed the division across the entire island with the basic unit of maneuver, his term, being a battalion. When the Jai landed, each battalion 'marched to the sound of the guns.' He went on to say, 'We couldn't concentrate force the way we wanted, but in a way it was better. The Jai never knew which direction a counterattack was coming from. Besides if we had been deployed as a whole division, that would have been too good of a target.' The first major battle was fought by that battalion deployed near the landing zone. For the most part they stayed hidden, and after the main alien column had pushed south, they made a mad dash for the beach. They never got close. Once they were spotted the Jai carrier simply fired a massive barrage of kinetic warheads.

The next two days were hell. I'd describe them, but I can't, not really. I don't really remember them. I mean I do, but in my head the chronology is jumbled, doesn't make sense, at least not until the last few hours. It's just a jumble of images, exploding tanks, singed Marines, MRAPs, and Bradley fighting vehicles getting vaporized. We shot miles of footage, but none it really tells the whole story. We got tape of gun flashes, explosions in the distance, that sort of thing. On the first night we were asked to help with the wounded. I'll never talk about that.

One incident has always stuck out in my mind. We were about thirty miles north of Reykjavik and the 8th Marines had just halted the Jai advance. From our position maybe a hundred yards behind the line we saw Marines concealed in the rocks, firing Javelin missiles and laying down machinegun fire as best they could. Anyone who stuck his head out got it shot off. The Marines held out like that for several minutes. Finally a platoon of M-1 Tanks crested the ridge on our right and came down toward the plain. Behind them a line of Bradleys took the ridge and lay down covering fire for a few seconds before they too descended the slope. A second tank platoon appeared, followed by a second Bradley platoon. Infantry deployed along the ridge and threw out a wall of lead. The tankers and Bradley crewmen fired their guns as long as they could. Amazingly commanders stood up in the cupolas of their tanks and fired the .50-caliber machineguns. But it was like feeding hamburger into a meat grinder. The tanks and Bradleys kept exploding; I doubt a single vehicle made it to the bottom of the ridge. Even after all their vehicles were destroyed, the infantry stayed atop the ridge and poured fire into the enemy. Eventually the entire ridge exploded in a ball of fire. In this way an entire Marine battalion was annihilated. I don't know what the hell I was watching, but it certainly wasn't war. I like to tell myself it meant something, and I know the Marines think it did. Heck they talk about Iceland the same way they do about Tripoli, Iwo Jima, Chosin, and Fallujah.

By the beginning of the third day more than four thousand Marines were dead, and the Jai had pushed all the way to the outskirts of Reykjavik. To the Marine's disappointment, Ureth, after consulting with Lutch, decided not to fight for the city. 'If they had any brains, they'd just bypass us,' Ureth said afterwards. 'If they went into Reykjavik, we'd get a lot of civilians killed.' So we—forgive me, but I was shot up just as much as the Marines were—we pulled back to the line of volcanic mountains running southwest from Reykjavik. Ureth figured the Jai would make dash for Keflavik and was going to make his stand there.

Denny, Scott, and I followed a battered, heavy weapons platoon up the mountain. The position bristled with machineguns and Javelin missiles. Where we were, you could see down the mountains and right to the coast about five miles away. Geysers and hot springs dotted the range, and the Marines hoped these would help conceal their position from Jai sensors.

When the Jai came out of Reykjavik that afternoon the entire north face of the mountain range came alive with fire. Once more groups of tanks and other vehicles flung themselves at the advancing Jai. From my perch, I saw several Jai vehicles explode. They called in their own air support, but the heat and steam from the open geysers played havoc with their sensors, hiding us better than any camouflage could. Between the withering fire from the mountain range and the Marine's kamikaze style armored attack, the Jai were forced to pull back. It was the first time they'd been forced to retreat.

The Jai doubled down on the attack and that evening sent an even larger force. One half of their armored thrust broke off from the main group and came right toward us. I counted forty-four armored vehicles of various types. They lashed the mountain range with cannon and laser fire. Even so, the Marines stayed put and fought back and once more unleashed a torrent of missiles and machinegun fire. It looked like the main thrust down the coast road was going to break through when General Lutch sprung a little surprise in the form of a flight of tank busting A-10 Warthogs. The ugly jets came in low and unleashed hell from their chain cannons. Denny zoomed in and got a great shot of a Jai tank as it was hammered by depleted uranium rounds and enveloped in a cloud of dust. When the cloud lifted you could see smoke billowing from several bullet holes. Of course the Warthog pilots were on a suicide mission, and not one made it back. But their appearance seemed to stun the Jai and they retreated. The group facing us on the mountain range withdrew as well.

Denny and I did a quick report with her footage of the Jai tank being destroyed as the lead in, but when we tried to send it out, all we got were error messages.

'Damn it!' Denny shouted.

'I guess the network is down,' I said.

'Yep,' said Scott.

'Can we go back to command bunker, send it out from there?'

Scott thought about it for a minute. 'Well, it's not like I can call and find out, so we'd have to head over there.'

Denny and I looked at each other and nodded. 'OK.'

We hopped in our Humvee and left the Marines on the mountain.

I took, and still take, a lot of heat for that. Every day of my life I wish I'd stayed up there, or tried to talk those Marines into coming with us or...I don't know. It wasn't cowardly. I'm a journalist, I had a report to file, and it was my responsibility to my craft to get my report out to the world.

That's what I tell myself.

By then it was nighttime. We pulled over several times for vehicles heading toward the front, or ambulances heading away. We were just a few miles away from Keflavik when we heard a massive explosion. Scott pulled over and we watched in horror as the Jai bombarded the mountain range from space. You could see the mountains several miles behind us, exploding in great geysers of fire and rock. The very ground beneath us shook. I thought the Jai were using nukes. Later we found out that they were just hitting the Marines with kinetic energy bombs, nothing more complicated that steel cylinders fired at tremendous speed. The whistle sound they made pierced the air like nothing I'd ever heard.

After annihilating our forces on the mountain range, the Jai laid down a 'rolling barrage' of whistle bombs from Reykjavik west down the peninsula toward the air base. By the time we got to Keflavik, Marines there and even Air Force personnel were digging trenches and fortifying buildings. Scott got us back into the bunker. No one noticed; there was too much happening. As we set up shop in an out of the way corner of the bunker I overhead General Lutch on the phone with Ureth.

'They're coming, though? Do you have anything left? Two battalions... OK...OK...Hold them as long as you can.'

A pair of red arrows on the flat screen map pointed right at Keflavik.

Denny edited the footage and then filmed me doing a quick report from inside the bunker. Very dramatic, I thought, and I figured a nice final calling card for an otherwise disappointing career in journalism. I expressed those sentiments to Denny.

'What do you mean?' she asked.

'I thought I'd be anchoring *Nightline* by now.'

'What's *Nightline?*'

'Never mind. Let's just say I ain't all that happy with where I've ended up.'

'You stupid old Balding Boomer,' she said. 'I'd kill to have your job. I've been watching you since we got here. You have any idea how much I admire you? Idiot.'

I blushed.

'Just get that report off to Roger, will you.'

We sent out the report on the military's transatlantic cables, thanks to Scott. After that things got dicey. The Jai flung missiles at Keflavik, nothing like those monsters we saw before, just missiles with warheads large enough to destroy buildings and what not. One by one they knocked the base installations to the ground. The command bunker shook with the force of each blast. When the bombardment finally stopped, Denny ran out of the bunker to get some footage. A worried Scott chased after her. Not knowing what else to do, and not seeing much point in doing anything else, I followed them. The base was aflame. Almost every building from airplane hangars to the barracks and rec hall had been obliterated.

'Only folks I ever saw who were this thorough about blowing stuff up was our guys,' I said.

'Shut up,' said Denny, 'Look at that.'

I looked over to where she pointed her camera. A few hundred yards away a pair of haggard airmen ran over to a flagpole. The flag atop the poll had been singed by an explosion that reduced a nearby building to smoldering rubble. Despite the heat from the fire the airmen lowered the burnt flag and attached the new one. While one airman raised the flag the other saluted. I'll be dammed if airmen, soldiers, and Marines all over the battered airstrip didn't do the same.

'You get that?' I asked.

'You think I'm some kind of amateur?'

'Yes.'

'Yeah I got it.'

I patted her on the shoulder. 'Good, then let's get back to the command bunker and send it out.'

'Hold on, I—'

'Let's do it now, Denny, while we still can. You just took the most famous footage since the firemen raising the flag at Ground Zero.'

Inside the bunker all seemed lost. Men slumped at their computer consuls. In one corner I saw an officer silently weeping. General Lutch stood before a flat screen projected map and looked as impassive as ever.

The news was not good. There was some rough, hilly terrain just south and southeast of Keflavik. This is where Ureth made his stand. Anticipating such a move the Jai blasted the position from space as their armored column moved against Keflavik. With the Marines out of the way there was nothing to stop the Jai from driving right on Keflavik. By the time we got our footage uploaded and sent off to Roger, a last ditch defense was being mounted in the village of Volgar, a few miles east of us on the coast. After meeting a torrent of missile and machinegun fire the Jai pulled back.

'Alright, they're stopped,' I heard Lutch say, 'But they're just waiting for air support. When that arrives it's all over…Yes, Madam President. No, ma'am, I don't think there's anything you can do. It means a lot asking, though, Madam President. I'll tell the men….My plan?…I'm going to nuke the base….no, ma'am, no, Madam President, we can't let the Jai have this base….thank you, Madam President.' He hung up the phone.

Scott laughed.

'What's funny?' I asked.

'You may be a cynical, gin-swilling son of a bitch, but you sure are gonna die a hero.'

Denny laughed too.

A light flashed on the map, and a dozen new icons appeared over the eastern end of the island. Then another dozen appeared.

'Damn, they're really going to paste us,' said Scott.

'Go out with bang,' said I. I wished I still carried a flask.

One of the airmen at the bank of terminals jumped up out of his seat and shouted, 'Yeeehaaaa!'

'What the?' Lutch said.

Before he could finish the airmen shouted, 'Listen, General!' He flipped a switch so the entire bunker could hear the audio.

A terribly English voice spoke, 'Hello there. Iceland Command, this is Typhoon Strike Leader, Royal Air Force.'

Lutch took the airman's headset, 'Strike Leader, this is Iceland, over.'

'I'm leading a squadron of Typhoon fighters. We're armed and ready for action.'

'Strike Leader, it's good to hear you. If you can, hit that fjord on the northwest of the island where the Jai have that big bastard parked.'

'Copy that, will do, Iceland. Tally Ho!' he said to the squadron. 'Weapons free. We shall fire a volley and close in.'

A second later the screen came alive with red blips as each Typhoon fighter fired off a pair of missiles.

'Iceland, be advised that a squadron of Tornado bombers is being me, where would you like them?'

'Strike Leader, there's a large Jai armored column scattered along the main highway from Reykjavik to my pos. Can you attack?'

'Certainly, Iceland. Also be advised, within an hour transports will be arriving.'

'What are they carrying, Strike Leader?

'Paratroopers, Iceland.'

'On behalf of the Marines, I thank you, Strike Leader.'

'No need, Iceland. And sorry for arriving late to the show. Just like you Yanks in the World Wars isn't it? Ha!'

'Very funny, Strike Leader...'

There was enthusiastic cheering throughout the bunker as men and women who a few seconds before knew they were about to die got another chance for life. Denny and Scott embraced one another and jumped up and down. After several seconds of this, Scott allowed himself a horrible breakdown of military discipline and kissed her. Fortunately, no one noticed. They were all watching as the RAF spread out across the island and dealt death to the Jai.

Me, I remembered my vocation, grabbed Denny's camera, and ran outside the bunker. There was news to be reported.

The Battle of the Atlantic has seemingly been won, if just, by Allied forces. The question is now, where will the Jai strike next?

Analysis from the Alexandrian Defense Group

Chapter 6: Airawat Kill Box

Arrival + 3 weeks

The Jai have changed their tactics. Instead of trying to overwhelm our air and space defenses they are landing forces on Earth and establishing bases from which to attack us. This effort failed on Iceland, but succeeded in Tunisia — an attempt to cut off Africa and Europe — South Africa, Tasmania, and Southern Pakistan. Of course, since the nuclear crises which transpired three years ago, Pakistan has no national government to speak of, which explains why the Jai landed there. From a large base outside of Karachi, which includes a landed carrier ship and two transports, the Jai have been attacking India...

Presidential Briefing, week five

Opposition Parties Slam PM's Slow Response to Alien Onslaught
Not for long, vows Defence Minister

Times of India

Sometimes it seemed Hyderabad still smoldered. On windy days a fine, black-gray dust rose up from the city and hung over the Thar Desert. The dust would eventually fall, wrapping thousands upon thousands of skeletons in a perverse blanket. Entire families huddled beneath the dust blankets next to whatever meager possessions the looters had left to the dead. They almost looked at peace, Manekshaw thought when he saw them. For the general that made the scene more demented still.

Manekshaw had been in the room that horrible night three years earlier when the Indian prime minister had consulted with the American president about the two nation's joint response to the nuclear crisis before them. Rogue elements supported by the Pakistani Inter Services Intelligence agency had already detonated one nuclear device at Camp Leatherneck in Afghanistan and

73

another in Jammu in India. Manekshaw had actually heard the PM say, 'Yes, Mr. President, I agree. A nuclear retaliation is in order.'

And so the combined might of the United States and India was unleashed on a sick and divided Pakistan. While the Americans were content to nuke a few military targets, including the ISI headquarters, India unleashed its full nuclear fury on its cousin, destroying Islamabad, Karachi, Hyderabad, and half a dozen other metropolitan areas. The world was aghast at what many felt was a disproportionate response, but the government held the support of the Indian public, and the United States exercised its UN veto in defense of its ally.

In the subsequent fighting the Indian army had acquitted itself well, soundly defeating the Pakistani army in several battles along the border, including the great tank battle at Jaisimlar, where Indian forces annihilated the Pakistani I[st] Armoured Division. Manekshaw could only look on in frustration as the battle he had trained and strived for his entire life was fought and won without him. Bollywood had already turned out a half dozen movies about the war and the Armoured Corps had gone on to great glory, but not Manekshaw. He had remained in the prime minister's office, briefing the government on the war.

Now that an uneasy truce remained between India and what remained of Pakistan it seemed to Manekshaw that he had missed his chance. Only after the great armored battles were over had Manekshaw gotten his wish and been transferred to the Armoured Corps, first to command a brigade, and then as Arrival approached, to command the elite I[st] Armoured 'Airawat' Division. Commanding the Black Elephants, as they were called in English, was a supreme compliment to his skill and dedication. The prime minister had even attached a hand written note to Manekshaw's promotion orders and citation, 'Good luck to the man who kept me so well informed during the last war,' it had read. 'I hope I do not need you again.'

India needed Manekshaw now. For a week the Jai had assailed India from their land base east of Karachi's ruins. Mumbai had been especially hard hit, as had Punjab and the west coast. Jai ground forces, several thousand strong, had crept east until they occupied a line on the edge of the Thar Desert on the border, seemingly in preparation for a push into northern India in what the national press was already dubbing a recreation of the Muslim and Mogul invasions.

On orders I Armoured Division had made its way south to the eastern edge of the Thar Desert. Manekshaw had arrived with his commanders ahead of the main body of the division to scout out terrain and choose where he would fight. He now waited for them west of Johdpur. He stood atop a scrub and rock-covered ridge, scanning the western horizon through his binoculars. Thin wisps of black smoke were evident in the distance. Mixing with the wisps of smoke from Hyderabad were plumes of dust, lots of them, as the desert to the west came alive with Jai vehicles. Behind Manekshaw was kilometer after kilometer of open land, boulders, and dry scrub. Beyond the open space, 27 kilometers to the east was a ridge and dry river bed which fell away to another open space, closed off on the north by a rock-strewn field and ending in a small, rock covered rise. At the end of that space was a shallow canal and a forest reserve originally planted by the British a century before.

'At the river bed, we hurt them,' said Manekshaw. 'At the forest reserve, we kill them.'

'Yes, sir,' said General Bawa, the commander of 43 Brigade. Bawa was a devout Sikh, sporting a handlebar mustache and turban. He even wore a ceremonial knife.

'Your regiments must make them pay, from here all the way back to river bed.'

'Yes, sir.'

'At the river bed, you must make them stop.'

'Aye.'

'Not for long, but stop they must.'

Manekshaw turned to General Mohamed, commander of I Armored Brigade. 'General, when we stop the Jai before the forest reserve, they will be reluctant to break toward the north. It is likely they will head south instead. You must stop them at all costs.'

'I will, General.'

Though it was not unheard of, it was rare for a Muslim to rise so high in the ranks of the Indian army. In the brief time he had known General Mohamed, Manekshaw had been impressed with his loyalty to the Indian state and his hatred for Pakistan. When Manekshaw asked him why, Mohamed had simply replied, 'They do not represent true Islam, sir. My wife is a beauty. I would not see her hidden behind a sack; we are not all blood thirsty Jihadists.'

'I will be waiting in the forest reserve with the division's two independent regiments,' Manekshaw said. 'The Jai will have air superiority,' Manekshaw said.

'Your units have been issued American made hand-held Stinger missiles, and our own anti-aircraft battalion has been reinforced, but these will be no more than a nuisance. Once the battle begins your brigades will not be able to move without incurring significant losses.'

'Questions?'

'Yes, General,' began Mohamed. 'Why won't the Jai simply blast the forest reserve in anticipation of our deploying forces there?'

'They might,' replied Manekshaw. 'I would. But if we deploy in the open, the Jai will spot our reserves and destroy them anyway. At least by deploying in the forest reserve we have a chance. It is not a good gamble but it's the only one we have.'

'General, permission to speak frankly?' Bawa asked.

'Yes.'

'Forty Three Brigade has some fine regiments, General. It will be a shame to see them used up this way.'

'Yes it will be, General. But it will be an even bigger shame to the Jai to lose those units approaching our position. So we will bleed them. We can build new tanks, we can train new crews. They cannot. Also do not forget that I once commanded one of your regiments.'

'Of course, sir.'

'Alright then. Return to your units. Luck be with you.' The generals saluted. Then Manekshaw shook both of their hands.

The two brigade commanders trotted down the slope of the ridge to their command vehicles. The armored cars sped east, leaving Manekshaw's car and two escorting cars behind. He looked west at the approaching dust plumes one last time before ascending the slope himself and getting in his own car, a Gypsy four wheeled drive off roader similar to an American Jeep. The trip took about half an hour. While regimental and battalion commanders talked back and forth on the division's communications net, Manekshaw reviewed his notes for the battle.

He had been privileged to see an initial report of the ground battle on Iceland written by the now famous General Lutch, who emphasized that frontal attacks on Jai forces were suicidal. Subsequent analysis of Jai ground forces and tactics showed thinking similar to a Western army's on the use of and coordination of armoured, infantry and air forces. The basic Jai unit of maneuver seemed to be 12 vehicles, each of these formed into a high echelon unit, roughly equivalent to a battalion of 48 tanks. Four of these battalions had been deployed on Iceland. The combination of tanks, mechanized vehicles, and infantry, with heavy air and naval support, had been almost unstoppable. Lutch believed they preferred to avoid using space based kinetic energy weapons if possible; feeling that it was against the conventions of their style of war-just as modern armies eschewed chemical weapons. Jai armor was similar to any earth tank, but they carried formidable countermeasures that could shoot down incoming ordnance before it impacted.

Manekshaw made his headquarters on the far edge of the forest reserve about 200 meters from the gun line. Under a bramble of branches was a plastic canopy shielding radios, computers, and other electronics from which he could listen in to the battle down to the battalion and squadron level and keep in touch with corps headquarters. He had a different radio phone tuned into each brigade and regimental command net. A pair of trucks were parked nearby as were several Gypsies. A company of military police stood watch over the headquarters. The company had dug several trenches to the rear, should the HQ come under Jai artillery fire. A kilometer further east in the desert a secondary HQ had been set up amongst a rock outcropping in case the staff had to evacuate.

Manekshaw sat down on a simple folding chair in the center of the HQ. He crossed his legs, folded his arms and followed the deployment of his division on a nearby computer screen. Little icons marked the positions of his brigade HQs and each of their three armored regiments. Airawat Division was deployed in a rough box formation with the left end being a very thin line and the bottom a very thick one. Blue dots lay just outside the east side of the forest reserve; these represented the division's logistic, medical, artillery and anti-aircraft battalions.

The Headquarters' communication officer, a young captain named Palit, brought Manekshaw the land line phone linked back to II Corps headquarters.

'General Singh for you, sir.'

Manekshaw took the phone. 'Manekshaw here.'

'What is your situation, my friend?'

'Just as we had hoped. The Jai appear to be advancing through the Thar Desert.'

'You shall deal with them?'

'I shall, General.'

'My 14 and 29 Infantry Divisions are deployed to your north. The Jai are demonstrating against them now, but I think this is only a ruse. I still have my armoured brigade in reserve, but will need it in case the infantry divisions get into trouble. So you are on your own.'

'Yes, General.'

'Is there anything else you need, General Manekshaw?'

'Not at this time, sir.'

'Then good luck, my friend.'

'And to you, sir.'

'And Manekshaw?'

'Yes, General.'

'Do not forget that you have the pride of the Indian Army out there in that desert.'

Manekshaw laughed. 'Of course not sir.'

General Singh hung up. Manekshaw handed the phone back to Palit.

'General?' Palit asked. 'May I ask why he called you his friend?'

Manekshaw smiled. 'He mentored me when I was a young officer out of the academy.' Manekshaw nodded to Palit. 'Much as I have done with you, I should think.'

'Yes, sir.'

'Singh commanded an armoured platoon in '65, fought in the battle of Khem Karan and commanded an armoured battalion in '71. General Singh was on the line at the Shakargahr Bulge.'

The captain's eyes widened like a little boy's as Manekshaw's once had when Singh first told him about fighting his armoured units against the Pakistanis.

'May I ask one more thing, sir?'

Manekshaw nodded his assent.

'How can you be so calm?'

The general smiled. 'The plan has been set, orders have been given, units are moving to their battle positions. There is little more that I can do. You see, Captain Palit, at this moment, I am the most useless man in the First Armoured Division. A mere observer.'

'Yes, General.'

Manekshaw smiled again. 'And let me assure, my young captain, it is hard work looking this composed.'

A million 'what if' questions ran through Manekshaw's head. Thanks to years of training he ignored these. He considered heading forward to the edge of the forest reserve and walking amongst the men there but thought better of it. It would look as silly as a retired cricket player taking to the pitch. As General Officer Commanding, his place was in his HQ. So instead, he walked over to a small table which held several cups and pots of hot water and made himself some tea.

Reports started coming into the HQ. A tech sergeant updated the division's status on a large computer screen. It showed several blue dots representing 43 Brigade's reconnaissance battalion and one red dot representing Jai forces.

'Put the radio chatter on the speakers,' Manekshaw ordered.

Palit pressed a button on his computer consol. A moment later the headquarters was filled with the excited chatter of the reconnaissance battalion.

'We have three enemy tanks...now four; my vehicles are positioned atop the ridge...oh my! One of my vehicles is gone, now two!' said the excited battalion commander.

'Get them out of there,' Bawa ordered.

'Now three! Gone!'

A second recon platoon became engaged and then a third. The battalion commander requested support from brigade, but Bawa held his fire and instead waited for the Jai to advance further. Manekshaw silently approved. One of the recon vehicles occupied a good position atop the ridge, hull down behind a rock outcropping. They hadn't been spotted by the Jai yet, and the crew was able to relay live feed of the Jai advance. The feed was automatically sent to Manekshaw's headquarters. It showed a line of turreted gray armored vehicles, Manekshaw counted twelve in all, advancing across the desert scrub toward the first ridge. The recon cameraman zoomed in on a pair of green vehicles on the Jai's southern flank.

'General, do you see that?' asked Palit.

'I do, Captain.'

Mankeshw stood up and walked to the computer screen. The camera held the image of a pair of BMP armored vehicles, the Pakistani flag trailing from their antennas.

'I do not believe it, the Pakistanis-'

Manekshaw held up his hand. 'Calm down, Captain. Inform II Corps of this development.'

Palit took a deep breath. 'Yes, sir.'

On the far horizon he saw missile contrails, Jai he knew, no doubt launched from the carrier ship floating off of Karachi. What was left of 43 Brigade's recon battalion pulled off the ridge back toward the dry riverbed where two armored regiments were dug in. When the Jai armored battalion topped the ridge it halted and surveyed the ground to the east. After a few minutes a pair of Jai bombers swooped in over the plain. The Jai bombers unleashed a barrage of missiles on the two Indian armoured regiments below. A dozen Stinger missiles reached out from the ground; the division's anti aircraft battalion fired a volley as well.

After the strafing run, the Jai tanks fired into the dry river bed.

'They are targeting my tanks one by one,' reported the commander of the Poona Horse.

'What about Hodson's Horse?' asked Bawa. 'Where is you GOC?'

'I do not know, General. I...' the voice was suddenly cut off.

'My god, General, two regiments,' said Palit.

'They're not gone yet. And Bawa still has 16 Cavalry atop the rise to the east,' Manekshaw pointed to the blue marker on the computer screen about a kilometer back from the river bed.

'Will you order General Bawa to move them up?'

'No,' was Manekshaw's reply.

As the bombardment continued, Manekshaw could do nothing. By the time the Jai were finished, the regiments reported their strength, 'This is Poona Horse, eleven tanks operable...this is Hodson's Horse, seventeen tanks...

'General,' said Palit, phone in hand, 'General Bawa asks that you release division artillery.'

'Yes,' said Manekshaw. 'Rocket batteries only. Shoot and scoot.'

Manekshaw waited until the Poona Horse commander reported. 'They are advancing down the slope...I do not believe this...those are Paki tanks. I count sixteen....nineteen. BMPs coming down the slope now.'

'Open fire,' Bawa ordered.

Manekshaw cursed Bawa as the surviving tanks in the river bed opened fire. *No*, he thought. *Save them for the Jai you fool.* A flurry of voices took over the radio net, 'Hit!' said one. 'T-72 engaged and destroyed!' said another. 'BMP engaged with heavy machinegun and is on fire.' said another. Then the tone of the reports changed. 'The Jai have us bracketed. They just destroyed Hodson-Four..and I...' the voice was cut off. 'Poona-One is gone, the XO is dead as well. This is Poona-Four, shifting fire to the ridge now...'

The remaining tank fire combined with the rocket barrage forced the Jai tanks on the ridge to back out of visual range. Poona-Four reported a smoke plume from the Jai line.

'What are the Pakistani's doing, Poona-Four...' asked Bawa. 'Poona-Four?'

'Poona-Four is gone!' someone shouted.

'Hodson's report. Who is now the GOC there?'

'This is Hodson-Eleven, General. I do not think anyone commands here. Both tanks on my flank are afire.'

'What about the Pakistanis?'

'The smoke is obscuring my vision, but I see burning T-72s and BMPs.'

'Very well, gentleman. Well fought Hodson Horse and Poona Horse, pull back behind 16 Cavalry. I will try and cover you.'

A combined 17 tanks and 13 armoured vehicles pulled out of the river bed and raced east toward the rocky rise occupied by 16 Cavalry. The Jai on the ridge returned to their firing positions and picked off several vehicles.

'General, Bawa for you,' Palit handed the phone to Manekshaw.

'General Manekshaw, there is a battalion of Jai tanks exposed on the ridge, I strongly suggest you release division artillery.'

'That will expose my artillery, General.'

'Yes, but we may severely damage that battalion and purchase valuable time as the next battalion has to move forward and take its place.'

Manekshaw thought for a moment. 'Very well. You will have your artillery fires.'

'Thank you, sir.'

'Captain Palit, order the artillery brigade to fire on that ridge, Three volleys only.'

'Shoot and scoot?'

'Yes.'

Moments after Palit relayed the order Manekshaw heard the nearby artillery batteries open fire. Artillery rounds exploded around and above the Jai armored battalion.

'I see smoke!' reported an excited recon commander. 'And another!'

The barrage continued past the three rounds to a fourth, fifth and then a sixth. Horrified, Manekshaw said. 'Captain, get the artillery brigade GOC and order him to stop his fires at once.'

'Sir!' Palit punched up the artillery brigade. 'Artillery brigade, this is HQ, you are ordered to cease fire immediately. You are ordered to cease fire immediately!'

'But we have them HQ!' replied the artillery commander.

'Give me the phone,' said an eerily calm Manekshaw. 'General you are relieved, put your XO on.'

After a few moments. 'XO here.'

'Colonel you are now the GOC of the artillery brigade. Your batteries will cease fire at once. Is that understood?'

'Understood, sir. Cease fire, all batteries, cease fire,' the colonel said.

Mankeshaw gave the phone back to Palit.

To his dismay he heard one of the techs report, 'Aircraft approaching, three Jai bombers...'

Once more missiles streaked into the sky. Manekshaw expected his ears to be split by explosions. But instead he heard the radar tech report, 'Hit, one bomber hit...its going down...The other two are peeling away.'

'New contacts. Missiles,' reported the radar tech. 'Originating from the carrier ship.'

The missiles slammed into the last plotted positions of the artillery batteries. One blast was less than a kilometer from the HQ and produced an impressive fireball. Reports flooded in to the HQ.

'They only destroyed one battery, General,' said Palit.

'Well, we are lucky for now, then,' said Manekeshaw.

While the divisional artillery redeployed, the Jai on the ridge, thirty three tanks in all, stayed put. A second battalion passed through their lines and advanced down the slope. A pair of Jai bombers orbited overhead. As the second battalion advanced, the first battalion fired into the river bed. Jai artillery walked a barrage toward the riverbed as well. Manekshaw feared it would hit 16 Cavalry, but the Jai cut off the barrage several hundred meters short of their position.

The second Jai armored battalion dashed across the open space and into the dry river bed.

'They're maneuvering amongst our destroyed tanks,' reported one of the recon platoons. 'It looks like they are taking up positions on the reverse slope.'

'I can't see them,' said 16 Cavalry's GOC. 'I can try to maneuver for a better shot.'

Bawa got back on the brigade command net. 'Colonel Aoroa, this is Bawa. You will hold your fire until the Jai advance out of that river bed.'

'Yes, sir.'

Good, thought Manekshaw.

'The Jai are firing artillery again,' Aoroa said. 'Ground and air burst. They are walking them forward. I may not be able to see their tanks come out of the river bed.'

'Our scouts in the north rock outcropping can tell you,' said Bawa. 'Fire blind if you have to, but make sure you fire as they're coming out of the river bed.'

They didn't have to wait long.

'Here they come,' said Aoroa, 'All tanks, open fire.'

Thirty nine T-90 tanks fired in unison at the advancing Jai armor. As the Jai tanks crested the riverbed, they exposed their undercarriages which were not armored.

'Hit!' reported one tank commander. 'Engaged and destroyed,' reported another. I see smoke.' A third tank commander chimed in. 'Yes, look at it burn.'

'Missile coming in!' shouted a squadron commander.

In the HQ they heard screams and static. One squadron commander shouted 'Keep firing, to hell with their missiles!'

'We're taking fire from the ridge again!'

Once more Indian tanks exploded into balls of fire. Jai bombers came out of the sky, braved the division's anti-aircraft and rocket fire, and bombed 16 Cavalry.

'This is Aoroa. My strength has been cut in half!' All listening could hear explosions in the background.

'What is the enemy's situation?'

'I can see several plumes, all tanks...' there was a loud explosion. 'That was close. I believe they have my position sir.'

A moment later Aoroa was cut off.

'What happened, General?' Palit asked.

83

'I think they just destroyed 16 Cavalry.'

The Jai, less a third of their tanks now, advanced to 16 Cavalry's position and a few hundred yards beyond before they stopped. The Jai unleashed another rolling artillery barrage, blasting everything for more than 500 meters past their lead tanks. Before them was open, rock-strewn, scrub-covered desert. The ground sloped gently away to the canal, three kilometers away, and beyond that the forest reserve.

'Shall we order the Royal Lancers and the 5th Armoured Regiment into position?' asked Palit.

'Not yet, Captain.'

Manekshaw listened to reports coming in over the command net.

'More Jai vehicles are coming down from the ridge,' said one recce commander. 'I count a dozen tanks and the same number of armoured vehicles.'

'Where are they headed?' asked the battalion commander. 'Due east, for the river bed.'

'New contact,' reported 1 Brigade's recon unit. 'I have Paki armoured and mechanized units, a mixed force of T-72s and BMPs.'

'What is their count?' Mohamed asked.

'Thirteen tanks, eleven BMPs.'

'Traitorous bastards,' said Mohamed. 'They will pay.'

There were murmurs of agreement across 1 Brigade's command net.

As Manekshaw waited, the third Jai battalion and their Pakistani allies turned right and advanced south toward Mohamed's brigade, which lay concealed behind scrub and beneath camouflage netting. They halted about a mile from his lead elements. Manekshaw was wondering what they were going to do when a fourth Jai battalion came over the ridge.

'New contacts advancing in column down the ridge. Two armoured columns, and a mechanized column,' reported a recon unit. 'They are advancing due east.'

'What count?' demanded the recce battalion commander.

'Twelve tanks in four columns; I see fourteen other vehicles.'

'So another battalion,' said Manekshaw.

Palit spoke, 'If the American report from Iceland is accurate, that is their entire force, at least opposite us.'

'Yes.'

'What do you suppose they are doing, General?'

'If I were the Jai commander, I would use that third battalion to cover my flank and advance the fourth right at us here in the forest reserve. I suspect they will hit our position with artillery and missiles first.' He watched the computer display as markers indicated the fourth battalion advancing down the ridge and toward the river bed.

'Let us give them something to think about shall we? Get me General Mohamed.'

Palit contacted I Brigade's HQ and handed the phone to Manekshaw. 'General Mohamed.'

'Yes, sir.'

'Attack those enemy forces opposite your brigade.'

'With pleasure, General.'

'Two regiments forward. Keep one in reserve to hold that battle line in case the Jai advance south. And if they do, General, hold as long as you can, I'll come out of the reserve with my two reserve regiments.'

'I thought the Americans recommended against frontal attacks, sir,' said Palit.

'They did, Captain, but sometimes they are necessary.'

Mohamed deployed his brigade's 7 Light Cavalry and 62 Armoured regiments in echelon. The Jai spotted both units as they formed up and fired several missiles. More than a dozen tanks were destroyed before the regiments could properly deploy. When they were ready, the regiments looked like two great 'L's with the short line facing west.

'Regiments advance,' Mohamed ordered.

When Mohamed gave the order more than 50 T-90 tanks advanced toward the Jai. Maneksahw watched a live video feed from Mohamed's headquarters. With their desert camouflage paint and the dust they kicked up around them the Indian tankers looked like they were reenacting a World War II era British battle in the Western Desert.

Jai artillery and missiles landed amongst the regiments as they advanced across the desert. Manekshaw listened to battalion and company commander's excited chatter as, one by one, their tanks were targeted and destroyed first by Jai missile and artillery, then by their tanks. Pakistani forces, now occupying the right side of the Jai line, added their fire to mix. To Manekshaw's irritation, the two attacking regiments directed the bulk of their fire at the Pakistanis.

Mohamed's voice echoed on the command net. 'All units, all units. Shift your fire to the Jai. Respond.'

'This is 7 Cavalry, understood.'

'This is 62 Regiment. Yes, sir.'

Dozens of T-90 tanks shifted their fire to the Jai tank line. Squadron commanders tried to coordinate their fire, 'Everyone target that lead tank!' One shouted over the din of battle. 'Third tank in line! Fire on the third tank in line!' shouted another.

The command net was filled with a cacophony of 'Hit!' and 'Target hit!' One tank sergeant said, 'I hit it, but he's still going!' another chimed in. 'Yes, they can take a massive punch!' Finally, 'Destroyed! Target destroyed!' one commander reported.

'We are taking heavy fire from the Paki tanks on our left,' reported 62 Regiment's GOC. 'I am detailing one squadron to deal with them.'

'Confirmed, Colonel,' Mohamed replied over the net. 'Do so.'

While one squadron from 62 Regiment broke left to engage with the Pakistanis, the rest of the two regiments pressed forward against the Jai tank line. The live feed on Manekshaw's computer showed a long line of green tanks in the distance, partially obscured by dust and smoke. Several tanks lay burning to the rear. The screen came alive with explosions. One tank went up in flame then another and another.

'Where is that fire coming from?!' asked one squadron commander. 'It must be missile fire!' shouted another. Then, 'Half my tank commanders do not respond!'

'Very well. All units halt! All units halt!' Mohamed ordered. 'Fire on the Jai tank line, two volleys.'

'And then what, General?' asked the commander of 62 Regiment.

'Then pull back.'

Manekshaw nodded his approval. 'Captain, order an artillery strike on the Jai line. Three volleys then change position.'

'Yes, sir.'

'And tell Mohamed the barrage is coming.'

'Yes, sir.'

A minute later one of the squadron commanders reported, 'The Jai line is getting hit by artillery. I can't see them.'

'Time to pull back,' ordered 62 Regiment's GOC.

'Agreed,' said Mohamed. '7 Cavalry, get out of there and regroup.'

As the two battered but still fighting tank regiments pulled back, 62 Cavlary's detached squadron reported. 'This is B Squadron. We engaged and destroyed four Pakistani tanks and two BMPs. The rest have withdrawn. Am pulling back.'

There were explosions near Manekshaw's HQ as the Jai homed in on the division's artillery. Secondary explosions told Manekshaw that at least one battery had been caught. I Brigade's surviving tanks rallied behind the brigade's reserve, 5 Armoured Regiment, which lay down covering fire.

Palit handed the phone to Manekshaw. 'Mohamed for you, sir.'

'Situation?'

'I have lost more than half my tanks. 7 Cavalry's GOC is dead,' said Mohamed. 'So is the XO. I am going to fold 7 Cavalry into 62 Regiment. Their XO is alive and in command.'

'Very good. Re-form at your discretion and be prepared to attack along a two-regiment front.'

'Yes, General.'

'Give your men my compliments on a fine action.'

'Thank you, sir.'

The Jai reformed as well. They kept their first battalion on the high ground but moved the second to a south facing position opposite I Brigade. The third and fourth battalions deployed just behind 43 Brigade's battle line, now a graveyard of tanks and armoured vehicles. One small force of four tanks moved east, north east, toward 43 Brigade's HQ.

'Get Bawa on the line,' he said to Palit. 'Find out why he is not moving.'

'Sir.'

Palit contacted 43 Brigade's HQ and spoke. 'General, the HQ says they are unaware of any enemy movement toward their position.'

'Give me the phone.'

'This is Manekshaw. Put Bawa on the line.' There was static for a moment as the officer on the other end handed the phone to Bawa.'

'Bawa here.'

'What are you doing, General? Get out of there.'

'Negative, sir.'

'What?!'

'I have already ordered my XO east, he will take command of what is left of my brigade.'

'Why are you doing this, Bawa?'

'I will not die with my dagger sheathed, General.' He paused for a moment. 'Will there be anything else, sir?'

'No,' said Manekshaw in resignation.

'Goodbye, General Manekshaw. It has been a privilege to serve under you.'

'Goodbye, General. Damn fool.' Manekshaw handed the phone back to Palit. 'Very well then. Captain, establish a link with 43 Brigade's XO, I want a status of forces report from him as soon as possible.'

'Yes, sir.'

When Palit got the XO on the line, he handed the phone to Manekshaw.

'This is Colonel Vijayan. I have nineteen tanks and ten BMPs. Where shall we deploy?'

'Hello Colonel. I want you on the far right flank of my line, between the forest reserve and the rock outcroppings north.'

'We can do it, General. Orders?'

'Stay there. You are my reserve.'

'Yes, sir.'

'Captain, patch me into the division net, I want to hear all my regimental commanders.' Palit pressed some buttons on a communications consul. One by one the regimental commanders and Mohamed reported.

'Gentleman. We shall hold the enemy here. The Jai are not to fight past the forest reserve. You will hold there at all costs, paying no attention to losses.'

'Yes, sir.'

'General Mohamed. You must not allow the Jai to breakout to the south.'

'Understood, sir.'

'Behind us lies India.'

'Yes, sir,' the officers replied.

'Good luck.'

Manekshaw handed the phone back to Palit, sat back in his chair, and looked at the map redoubt displayed on his computer screen. The Royal Lancers and 5 Armored Regiment were deployed inside the forest reserve. More than 90 tanks in all. These were supported by a battalion of BMPs. The positions bristled with anti-tank guns, missile launchers and heavy machineguns. Behind them the division's surviving artillery, three gun batteries and a rocket battery, waited in support. To the south was General Mohamed with 7 Tank Regiment and his ad-hoc regiment. He was already trading fire with the Jai.

Manekshaw knew the battle had begun in earnest when 5 Armoured Regiment's GOC reported, 'Rolling barrage heading our way.'

Manekshaw stood up, 'I suggest everybody head for the trenches.'

The HQ company dropped what they were doing and trotted over to the trench line they had dug before the battle. Manekshaw made sure he was the last in. He had been under fire before, in the Kargil conflict of 1999, but that was nothing like this. The very ground seemed to shake as the Jai hit the forest reserve with artillery and missiles. Manekeshaw saw the dirt on the lip of the trench shake and felt a heat blast. Instinctively he closed his eyes in anticipation of the next blast, but breathed a sigh of relief when the next blast landed outside of the reserve in the open ground beyond. After yet another blast even further out of the forest reserve, Manekshaw and the HQ company got out of the trenches. Trees around them were felled, many burned. Some still stood but had been singed. The HQ, however was intact, save for the plastic canopy which had been blown over in the blast, and few computers which had been knocked off their tables. In the distance there was screaming, and through the trees could be seen several burning vehicles. Manekshaw's chair was also knocked over. He picked it up and sat back down.

Then Manekshaw heard the order delivered over the command net. 'Open fire.'

The entire forest reserve seemed to erupt as the two Indian regiments fired every weapon at hand. Tanks, missile launchers, anti-tank pieces, machineguns, even small arms, created a wall of fire for the Jai to fight through. Missile and gun teams concealed within the northern rock outcroppings joined the fusillade. The command net was alive with reports from various officers. Manekshaw could not possibly follow it; all he could do was sit, and listen, and wait. He heard snippets, but not enough to get a clear picture. 'Target destroyed!' he heard. A second later. 'I have five MGs trained on that tank. It has stopped and its crew is bailing!' and then, 'They're shooting down our missiles before they hit!'

The forest reserve exploded as the Jai returned fire. Fireballs that were once Indian tanks reached into the sky.

'Get me I Brigade,' Manekshaw said over the din.

Palit contacted I Brigade's HQ and handed the phone to Manekshaw.

'General Mohamed, attack now. I'll cover with artillery.'

'Yes, General.'

'And good luck.' Manekshaw looked at Palit. 'Get me the artillery brigade.'

He pressed some more buttons on the consol and nodded at Manekshaw.

'This is Manekshaw. Fire everything.' He was cut off by a nearby explosion. 'Fire everything in support of I Brigade.'

Jai artillery exploded around the HQ. 'Let's get out of here!" Palit shouted.

'I agree,' replied Manekshaw. 'Everyone out! Get in the lories!'

The HQ Company packed up their gear and piled into the lorries parked nearby. Manekshaw got in the back. Next to him was Palit with the radio phone and power pack. As they drove out of the reserve and into the open desert. Manekshaw was able pick up I Brigade's command net.

'Keep advancing! Keep advancing!' Mohamed ordered.

'Our artillery is scattering them,' reported a commander.

'Two tanks! We just destroyed two of their tanks!'

'Bombers coming in. Get those Stingers in the air!'

Manekshaw saw dozens of missile contrails rise up from the forest reserve and the area around it. Tracers from 50 caliber emplacements reached out as well, filling the sky with smoke and light.

'We got one! We got one!' someone shouted.

Manekshaw didn't look up to watch the Jai bomber crash because he heard General Mohamed report, 'They are falling back. The third Jai battalion is falling back toward the fourth. All units advance toward the Jai line. We shall hunker down amongst their own burning vehicles.'

The two regiments advanced, losing a tank here or there to Jai fire, and half a squadron to a carrier ship launched missile barrage. Despite the casualties, within two minutes they took up positions among the burning and dead hulks of Jai tanks.

'Report tank strength.'

'This is ad-hoc regiment, 23 tanks.'

'This is 7 Cavalry, 28 tanks.'

'We shall hold here. Fire all weapons in support of the forest reserve.'

The Jai were now taking fire from three sides. On the extreme right flank, the remains of 43 Brigade added its fire to the battle. The assorted phones tuned to the various squadron and battalion nets drowned each other out, becoming an unintelligible jumble of commands and reports.

'Turn them off, Captain, just turn them off.'

One by one, Palit switched off the receivers. 'But how will we follow the battle?'

'Well,' began Manekshaw, 'if we see the Jai come through the forest reserve toward us, I suppose we shall know we lost.'

Mankeshaw leaned back and listened to the awesome roar of the Airawat Division. Manekshaw laughed. *Well, Manekshaw, old boy*, he said to himself, *you have your great tank battle now!* He heard a volley of Jai missiles incoming, but instead of striking the forest reserve they continued north toward 14 and 29 division. *Now why would they do that?* He wondered.

The din of fire drew closer and peaked, and for a minute reached a plateau, and then suddenly slackened off. Manekshaw looked toward the forest reserve and saw burning vehicles and trees, but could also make out muzzle flashes and missile contrails heading west toward the Jai.

'Turn the receivers back on. I want to know what is happening.'

'Yes, sir.'

'Get me Mohamed.'

One by one Palit switched the radios back on. The truck filled with the chatter of tank and infantry commanders.

'The Jai are withdrawing!' reported one commander.

'Keep firing. Keep shooting!' commanded another.

'General Mohamed, sir.' The captain handed a phone to Manekshaw.

'Mohamed.'

'General Manekshaw, the Jai are pulling back. We are keeping up the pressure.'

'Well done, General.'

'Thank you, sir.'

'I want you to fall back to your original line. Be prepared to defend if the Jai come toward you.'

'Yes, sir.'

Palit pointed to the dust clouds to the north. 'General, the Jai turned our flank!'

'Settle down, Captain. I served out here long enough to know Indian army lorie dust clouds when I see them.' Manekshaw furrowed his brow. 'Now why would they be here?'

Manekshaw walked out from his impromptu headquarters toward the approaching vehicles. He counted six trucks and two BMPs. As they approached he could see that the trucks were packed with soldiers, men were even holding on to the side running boards. Several wounded soldiers lay across the engine compartments of the BMPs. When they drew near Manekshaw held out a hand. The lead truck stopped. A tired looking officer, his left arm in a sling, got out of the passenger side. His helmet was gone and his hair was dried and caked with blood. He walked over to Manekshaw and saluted. Manekshaw returned the salute.

'Major Donijay, 14 Infantry Division.'

'Why are you here, Major?'

'The Jai broke through our position.'

'What?'

'Yes, General. They routed us, and 29 Division to our north.'

Manekshaw turned to Palit. 'Get me II Corps, immediately please.'

'Yes, sir.'

'What are the Jai doing now?'

'Last report, before 14 Division HQ went off the air, was that the Jai were pushing northeast.'

'Are there more of you?' asked Manekshaw.

'Yes, General. Thousands will be coming.'

'I cannot raise II Corps, sir!" Palit shouted from the truck.

Behind the first wave, Manekshaw could see more dust clouds, and more trucks fleeing south.

'Major. I need you to take charge and organize these stragglers.'

Major Donijay straightened. 'Yes sir.'

'I want lists of who we have, and what we have. Organize them into ad-hoc units. You are GOC until further notice.'

'Yes, sir.'

Manekshaw walked back to the truck. 'Still nothing from II Corps, Palit?'

'No, General.'

'Very well. Get General Mohamed, tell him he is the GOC of the division.'

'For how long?'

'At least until I can get things organized here.'

'After that, then what?'

Manekshaw rubbed his chin, 'Prepare to pull back east, southeast. We shall try to protect the interior of the country.'

'What about the other Jai forces advancing northeast?'

'We can't stop them.'

Chaos Reigns as Jai Advance into Northern India
Indian army retreats

Russia Today

Government in Disarray, Defence Minister Resigns in Shame

Times of India

Chapter 7: The French Interrogator's Alien

Arrival + 4 weeks

...To say that we have won the first round of this war is not accurate. No military that has sustained the losses we have sustained can say they won anything. But we have not lost either. In fact...

Excerpt of memo from CINC Space
Command to the Secretary of Defense

'...Privately, Brian, White House sources are saying that the Jai have paused their offensive.'

'Is there any indication as to why, Anne?'

'The Pentagon feels that the Jai were unable to attain their goals during the first weeks of fighting.'

'Has the United States or any other nation captured any prisoners?'

'So far, Brian, government officials aren't saying anything on the matter of alien POWs, but it stands to reason...'

NBC News

Croix sat groggily in the backseat of a non-descript white car sent for him by the Ministry of Defense. The driver had rousted Croix from a pleasant wine-induced slumber and insisted he come with him. They had driven west for some time, past blacked out towns and villages, passing with ease through the various military roadblocks. Now they were on a country road; Croix could see a castle in the distance. Behind the castle the sky glowed orange.

'Did they hit LeHarve?' Croix asked.

'And Bordeaux, Captain.'

Croix shook his head.

'Are you taking me to that castle?'

95

'Yes.'

Croix laughed.

At the Castle's gate was an AMX 30 tank. He noticed that several soldiers manned the gatehouse. The towers were adorned with heavy machineguns. A grim looking officer waved the car through. In the courtyard were more soldiers, another tank, and several machineguns. Soldiers walked the ramparts as if they were medieval sentries. More soldiers manned the keep.

When Croix stepped out of the car, a familiar face greeted him.

'Duceppe,' Croix said wearily.

'Croix.'

Croix saluted. Duceppe returned it.

'Why do I smell wine on your breath?'

'My companion and I were sharing a bottle.'

'Were you?'

'Yes, a lovely young lieutenant I met a few days ago. She's very concerned about the state of things.'

'I don't blame her.'

'She needed reassurance and comfort.'

'Well, it is good you were there.'

'It *was*,' Croix replied.

Jet engines screamed overhead and faded south.

'So the air battle continues?'

'The Jai hit the Riviera tonight. Italy was attacked as well. They seem determined to severe communications across the Mediterranean.'

'Did you bring me here to give me this update on the war?'

'You have someplace better to be?'

'I just told you about it.' He sighed. 'I just spent the last week interrogating captured Algerian Jihadi. They think the aliens were sent by Allah.'

'Preposterous.'

'You may not believe it, Duceppe,' he pointed back toward Paris, where the Arab sections of the city were in flames, 'but they do.'

'And what do you believe?'

'What do I believe? What kind of question is that? What do I believe?!'

'Well?

'I believe I am entitled to some rest.'

'I am sorry, Croix. Is this war an inconvenience for you?'

Croix laughed again. 'It's bad enough you pull me out of bed, but to bring me to a castle, Duceppe, really? I'm surprised you didn't find a dark castle on a hill someplace, at least that would have complete the scene. This is amateurish.'

'It has underground rooms in case of air attack and is easily defended.'

Croix nodded and had to admit his colleague had a point.

Duceppe took Croix into the keep, past more soldiers and through the castle's winding medieval passages. There were stairs and a definite sensation of slow but steady downward movement. Croix lost all track of where he was. Duceppe led him to a low-ceilinged room. A few tables had been set up in the corner. There were several computer monitors and speakers. A small man in civilian khakis and button down shirt sat at one of the tables. Several notebooks were in front of him. Croix could see a page; it was filled with scribbling.

'Who is he?' Croix asked.

The man turned from his notebook and said, 'I am Dr. Martin Rothois, psychiatrist.'

'Must be a pretty important Jihadi to keep him down here and have a shrink on hand.'

'It's not a Jihadi.'

'Than who?'

'We have a Jai.'

'You are joking.'

'See for yourself.' Duceppe pressed a button, bringing an image onto the monitor. There sat a Jai. The Jai prisoner was detained in a small, nondescript room—once a cell obviously—which had only a table and two chairs. It sat in a chair and was handcuffed to a wrought iron bar welded into the table. Croix was surprised by how human the prisoner seemed. He was slight of frame, but no smaller than a lot of African immigrants that Croix had seen on the streets of Paris. His head was thin and elongated, but otherwise similar to a human's. Two eyes, two ears, nose, neck, and hair atop, though this was tougher and bushier, almost like an African's. Its skin was gray/green and smooth. It wore clothes too, a pair of blue overalls atop a long-sleeved white shirt.

'Why me?' Croix asked the commander as he looked at the Jai. 'I'm counter-intelligence. I interrogate Muslim Jihadi, not aliens.'

'Which makes you the right man for the job,' Duceppe replied. 'You deal with foreign cultures.'

'Yes foreign, not alien. I should be talking to captured Algerian terrorists, not this thing. I don't even speak its language.'

'Oh, do not worry.' Duceppe pressed the intercom button. 'Can I get you anything? Are you hungry?'

'Yes, Iwouldllikesome food,' the Jai replied in slightly broken English.

'My god, it speaks English.'

'Yes. The Queen's English.'

'How?'

'We would like for you to find out.'

Croix pursed his lips as he stared at the Jai.

'Ahhh. . .' Duceppe said. 'I see that ego of yours is getting to work.'

'Quiet!' Croix snapped without taking his eyes from the monitor. After a few moments, 'What have you learned about him so far?'

'Not much. He is not talking.'

'What about the shrink?' He turned to Rothois, 'What do you think?'

Rothois adjusted his glasses. 'So far he seems rather human.'

'What does that mean?'

'He is reacting the way a human would react.'

'So he may respond to the same pressures?'

'It is not out of the question.'

Croix turned to Duceppe, 'How long have you had him?'

'Since this morning.'

'Any harsh methods?'

'None.'

'Why ask?'

'I was with the Americans in Afghanistan, remember?'

'Alright.'

He looked at the Jai for a few moments until a soldier brought a pre-wrapped sandwich and a bottle of water for the Jai. 'I'll bring them in,' Croix said.

Croix nodded. A guard walked over and unlocked the door. Croix opened it and walked in. He made eye contact with the alien, his eyes were a deep blue. Croix walked to the table sat down across from alien. He put the sandwich and bottle of water on the table and never broke eye contact.

'You wanted something to eat?' he asked.

'Yes,' the alien replied. 'What is that you bring me?'

'Water and a sandwich.'

'Meatwithbread?'

'Yes.'

The alien reached out and took the sandwich. He unwrapped, sniffed, and took a large bite. He chewed quickly and swallowed. Croix watched every move and reaction. They seemed, while not exactly what a human would do, surprisingly human nonetheless.

'Taste good?'

The alien bobbled his head right to left. 'Yes.'

The Jai took another bite and chewed quickly before swallowing.

'Alright, let me know if there is anything else you need.' Croix stood up. 'I will be back soon.'

He knocked on the door. The guard opened it and let him out.

'What was that?' asked Duceppe.

'I will go back in soon.' Croix replied. 'What was I supposed to do? Give him the sandwich and ask him the North Pole Ship's biggest weakness?'

Duceppe said nothing. Croix waited for a few minutes and watched the Jai finish the sandwich. Croix went back in and sat down. He looked into the alien's eyes.

'More?' He asked.

'I am fine.'

'Did they treat you well? The guards?'

'Yes.'

'You have not been abused?'

'Abused?'

Croix punched and slapped the air.

'No.'

'How did they catch you?'

'My ship crashed.'

He considered pressing for more information about the Jai and the ship but decided not to push too hard. Instead, 'I am sorry, I've been rude. What is your name?'

The Jai said nothing.

'Your name?'

Again nothing.

'I am curious about you, about your language.'

Nothing.

'Telling me your name cannot hurt your cause. You are not giving me any information we can use to bring down your ships.'

'What is your name,' the Jai asked without inflecting the question.

Croix smiled. 'You are right. My name is Croix, Gilles Croix.'

The Jai waited a few moments and spoke, 'I am Kle na Gipong.'

'Kle na Gipong.'

'Yes.'

'Shall I call you Kle?'

'Yes.'

'Gipong is your last name? The name of your father?'

Kle thought about this for a moment. 'We take the name of our mothers.'

'I see.'

Croix looked at his watch. 'Will you excuse me? I have to check on something.' He stood up. 'I'm going to bring you back something, though. You will love it.'

Outside, Duceppe said, 'He did not tell you anything we did not already know.'

'Except his name. I learned his name.'

'His name?' Duceppe mocked.

'He has now given me a bit of information. The next bit will be easier to coax. And the next after that easier still. Get me a couple of cups of tea.'

'How do you intend to get more information?'

'By getting him to open up. I will talk about myself; then he will talk about himself.'

'You will tell him lies?'

'No. When you talk about yourself, always the truth, otherwise it's hard to keep track of your personal lies. I learned that when I was with the Americans. And give me the keys to those handcuffs.'

'Why?'

'I will take them off as a reward.'

On Duceppe's orders one of the guards tossed the keys to Croix.

When the tea was ready, Croix poured two cups and walked into the room. He put a cup in front of Kle. 'Try it,' he said.

'What is it,' Kle asked, again with no inflection.

'Tea. It's a hot drink.'

'You,' Kle said.

'You want me to drink first?'

Kle bobbed his head right then left.

'Alright.' Croix took a sip from Kle's cup, and then one from his own.

Kle took the cup and blew the steam off. He cautiously took a sip. He gestured with his shoulders and set the cup back down on the table.

'You like?'

'Is drinkable.'

Kle didn't say anything else. Croix just stared at him, trying to get a read on him. Croix took a sip and said. 'My mother was a tea drinker. Her father hated that.'

'Why.'

'He thought it was a French thing to do. They were Algerian.'

Kle stared at him. Croix got the sense that Kle didn't understand. 'We used to occupy Algeria; there was a war. My mother came to France afterwards.'

'Algerian or French.'

Croix thought he was asking a question. 'Yes, I suppose I was both. My mother taught me Arabic, taught me about Algeria. Hard to learn.' There was silence. 'Was it hard for you to learn English?'

Kle bobbed his head left then right.

'Does that mean no?' Croix imitated Kle's head bobbing.

'Yes.'

'How long did it take?'

'I couldspeak it within severalof your months.'

'How? I mean, how did you pick it up? Where did you get it?'

'We read your...electronic...noise.'

'Why English?'

'Everyone seem to speak it. Other languages toohard.'

'That would make it easier to occupy the planet then, if you already know English.'

'Yes, they wanted tomakesure we all able to speak with you whenwe occupy planet.'

Kle abruptly stopped talking. Croix got the sense that he realized where the conversation was headed. The alien sipped his tea.

So they wanted to take the planet, Croix thought. *I've got to make him think we already knew that.*

'What is wrong?'

'I talk too much.'

'How?'

Kle remained silent.

'Kle, we already knew you were here to take the planet from us.'

'You did.'

'Yes.'

More silence.

'Kle,' Croix began, 'you do not have to tell me anything you do not want to.'

'I have to...' he spoke in his own language. 'Relieve. Relieve waste...'

Croix thought for a moment, 'Oh, you have to relieve yourself. Go to the bathroom. Expel waste?'

Kle bobbed his head right to left.

'Alright.'

Croix stood up. 'Open the door.' He said.

Croix stuck his head out of the door, 'He has to take a piss.'

'I suppose he would,' replied Duceppe.

'You did not think of this.'

'It never occurred to me, no.'

'Which is why I am in here, and you are out there.'

'Oh, touché.' Duceppe shouted for a bucket and some toilet paper.

'A bucket? That is what you are going to do for him.'

'Until I know more, yes.'

'Know more about what?'

'About your alien friend. One never knows what he may be plotting.'

A guard walked into the room with a bucket and some toilet paper.

'Are you afraid he may have a death ray up his posterior?'

Duceppe shrugged. 'One cannot be too careful.'

'Apparently not.'

'What would your American friends do?'

'Their army would take him to the latrine. The Marines wouldn't let him go until he told them something useful.'

'Typical.'

'They won, didn't they?'

Croix took the bucket and walked into the cell. He handed the bucket to Kle. 'I would like be alone.'

'Oh. Of course.'

Croix left the room.

'We have learned something else,' Rothois said. 'He wants privacy, just like a human.'

'You see, my new friend and I are making progress.'

'Croix?' Duceppe began.

'Yes?'

'Remember, you work for us, not him.'

Croix stood strait. 'What are you implying?'

'I am implying nothing. I am telling you I don't want to turn on the television in a year and see you testifying on this alien's behalf.'

'Ah, the banlieu affair.'

'You said a gang of Algerian rioters were not to be blamed for their actions.'

'I did what I felt was right.' Croix walked to the door. 'Anything else?'

'Watch yourself, Croix.'

'But of course.'

'What is your plan?'

'Now I will go in and tell him a lot of lies.'

'You said no lying.'

'I said no lying about myself.'

'Ah. A distinction I did not think of.'

Croix did his best to look saddened and walked back into the room. He sat down and said, 'I am afraid I have some bad news. The French air force shot down one of those big ships of yours.'

There was a change in expression, Croix couldn't tell exactly what though, but it might have been shock. 'I donot believe you.'

'Why not? Have not the Americans and Russians already done the same?'

'We lose ships, yes.'

'So why do you think France could not shoot one down? I can get a photograph if you like.'

'Yes.'

Croix stood up and walked out.

'Get the photograph the Russians sent out, the one of the Jai carrier ship cracked in half and smoldering on Kamchatka.'

'Where am I supposed to get it?' asked Duceppe.

'Find a computer.'

One of Duceppe's men found the pic on the internet and printed it out. Croix took the pic and walked back into the cell. He sat down and pushed the pic across the table.

'You must understand that we will win this war.'

Kle said nothing.

'We will use nuclear weapons on our own planet, in our own atmosphere.'

'Yes we know, we saw.'

'Saw?'

'Yes.'

'What do you mean?'

Kle stopped talking.

'What do you mean, you saw?'

'That war you fought before we arrived.'

'You mean against the North Koreans?'

'You used nuclear weapons. Destroyed country on. . .' Kle searched for the word. 'Bit of land.'

'North Korea. The war with the North Koreans?'

Croix tore out a piece of paper from his note pad and drew a rough sketch of north Asia. When he was finished he pointed to Korea. Kle tilted his head right then left.

'Doing that with your head, does that mean yes?'

'Yes. We did not think you would do that.'

'Why not?'

'Hurt your planet.'

'So you wanted the planet for yourselves.'

Kle almost said yes but stopped himself.

'You came to stay didn't you?' Kle said nothing. 'Didn't you? Come on, Kle, you already said you did. Just say it.'

'Yes. We plan to stay.'

'Why?'

Kle didn't speak.

'I can surmise.'

'Sur-mize?'

'Guess.'

Nothing.

'To rule.'

Kle said nothing, but he did look up at the ceiling,

'There must be many of you to be able to do that.'

Kle said nothing.

'Alright Kle, I have to get something to eat, I will be back. May I get something for you?'

Kle nodded his head left then right.

When Croix stepped out Dr. Rothois spoke. 'That gesture, looking up at the ceiling. That must be the same as when we look down at our laps or feet.'

'You mean—'

'You discovered some information from him, and he is ashamed.'

'Yes.'

'What next?' Duceppe asked.

'I am going to get him to tell me how many Jai are in those ships.'

Croix walked back in and sat down. He tried to suppress a smile and then laughed.

'What that.' Kle asked without the proper inflection.

'This is called laughing.'

'Laughing.'

'Yes. We laugh when we think something is funny, humorous. Not as it should be.'

Kle bobbed his head right then left. 'Whatfunny.'

'Oh I should not tell you.' Croix looked down and then fixed Kle's gaze. 'Oh, very well, I do not see what harm it can do. You are funny.'

'I am funny.'

'Yes.'

'Why.'

'What you said, ruling the Earth. You cannot do that. You do not have enough soldiers, enough ships and vehicles.'

Kle said nothing.

'We can overcome anything you Jai have.' Croix pointed at Kle and laughed some more. 'I am sorry.'

Kle made a fist and slammed it on the table.

'Do not get mad at me,' Croix said. 'It is not my fault you are weak.'

'We have tens of thousands of soldiers,' Kle said, louder than Croix had ever heard him speak.

Croix gave a nonchalant shrug. 'There are seven billion of us.'

Kle stood up.

'We have six four,' he said something unintelligible in his own language, 'each has one six ships.'

Croix smiled. 'We shot down your ship quite easily.'

'I flew squadron over channel. We shot down many of you aircraft, shot down ship on water, and destroyed port, I—'

Kle stopped talking. Croix looked up from his note pad and tried to hide his surprise. He threw the pen and paper on the table and folded his arms in mock disgust.

'Kle, I cannot help you unless you are completely honest with me. Why did you not tell me that you commanded a squadron of ships?'

'I do not.'

'Yes, you said so.' Croix turned to the mirror. 'Play back the audio of Kle saying he led a squadron.'

A few seconds later the audio ran, '*I flew squadron over channel.*'

'You command a squadron of fighter ships. Not only that, you told us how many of these big carriers are in your fleet, how many fighter ships they carry, and gave us some idea how many ground troops you have.'

Kle looked stunned.

Croix stood up. 'I will leave you alone. I want you to take a moment and think about what this means. Take your time.'

Croix stepped out of the room. Once the door was closed, Duceppe clapped.

'Very nicely done,' he said.

Croix took a sarcastic bow.

'We did not suspect that he was a squadron commander.'

'Which is why you brought me here.'

'Do not let it go to your head, Croix.'

They watched Kle. He sat in the chair, hands in his lap and stared at the ceiling.

Rothois spoke, 'I would say the man,' Croix and Duceppe looked askance at the doctor. '...well, Jai, is suffering now. A great internal battle is occurring within.'

Croix smiled. 'That is what I do.'

'Go back in?' Duceppe asked.

'Let him think about things for a few more minutes.'

'Do not wait too long. He may decide he doesn't want to help us.'

Croix looked over at Duceppe in irritation. 'Do you not think that I know what I am doing?'

Croix waited five more minutes out of spite for Duceppe.

When he sat back down in the interrogation room he began, 'I would like to help you, Kle. I would. But you need to be completely honest with me. You should have told me that you are a squadron commander.'

'I do not want you help.'

'You may not yet know it, but you do.'

Kle did not speak.

'As I said before, we are winning and will win this war. When that happens, you will be trapped here on Earth. Not as a ruler but as a prisoner.' Croix waited a few moments for the sentence to sink in. 'When that happens, when we win, and the survivors of your fleet are trapped on Earth, there will only be two kinds of Jai prisoners, those who helped us, and those who did not.'

'We may win,' Kle said.

For the first time, he doesn't sound confident, Croix thought. Croix nodded 'Perhaps. But if the Jai win, you will still lose. We are already writing a press release about you.'

'Press release.'

'A message that will be broadcast all over the world.' Croix cleared his voice and did his best newscaster impersonation, 'A Jai squadron commander named Kle na Gipong has been aiding our efforts against the invasion.'

Kle said nothing. He looked up at the ceiling again.

'I presume that the Jai have a punishment for treason. Ours is death.'

Croix waited, but Kle said nothing for a long minute.

'Alone.'

'Alone?'

'Yes. I want alone.'

Croix nodded and stood up. 'Take your time. You have a lot to think about.'

Outside Duceppe asked. 'Think he will turn?'

'He is talking himself into it now.'

Rothois nodded. 'I think so too.'

'Get someone from the air force here. Navy as well.'

'Why?'

'He will be divulging much technical data. I will not know what it means. I will not know what follow up questions to ask.'

'Good thinking, for you, Croix.'

Duceppe picked up the telephone and asked the operator to get him the nearest air force base. When Duceppe got off the phone, Croix asked if he could use it.

'Want to call your woman?' Duceppe asked.

'Yes.'

Croix hit the number for an outside line and then dialed his apartment. It rang once before she picked up.

'Hello Huguette.'

'Oh Gilles,' she began. 'Terrible things are happening. There was a huge explosion and then jets overhead, they shattered one of your windows. I hung a towel over it.'

'Calm down, my dear,' he said. 'How are you?'

'Scared. When will you come back?'

'I do not know yet.'

'Please, Gilles, I do not want to be alone.'

As they spoke Kle put his head in his hands and started moaning.

'Is he crying?' Duceppe asked.

'If he were human that would not be out of the question,' said Rothois.

'Darling, I must go,' Croix said.

'No please,' Huguette said. 'Just talk to me a while longer.'

'I can't. I will telephone later.'

'Please.'

Croix hung up. 'I am going back in,' he said.

The guard opened the door. Croix slowly walked into the cell. He reached into his pocket and took out a wad of napkins.

'For your face,' he said.

Kle took the napkins and wiped his face.

'I have...' he began. 'I...'

Croix stopped him. 'I know, Kle. I am a soldier too. And now you, like all soldiers eventually must, have to make a decision.'

'I have. What would youwant know.'

Croix reached out and touched Kle's hand. 'Thank you, Kle. You are doing a great thing. It must be hard for you.' Croix squeezed his hand.

Outside, Duceppe made dramatic gagging sounds.

Rothois said, 'It's working.'

An hour later, Croix sat back in his chair and rubbed his face. 'Alright, let me see, one more time, if I have this right.' He picked up his note pad and read.

'What we call Tau Ceti is your home world.'

'No,' said Kle, 'it is not our home world.'

'Ahh,' Croix made a show of scratching something from his note pad and scribbling something new. 'Your home world is close by though.'

'No, it is over four hundred light years away from Earth.'

Croix scratched something out again. 'I apologize for the continued errors.' He smiled inwardly. *His story is holding up to scrutiny*, he thought.

'You are the youngest son in a great family on Tau Ceti.'

'Yes.'

'What did your father do?'

'He was a great....lord. He owned many...farms.'

Story is still not changing, 'You joined the military because there was no land for you.'

'I couldwork with brothers.'

'And you did not want to do that.'

'No.'

'So the military was your only option.'

'Yes.'

Croix felt it was time to reinforce and reassure Kle a bit more. 'This is a decision that is often made on Earth. My father went to Algeria because his brother inherited everything,' Croix made a show of flipping more pages in his note pad. 'Now, this military expedition of yours, the purpose is to come to Earth and take over.'

'Take over.' He asked without getting the inflections right.

'Rule.'

'Yes.'

'Now, this was not organized by the government, by the lords.'

'No, a rich lord and a general put fleet together, combined one of his great ships-'

'The ships orbiting our poles?'

'Yes. Put great ship together with another great ship.'

'This owner of the other great ship, he was partner?'

'Yes, but not...equal. I do not understand details of their force.'

'Of their agreement?'

Kle nodded his head right then left.

'The leader, what is his name again?'

'Zetroc Nanreh.'

'So this Zetroc Nanreh, he was going to conquer Earth and make himself ruler.'

'Yes.'

'What do you get?'

Kle said nothing.

'You are commanding a squadron of bombers.'

'Yes.'

'You are risking your life.'

'Yes.'

'What do you get for this?'

'Land. Lord. I become rich.'

As he spoke those words Kle looked up and started wailing again.

Croix stood up. 'I will leave you for a moment.'

'Yes.

When Croix walked into the other room Duceppe looked visibly angry. 'So we're just the victim of some petty lord's feudal adventure,' he said.

'It would appear.'

'The gaul, the nerve...'

'Settle down, Duceppe, the same has happened in our history. Algeria for instance.'

'Shut up.'

'Try not to take it personally.'

'Still I do not understand. How long would they have stayed? Where are their women? Why would someone risk his neck...?"

Croix held up his hand.

'What?'

'I am going back in.'

By then Kle had composed himself.

Croix sat down and asked. 'Kle, you said you joined the fleet to become rich.'

'Yes.'

'You could have done the same back on Tau Ceti, no?'

Kle said nothing.

'You could have worked for your brothers. You could have become rich that way.'

Kle looked up again.

'Why did you really join the fleet? It was your brothers, your father, that was the reason wasn't it? You wanted to prove yourself, did you not?'

Kle wailed once more, this time his cries filled the room.

Croix stood up again. 'I will talk to you more later. We want technical data.'

Kle nodded as a human would.

Outside, Duceppe asked, 'Why did you go back in there? Who cares why he joined.'

'People are endlessly fascinating, Duceppe. Even if they're aliens.'

French Forces Stop Jai in Battle over Bay of Biscay
Maintain tenuous lifeline across Atlantic

Paris: French air and naval units today reversed their fortunes and shot down several Jai ships and, in the words of a government spokesmen, severely damaged a carrier ship. Speculation is rampant that the French military has come into information or discovered some weakness in the Jai ships, but no one is sure how...

Sky News

This Time, France stays in the Fight

The Spectator

Massive Battle over Mediterranean as NATO attacks Jai Landing in Tunisia

Paris: French air and naval forces, accompanied by British forces, possibly out of Gibraltar, and Italian forces from Malta, launched an attack on the big Jai base in Tunisia...

The London Times

Chapter 8: Rising Again

Arrival + 5 weeks

SEC DEF: There's no getting around it, Madam President; they've punched through the Aleutian line of defense.

POTUS: But how?

SEC DEF: They spent two days systematically reducing our defenses there. First Shemya, then Unalaska Island fell. Once those were gone it was easy to roll up the rest of the chain.

POTUS: What about this missile base at Fort Greeley?

SEC DEF: It lobbed dozens of missiles at the Jai and did damage, but they hit Greeley with everything they had. Greely put up a heck of a fight.

POUTS: What next?

SEC DEF: The Northern Pacific is wide open. I've already ordered reinforcements to Hawaii, a squadron each of F-16 and F-22 Fighters are on the way.

POTUS: Aren't we weakening the Continental United States?

SEC DEF: Yes but if they attack down the Continental United States, the forces in Hawaii can be sent back. Besides, they may not attack the West Coast, the Jai may hit China and Japan. And if they do, we need to be in a position to help.

Presidential transcript, White House Bunker File

Captain Hiroshi Takahashi didn't sleep. He tossed and turned and awoke every few minutes as he was tormented by the memory of alien lasers, missiles, and kinetic bombs piercing the air and drowning sailors. He lay fitfully on his bunk like this for over an hour until he heard a respectful knock on his door.

'Enter,' he said.

'Kiki Shima nears, Captain,' said his steward.

'Thank you.'

Without another word the steward placed a cup of tea on Takahashi's desk and left. Takahashi sat up and rubbed his eyes. He took the teacup from the desk, took a sip and carefully placed the cup back on the saucer. Next to the teacup was a copy of *Japan Pro Baseball Handbook and Media Guide*, the only non-military history book on a desk shelf filled with the likes of *The Influence of Sea Power on History* and *Midway: the Battle That Doomed Japan*. In peacetime his steward would have left a summary of the day's box scores and hand written notes on the performance of Japanese baseball players in America. Takahashi donned his coat. He checked that the array of campaign ribbons were in place, straightened them, and walked out of his Spartan cabin to the bridge. Kiki Shima loomed on the starboard side. The towns there were dark, but a fire raged where the island's airport had been. He recalled that a squadron of F-15J Eagles had been stationed there.

Takahashi stood on the bridge of the *Kongo* and sipped his tea, as for the first time since the Second World War, a fleet of ships steamed into battle under Japanese command. He'd always wondered about a moment like this. He wondered if the upcoming battle would be Tshushima or Midway. It would be his second battle in as many days. Most of the fleet, including the *USS George Washington*, were at the bottom of the Pacific after a ferocious battle. A single man nearing his fiftieth year, the navy was all Takahashi had, and it pained him deeply to watch a great ship go down, even if it was part of another navy.

The four surviving ships of the task force had one by one staggered into the White Beach naval base on Okinawa. Miraculously all four ships were rearmed, patched up, and sailing before dawn. As the crews worked feverishly, the big American airbase at Kadema burned on the horizon, the result of a concentrated alien assault. Because there was nothing left at Kadema to defend the base commander gave *Kongo* their last surviving THEL. The laser module had been welded to the top of *Kongo's* forward gun while the two trailers were lashed and bolted down to the deck behind.

As Takahashi stood on the bridge, those four surviving warships cruised north toward an alien carrier ship, designated OMEGA, on station off of Kyushu's southern point. JDF *Kongo* was in the lead with *Chokoi* six miles to stern. *John S. McCain* was three miles to starboard, *Shiloh* three miles to port. Six F-15 Eagles, deployed in groups of three, patrolled to the stern, just below the horizon. F-18 Super Hornets, survivors from the battle group, were armed and ready at the Naha airport on Okinawa. The squadron made 12 knots; a ruse meant to deceive the aliens. When the sun disappeared entirely, Takahashi ordered the fleet to a course of 015 toward OMEGA. The squadron made thirty knots.

The Officer Of the Day reported, 'Captain, reports are sketchy, but there seems to be a large battle developing over Manchuria.'

'What do we know?'

'It sounds like a joint attack by Russian forces on one end and Chinese on the other.'

'Who's winning?'

'The Russians have taken heavy losses, sir. We heard a transmission about a squadron of Backfire bombers being blown out of the sky.'

'Is there any indication that the carrier ship off Kyushu is responding to our movement?'

'Not yet, Captain.'

He sipped his tea. 'Very well. Proceed.'

'Yes, sir.'

Takahashi sat down in the captain's chair. Lying on the armrest was a manila folder, the report on the previous battle he had ordered his Tactical Operations Officer to compose. He picked it up and began reading.

The battle had begun when a Jai carrier ship spotted the task force sailing north. At one hundred miles the ship began a standoff missile barrage. The American and Japanese Aegis missile systems brought these down without too much trouble, except for one that slammed into USS *Thatch* and set her afire. Under cover of this barrage the Jai launched two waves of six bombers. *George Washington's* carrier air wing engaged. More than half of the jets were shot down before they ever got a shot off. But once the Jai were in range, the Super Hornets did some damage. The ship's own missile barrage destroyed one bomber. The American pilots claimed a second, but intelligence was unable to confirm it. The Jai bombers closed in and attacked the fleet. Another bomber was shot down, but the fleet lost two destroyers sunk and two more ships damaged. Having expended their ammunition, the bombers drew off, at which point the carrier ship closed and bombarded the fleet with kinetic warheads. Takahashi shuddered at the memory of those horrible bombs. Through his binoculars he had seen desperate American and Japanese sailors floating in the water, waving for *Kongo* to rescue them. Takahashi had had to ignore their pleas, and instead maneuvered for the safety of the ship.

'Captain, OMEGA is losing altitude and accelerating.'

'Order General Quarters. I'm going to the CIC. OOD, you have the bridge.'

As general quarters sounded Takahashi made his way down to the Combat Information Center. The room was crammed with computers and video screens, all relaying data to their operators. The Tactical Operations Officer was leaning over a radar operator's shoulder, watching as real time data on OMEGA streamed in.

Takahashi took a seat in the chair reserved for the captain, 'Report.'

The TAO responded instantly. From bitter experience he had learned that Takahashi was not to be kept waiting. 'OMEGA is losing altitude at just over a mile per minute.'

'Course?'

'Heading away from Kyushu on an intercept course with us.'

'Very well. I want to know when OMEGA is within one hundred miles.'

'Yes, Captain.'

A mind trained by the pursuit of an MA in statistics wondered what the Jai carrier ship was up to and plotted possible reactions until. . .

'Captain we are now within one hundred miles of the target, altitude ninety miles and dropping.'

He picked up the satellite phone, punched a button, and heard *Chokoi's* captain answer on the other end. 'This is Takahashi. Fire one SM-3 at OMEGA.'

Moments after the order was relayed, one of *Chokoi's* four SM-3 missile hatches flew open. There was a quick burst of flame, and then a contrail as the missile, originally built to intercept ICBMs, streaked into the air. *Kongo's* radar operator tracked the missile as it sped toward OMEGA, accelerating and gaining altitude. After the missile closed to within ten miles, one of OMEGA's lasers stabbed out and obliterated the target, leaving a cloud of smoke and debris.

'Missile destroyed.'

'Captain?' asked the TAO. 'May I ask what that accomplished sir?'

'Since you already have I will answer. OMEGA knows we are coming. More importantly, they may think we had only one SM-3 to fire.'

The TAO nodded in comprehension.

'They will at least have to consider that possibility, and I believe—'

'Captain, I have three contacts, Jai bombers, sixty-five nautical miles, altitude thirteen thousand meters and closing fast. Designated XRAY One, Two, and Three.'

'Commander, deploy strike groups at your discretion.'

"Yes, Captain.'

The TAO spoke into his mic, vectoring Strike Group Bravo twenty miles behind Strike Group Alpha's aft, starboard flank. Both groups accelerated to mach one on a course taking them between the task force and the Jai bombers. He then ordered Naha base to scramble the rest of the surviving aircraft.

'Captain, I have eight new contacts. Judging by their altitude and speed, they are anti-ship missiles.'

The TAO spoke again. Seconds later *Kongo's* deck ignited as an SM-2 missile was launched from its silo within the hull. This was followed by three more missile launches, each at one second intervals. To the stern *Chokoi* fired off a quartet of missiles as well. Takahashi followed the contrails as they streaked off to an unseen point ahead. There was a flash in the distance and then a second. *John S. McCain* and *Shiloh* fired volleys next, more flashes. Finally, there was an explosion to port, as *John S. McCain's* point defense brought down a Jai missile.

'All missiles destroy—'

Before the tech could finish his sentence radar picked up another quartet of missiles fired by XRAY-One. Before the port bomber could fire, the TAO ordered Alpha and Bravo wings to break to port and accelerate towards it at mach two. Alpha made directly for XRAY-One, while Bravo looped around to its south, and then broke north. They flooded the air with missiles just before Alpha lost a pair of Eagles to a Jai laser. Because of the incoming missiles, XRAY-One could not engage the other jets. Instead, it banked away and climbed while its own point defense dealt with the incoming threats. XRAY-One knocked missile after missile from the sky, first with a pair of fore and aft laser batteries, then with kinetic point defenses that used small pellets to shatter the incoming targets. However, there were far too many incoming missiles for the bomber to destroy them all. One missile from Alpha exploded 30 meters aft of XRAY-One, while one from Bravo detonated under the joint that connected the wing to the fuselage. Alpha Flight leader reported a smoke trail and said he could actually see the stricken aircraft losing altitude.

Seeing an opportunity, Takahashi gave quick orders. 'Send Alpha and Bravo against XRAY-Three and concentrate all SAM fire on XRAY-One and XRAY-Two.'

As Alpha and Bravo engaged XRAY-Three, *Kongo* and the other ships in the task force fired a volley of SAMs at XRAY-One and Two. Since XRAY-Two was closer, it received the volleys first. Unused to being the lone target, the ship's defenses were overwhelmed. Three missiles detonated aft of the ship, while a fourth exploded just above the cockpit. XRAY-Two spiraled down to the sea trailing smoke.

'Target destroyed!' reported the fire control officer.

XRAY-One banked to port, a maneuver which bought crucial seconds for its point defenses to knock down the incoming SAMs. The Eagles pressed home their attack on XRAY-One, but their Sparrow missile barrage failed to penetrate the Jai's defenses. They were forced to close to ten miles to engage with Sidewinders. XRAY-One shot down one Eagle with a laser burst, and then another with a missile. But the two remaining jets closed to within range and launched all eight of their Sidewinders. XRAY-One shot down half of the missiles, but the others hit their target, exploding to the aft of the bomber and separating the tail section from the fuselage. It crashed into the sea.

'XRAY-One has been destroyed, Captain.'

'XRAY-Three coming in fast, four missiles in the air, make that eight, make that twelve and still coming, sixteen…now twenty.'

All four ships in the taskforce flung SAMs into the air.

The TAO reported 'Strike groups Charlie, Delta, and Easy now in range, am ordering them to fire on incoming missiles.'

'Negative,' said Takahashi. 'They are to attack XRAY-Three; we'll fend off the missiles.'

'Sir.'

The TAO issued orders to his fighter groups-surviving Super Hornets from *George Washington*, sending them to under five hundred feet and maximum speed with orders to engage at their discretion. In the meantime, contrails reached up from ships towards the incoming missiles, now closing at a mile per second. The radar controller dutifully reported the time to impact and count as both decreased, 'Fifteen seconds…eleven missiles left…fourteen….thirteen…twelve…ten missiles, make that nine….five seconds.'

'Shall the THEL battery fire, Captain?' asked the XO.

'No.'

'But, Captain, it—'

'I said no.'

Takahashi could actually see explosions in the sky. *Kongo's* point defense went live, sending a hail of bullets in the air. A missile exploded in a fiery ball of steel less than a half mile from *Kongo*, but its momentum carried the debris into the fore of the ship, showering the forward gun and SAM launchers with shrapnel. The bridge's Plexiglas window buckled and cracked under the force of the impact, sending the entire bridge crew flying to the floor. As he scrambled to his feet, Takahashi heard a large, loud explosion to port, and through the shattered window he saw *John S. McCain* trailing smoke from two hits, one on the fore, the other just aft of the bridge. Flames rapidly spread as the stricken ship listed to starboard.

The XO spoke. 'Captain, the THEL trailers.'

Takahashi looked forward and saw the trailer farthest forward, housing the guidance system, had been peppered by shrapnel.

'Get down there, find the damage sustained by the THEL, and get it fixed.'

'Yes, sir.'

Before Takahashi could issue any more orders, strike groups Charlie, Delta, and Easy roared overhead. The Super Hornets attacked at supersonic speed, knocking the already broken bridge windows out of their holdings. There were more flashes of light off in the distance as they fired a volley of Sidewinders at the closing bomber. They pressed ahead despite the XRAY-Three's deadly accurate lasers, which systematically vaporized a first, second, and then a third jet.

'A hit, Captain, and now a second and a third!' reported the TAO with growing excitement as his jets savaged the Jai bomber. 'That's it, XRAY-Three destroyed.'

'Are there any more bombers?'

'Not yet, Captain.'

'Very well, get me a status report on *John S. McCain*.'

A few moments, and then, 'Dead in the water sir, dozens killed, weapons systems still functioning, so says the XO. Captain Reynolds is dead.'

'Very well. Order *Chakoi* to come up beside us and *Shiloh* to fall back three miles.'

'Yes, sir.'

The fleet took up its new formation, leaving the wounded *John S. McCain* behind.

'I want an update on the THEL' said Takahashi. 'Where are the repairs? How long?'

The XO returned to the bridge. His face was covered in soot and his shirt torn. In his hand was a spanner wrench.

'Report.'

'Captain, the first trailer housing the fire control system was heavily damaged. We are salvaging the equipment and setting it up in the second trailer.'

'Will that configuration work?'

'It will be crowded.'

'What about the THEL unit?'

'When I supervised its installation I had a metal plate bolted to fore. It protected the THEL from the blast.'

'Excellent work, XO. How long before the unit is ready?'

'Soon, Captain. That's all I can say.'

'Make sure it is very soon.'

'Captain,' said the OOD, 'OMEGA is turning to face us and accelerating.'

'Is it descending?'

'Not yet, Captain.'

'Where are the bombers?' the XO asked. 'Maybe we destroyed them all? Are they over Japan?'

'Right now, they are not here, that is all that matters,' said Takahashi.

'OMEGA firing.'

'Commander, you are free to fire the THEL as you see fit.'

'Yes, Captain.'

As the kinetic bombs closed in the TAO issued orders. The THEL laser fired a three-second burst, and then another. The extreme heat generated by the laser did not actually harm the projectiles; instead it fried the bomb's guidance system. Unable to track their targets, and with their circuits warped, both bombs went haywire, flying miles off course and slamming harmlessly into the sea. A second volley followed. This one fared no better than the first. Then a third, this time of four whistle bombs. Once again, the THEL lined up each incoming target and fried their guidance systems.

OMEGA fired a barrage of missiles. Methodically, SM-2s reached out from *Kongo* and *Chokoi*, one by one downing the incoming Jai missiles until there was only one left for *Kongo*'s point defense to deal with, a burst from *Shiloh* brought it down more than a mile away, peppering the water before *Kongo* with a wave of falling debris. The Jai ship continued to close, but fired no more missiles.

'Are they dry?' the XO asked.

'Perhaps.'

'They did fire many, many missiles in the battle last night.'

Takahashi watched as OMEGA closed to within ninety miles, and then eighty, wondering and waiting for another barrage. None came.

TAO. 'Fire all four of our SM-3s, in echelon, staggered by two seconds.'

'Yes, sir.'

'And order *Chokoi* to do the same.' He turned to the air control officer. 'I want Charlie, Delta, and Echo to close in fast behind the SM-3s. Close in and engage.'

'Yes, sir.'

Pillars of flame jetted out from *Kongo*'s deck as one by one the SM-3 missiles were fired into the sky. Thin contrails were left in their wake as they gained altitude and speed until they travelled at 1.6 miles per second. A second volley of three from *Chokoi* followed close behind. As per orders the Super Hornets followed behind at mach one. OMEGA's formidable point defenses went to work. When they were within range, small, powerful lasers opened fire, bringing down two of *Kongo*'s missiles, and three of *Chokoi*'s. But two got through and close enough to launch their Kinetic Energy Warheads. Both KEWs impacted just to the fore of the carrier ship's engine compartment with the force of a Mack truck slamming into a wall at six hundred mph. The SM-3s bored into the carrier's hull, smashing bulkheads and collapsing decks. One of the warheads cut a fuel line, causing an explosion which sent a fireball scorching out the entry point.

'Two hits!' reported the TAO.

'We nailed it!" the XO shouted. 'Look at that ball of fire.'

'OMEGA is descending.'

'How fast? Is it crashing?'

'It looks like the descent is controlled sir.'

TAO reported, 'Strike groups closing sir.'

Takahashi watched the display as the remaining aircraft, eleven in all closed with the Jai ship. Three of the dots representing aircraft winked off the screen in quick succession, then a fourth. But the survivors got within Sparrow missile range, firing a combined nine in all. Rather than bank away, the pilots pressed their fighters forward, passing under the Jai carrier at maximum speed. OMEGA shot down another Super Hornet as they passed beneath. The ship's point defenses went back to work, shooting down all but the last missile, which exploded mere feet from the hull and opened up a gap large enough to drive a garbage truck through. Amazingly the seven remaining Super Hornets swung back around and fired a combined volley of twenty-eight Sidewinder missiles. The carrier's point defense were so busy with the incoming missiles that all seven Super Hornets were able to fly back underneath the ship, though one more was brought down by a laser as it flew away.

'Four more hits, Captain,' said the TAO.

'Well done, Commander,' said Takahashi.

'Surviving Super Hornets say they are dry. I'm sending them back to Naha to rearm.'

Takahashi nodded.

Tense minutes passed until the fire control officer spoke. 'Captain, at present course and speed OMEGA will be in range of our SM-2 missiles within two minutes.'

'I know,' he said.

'New targets, two bombers. Twenty miles and closing. Designate XRAY-Four and Five.'

'How?' asked the XO.

'They must have kept them in reserve aboard ship,' Takahashi said dispassionately. *Damn.*

XRAYs Four and Five flew in echelon a mile or so apart. They concentrated on *Chokoi*, alternating missile fire and laser bursts from their nose cannons. *Chokoi* responded with a counter volley, the first of which was aimed for the oncoming bombers, not the missiles, Takahashi noticed. Those not brought down by the SAMs were blasted from the sky by *Chokoi's* point defenses, except one, which slammed into the bridge. A split second later a laser blast sliced through and exploded the gun. The Jai bombers triumphantly screamed over the stricken cruiser. Even in its death throes *Chokoi* fired off a trio of SAMs, scoring a hit on the lead bomber as it passed to the south. *Kongo's* fire control officer fired a pair of missiles at the now damaged bomber, as did *Shiloh*, trailing behind the two cruisers. XRAY-Four took two more hits and exploded in the sky, leaving XRAY-Five to continue south until it too was unexpectedly hit by a pair of SAMs.

'XRAY-Five just took a pair of hits, Captain. It's going down.'

'Where? Who fired?'

'They weren't from us…wait, a third now. The missiles were fired by *John S McCain*!'

The bomber's point defense took out the first two missiles, but could do nothing about the third, which exploded less than twenty-five meters in front of the nose, which was smashed by the force of the explosion. The bomber cart wheeled forward and tumbled end over end into the ocean.

'Any more bombers?'

'No sir, none spotted, just OMEGA,' the radar operator punched a few buttons. 'It's slowing down and beginning to turn, Captain.'

'Turning?' asked the XO.

'Yes, Commander.'

'He doesn't want to fight, Captain!'

Takahashi nodded. 'Well I do. Target OMEGA. Signal *Shiloh* and tell her to do the same.'

'Yes, Captain.'

A pair of SM-2s rocketed out from *Kongo*, then another pair, and another. *Shiloh* added her own missiles to the volley. The carrier's defenses were swamped. Each salvo managed to get closer than the last. A torrent of laser blasts brought down a half dozen missiles inside of a mile, staving off disaster, but only for a few moments. The fourth volley detonated amidships, the fifth forward of the engine compartment. A sixth volley, this one from *Shiloh*, exploded above OMEGA, showering its hull with shrapnel. Two more missiles followed. These ripped a great gash in the hull. A lucky volley from *Kongo* exploded less than fifty feet from the thrusters, shredding one.

'It's going down, Captain, losing altitude quickly.'

They could see the carrier now, off in the distance, a flickering white light trailing a thin wisp of smoke. Bursts of yellow light went off around it. The ship wasn't crashing, but it was dropping altitude as quickly as possible, until it settled down in the water, forty-five miles north, northeast of the squadron. OMEGA did not sink. Rather it floated like an ocean going vessel. Internal propeller screws deployed, and in moments, the spaceship was underway.

'OMEGA is in the water, Captain, steaming away from us at twenty-two knots.'

'Captain, we can—'

Takahashi held up his hand and said, 'I know, Commander. Fire the Harpoons, all of them, now.'

Only three harpoons got through, but they were enough, the first two impacted just aft of the carrier's bridge, causing a cataclysmic explosion which lifted the ship out of the water and ripped a thirty foot gash in the hull below the water line. This time *Kongo's* bridge crew did clap and cheer. Even Takahashi smiled.

Later, *Kongo* approached the area where the Jai carrier had landed. Slowly bobbing up and down in the water, like a cork, was the fore of the ship. Takahashi scanned it with his binoculars and saw dozens of human-like beings hanging on. Some clung to wreckage floating in the sea. Many just floated face down in the water. He couldn't help but feel sympathy for the stranded Jai and for the ship. It was always sad to see a great vessel destroyed, even if it was your enemy.

'Survivors, Captain,' said XO.

'Yes.'

'Shall I order the gun to open fire?' asked the TAO

Takahashi lowered his glasses and gave the officer the icy glare which had earned him his reputation. 'Negative.'

'What then, sir?'

'Dispatch a launch and our helicopter. Pick up survivors.'

'Simply put,' said the American ambassador to Japan, 'the nation hasn't seen this kind of devastation since the Second World War.' Indeed, Tokyo, Osaka, Yokohama have been all but destroyed by Jai attacks. Much of the Japanese air force has been destroyed, and one high-ranking source, speaking off the record, said that more than half the Japanese navy lies on the floor of the Pacific.

A major counterattack was planned, but according to American sources, had to be called off at the last minute because Chinese commanders refused to cooperate with Taiwanese forces.

As of this writing, the Jai seem content to bombard Siberia.

On a side note, Allied forces were able to exact a measure of revenge the next day when a combined surface task force engaged a Jai carrier ship and brought it down. . .

The Daily

Chapter 9: Guitars and Stars

Arrival

Civilians are strongly urged to stay in their homes.
What to do in Case of Alien Attack, US Printing Office

I actually didn't stay put during the war. How could I? I parked the missus and the kids with my brother, borrowed his motorcycle, and toured the country. Mostly I talked to people, in rest stops, in bomb shelters, in bars. Heck after a few weeks it was amazing how normal the invasion seemed. A lot of schools stayed open, a lot of businesses remained open. The internet worked at least some of the time. I was able to keep blogging. Here's an example of a day's blogging as it unfolded during the third week of the war:

Ok, I don't get it. You aliens bent on world conquest, you're at war with the United States. So why not hit Oak Ridge? Just askin'.

Posted 9:45 p.m.

Good dinner tonight, some local venison with some canned veggies that came into the grocery last night. Could be worse.

Posted at 7:47 p.m.

Went out chopping wood for the fire tonight, saw a great blue streak high up in the sky, definitely one of theirs.

Posted at 5:01 p.m.

Power out for a couple of hours, briefly on, then out again for another hour.

Posted at 3:43 p.m.

Report on radio of nuclear blast off Florida. . .stay tuned. (Update: not a nuke, just a really big bomb.)

Posted at 11:09 a.m.

So I'm staying with a friend outside of Memphis right now. Things ok here; the Jai haven't hit the area, at least not yet. There are performances at the Opry every night, usually by the same acts who were caught in town at Arrival. Gas is too expensive for a large music act to travel. One singer told me the army confiscated his tour bus. Admittance is usually some donated food or canned goods.

Posted at 9:01 a.m.

Up bright and early. Don't be impressed; we were all woken up by sonic booms.

Posted at 5:03 a.m.

Most people tried to stay out of the military's way. Those who could helped however they could, digging ditches, bringing food, that sort of thing. Plenty of people I met let soldiers stay in their homes as their units passed through. A lot of towns put on dances for the soldiers. Soldiers I met were grateful, but wary, I think they just wanted folks to let them go about their jobs without having to worry about civilians hanging around. Some people got caught in the middle of the fighting, though. . .

Before, During, and After: Blogging the Aliens

'Madam President, in order to proceed, I need your nuclear authorization code.'
'Yes, General, the Football is right here, one moment. Authorization code Lima-Tango-Tango-Bravo. . .'

Grant sat on the blanket in the cool October night contentedly strumming his guitar. The notes drifted across the hill, but there was no one to hear except for Kristin, who was busy gathering her clothes. Two hours before he had been playing guitar in Cal's Drinkery, where a hundred people had gathered to watch Arrival. Since everybody was glued to the TV, no one had really noticed him, except for two girls playing pool near the stage. One of them wore snug jeans and sandals, and when she bent over to shoot, Grant saw she had a sunburst tattoo above her tailbone. She was shapely, with big brown eyes and long brown hair. Seeing the girls look over at him, Grant switched from testosterone-fueled classic rock to more 'sensitive' songs. It was Led Zeppelin's 'Tangerine' that finally drew Kristin over to the stage. Grant and Kristin chatted for a while, and then ditched her roommate for the hill overlooking town, 'To get a good view of the aliens, if they come our way,' he had said.

'You want to go back to the bar, watch the arrival?' Kristin asked as she pulled her sweater back on.

'Not yet. I like it up here,' he said. 'With you.'

Kristin smiled at him. 'You sure don't seem very excited about the aliens.'

Grant shrugged and tried to look as if he was too cool to take an interest in the alien's arrival.

'My roommate,' Kristin began, 'she made us go through all this...what do they call it?'

'Disaster preparedness?'

'Yeah! She had all these pamphlets from like, the government, and she stored canned food, and water...'

Grant shrugged indifferently and resumed playing. He was only half aware that he was playing 'Shook Me All Night Long' when Kristin said, 'Play something nice.'

'What, you don't like AC/DC?' He started to sing some raunchy lyrics.

She flashed that flirty smile that Grant had noticed at Cal's. 'You better be singing about me.'

Grant smiled. 'We'll see what you can do, later.'

'Later!' she reached across the blanket slapped him on the arm. 'We'll see about later!' Judging by the gleam in her brown eyes, Grant figured there would be a later.

He was distracted from thoughts of that pleasant pursuit by a series of quick, yellow flashes in the eastern sky. A minute later there was a distant thunderclap, then another.

The combat veteran looked worriedly to the east.

'Are those the aliens?' Kristin asked.

Before Grant could answer there were flashes to the north, a whole string of them lighting off higher and higher into the sky. There were more explosions, not thunderclaps, but booms. Grant recognized them from his time in the Middle East. 'Those are sonic booms,' he said as he looked up. 'Air force jets.'

'What's going on?' Kristin asked

There was another string of flashes high up in the eastern sky, followed by orange streaks coming up from the ground. In response, green beams lashed downwards. The horizon started glowing orange.

Grant didn't know how long he'd been watching when he felt Kristin fold her arms across the back of his shoulders. 'That's some show the aliens are putting on for us.' The northern horizon lit up like the eastern sky. 'And look over there!'

In the distance a green laser reached down from the sky and touched the ground. It was followed by another laser and then another. Grant stood up and zipped his guitar inside his gig bag. As he was lacing up his boots Grant looked at Kristin, who simply stared at the light show. 'We gotta' get back to town, back to the bar.'

'Yeah! Maybe we can see the show on TV.'

Grant didn't feel like expending the mental energy explaining to Kristin what he thought was happening. 'Okay, whatever.'

Kristin folded the blanket while Grant rolled up his sleeping bag. The lightshow to the north grew more intense. There were more sonic booms, and this time he saw a cluster of blue dots heading east. Suddenly, there was the steady beat of helicopter rotors, lots of them. He looked up to see a dozen Apache gun-ships not more than a hundred feet above the ground. They flew past the hill and over the town, where they hovered. As if someone flicked a switch, the gun-ship's noses spat fire and missiles streaked out from under their stubby wings. Then there was a strange howling sound; this was followed by a high-pitched whistle. Knowing that the whistling could only be some kind of ordnance, Grant ran over to Kristin and tackled her. A moment later there was a tremendous explosion which bombarded the hill with a searing blast of heat and seemed to suck all the oxygen out of the air. Grant looked up; the gun-ships were gone, and the town below was engulfed in flames.

'Holy Christ!' Grant shouted.

Kristin stood up and looked at the flaming town. 'Oh my god...' she whimpered. 'The town...Kelly...'

Grant heard that strange whistling sound again and dived back to the ground, pulling Kristin down with him. Another ear-splitting explosion ripped the sky above them, and Grant felt a blast of heat against his back. There was the familiar sound of missiles followed by a series of smaller explosions. Then came the screeching sound of something large tearing through the air followed by a ground shaking blast. Grant knelt up and looked around. A mile or so away, on the hill at the opposite end of town, there was a fiery wreckage. Before he could figure out what it was, he was slammed to the ground by the sonic boom of a flight of F-22 Raptors.

A second later the sonic booms were cut off by a string of explosions. These were replaced by the whistling sound.

'Head down!' Grant shouted as the sky overhead exploded again.

Throughout the night, Grant and Kristin were trapped on the hill as the battle between the aliens and the United States Air Force played out overhead. By the time the sky turned gray, the fight had shifted elsewhere, leaving the pair to survey the smoldering remains of the town. An airburst had flattened it. The Wal-Mart at the edge of town was a massive pile of rubble, as were the Best Buy and Shop Rite next to it. Grant didn't even know where to begin looking for Cal's Drinkery and the little one-room apartment above it that had been his home for the last year. The town's gas lines had exploded, as had the service stations, leaving small fires throughout. Here and there a few dazed persons wandered the rubble-strewn streets or squatted by the remains of their homes. An ambulance wove through the rubble. On the opposite end of town a medivac helicopter landed.

'We have to get out of here,' Grant said.

Kristin didn't move, she just stared at what had been her home.

Grant pulled Kristin to her feet. 'We have to go.'

Still stunned, she stared at him, or through him, crying. Grant took Kristin by the shoulders and shook her. She reached up and pushed Grant away from her.

'Stop it!' Kristin shouted.

'We have to get out of here!'

Kristin looked at the smoldering town, and at Grant. She nodded.

They hurriedly packed everything on Grant's Kawasaki. He put on his helmet and gave Kristin his spare, a gift from his older brother marked 'Devil Dog' with an image of a bull dog painted on one side and the Marine hero Chesty Puller on the other.

'Where are we going?'

'You have any family nearby?'

'My father's in Philadelphia...'

Grant shook his head. 'Big city is a bad idea right now.'

'I want to be with my father,' Kristin said in a tone of voice that suggested to Grant that she was used to getting what she wanted from men.

'Look, Kristin,' Grant pointed to the flashing eastern sky. 'That's what's going on in New York right now. What do you suppose is happening in Philly?'

'But my father's a cop.'

'Then he's probably way too busy for us. Best thing you can do for him is to stay out of his hair.'

Kristin looked crushed for a moment, but then nodded her head in understanding. 'Where do you want to go, then?'

Grant thought for a second. *I haven't been up to the family home in years. I don't know where else to go. Crap.* 'My family has a home in the mountains of Western Massachusetts. We can hole up there until this thing blows over.'

Without waiting for Kristin to respond, Grant started his Kawasaki and gently rode down the hill to the main road.

Figuring it was a good idea to stay off the highways, Grant took them north along back roads. He had played guitar or done some contracting side jobs in half the places between Hackettstown and the New York State border. He knew the back roads well, and plenty of people along the way.

The going was slow. A lot of places didn't want people coming in and closed off the main arteries. A telltale sign was traffic backups. Once he saw these Grant would dart down a side road, navigating by the sun as he went. Outside of Ogdensburg he heard a great rumble in the distance; he and Kristin stopped and dove into a side ditch. They looked up in time to see a great ship the size of a jumbo jet speeding across the sky, a yellow streak of flame roaring out of the tail. Air force jets followed it, piercing the sky with a series of sonic booms as they went.

As the sky started to turn dark they stopped on a side road, just short of the border with New York, where they stretched and relieved themselves.

'Is your family at this house?' Kristin asked as she came out from behind a bush.

'My older brother's already up there with his family, so it's a good place to go. Whether or not Bradley wants to see me is another matter.'

Kristin put her helmet back on, 'Why?'

'Family, you know how it is.' Grant started the motor cycle. 'But I got as much right to be there as he does.'

'What about me?'

Grant didn't answer.

When they got to the New York State border they were confronted by a large traffic jam. At the head of the backup, Grant saw police cars and flashing lights. There was a pair of State Troopers walking down the road; one held a baton, the other a shotgun. Each time they got to a car, the officer with the baton leaned inside the window and a second later the car started turning and heading back the way it had come.

'Are they going to send us back?' Kristin asked.

'Not if I can help it.'

Grant reached into his back pocket and took out his wallet. When the troopers got to him he flipped it open, showing his military ID.

'Okay, turn the bike around, I don't want any argument,' said the cop.

'Officer, I'm a sergeant in the Marine Corp Reserve.' He indicated his wallet. The officer took the ID and examined it.

'Grant Canavan?'

He nodded. 'My unit is assembling up around Groton, Connecticut, you know, to protect the big sub base. I've been ordered there pronto.' Grant was grateful for his helmet. The officer would never have believed his story if he'd seen his shoulder-length hair.

'This is your lucky day. We've been ordered by the governor to stop people from coming in, but to let military personnel through.

He turned to face the road block and whistled. 'Hey, let the motorcycle through! He's a Marine.' The officer turned back to Grant. 'Who's this?' he indicated Kristin.

'My wife. We were honeymooning when this thing broke out.'

'Alright, go on through.' He waved them through with a flashlight. Grant felt Kristin's kiss on his cheek. 'Your wife?'

He shrugged.

Going through New York State they saw a lot of cars stopped on the side of the road. People were camping out, waiting, or gathered around a transistor radio listening for news. Grant's first immediate problem was getting across the Hudson. He decided to try the Tappan Zee Bridge. As they approached there was a steady stream of cars coming the other way. Once they got on the New York Throughway, the westbound lanes were jammed up. Not only was there a lot less traffic on eastbound lanes, but hundreds of cars were pulled over on the shoulder. Less than a mile on the thruway, at the gigantic Palisades Center Mall, there was a line of Humvees parked bumper to bumper across the road. In the middle was an APC; a soldier atop it pointed an M-60 machinegun straight ahead. As Grant drove up very slowly, another soldier with an M-16 cradled in his arm stepped forward. Two more were behind him, rifles at the ready. Judging by the man's age, he was nearing forty, he must have been National Guard.

'No one goes through. Turn around.'

As Grant reached around for his wallet, the guardsmen responded by chambering rounds. 'Easy, just getting my wallet.' He opened it and handed it to the Guardsmen. 'I'm a Marine. My unit's assembling at Groton.'

'You an officer?'

'Nope, E Five.'

'Sorry, Sergeant. We had some trouble earlier.' He nodded to the burnt out shell of an SUV on the side of the road. 'No one gets across except key personnel.' He handed Grant his wallet.

'Any news?'

'TV and radio are starting to get iffy. Satellite's out. No more DirecTV, I guess. A bunch of B-1s flew over us an hour ago. There was some loud explosions after that. Fighter jets all over the place. Saw a bunch of F-16s dog fighting this big alien ship, must have been the size of a seven thirty-seven. Kept knocking the Falcons out of the air, but they got him eventually, crashed up there,' he pointed north. 'Bunch of army helicopters flew up there not long after.'

'What's the holdup?' someone at the roadblock shouted.

The guardsmen turned around. 'Sorry L-T!' he turned back to Grant. 'Okay, Sergeant, turn her around.'

'Alright.'

Grant rode the bike though the gap in the highway partition and joined the jam on the other side. As angry motorists looked on, he wove through traffic until he came to the ramp for the Palisades Parkway leading to the Bear Mountain Bridge.

Soon after getting on the Palisades, they saw dozens of contrails heading west.

'What are those?' Kristin asked.

'Missiles.'

'Are those ours?' Kristin asked.

'I saw plenty of Tomahawk missiles in the war,' he said. 'Those aren't Tomahawks.'

It wasn't until after two p.m. that they got to the exit for the bridge. Here too, they were stopped by a National Guard roadblock. Once again, his Marine gambit didn't work.

'Sorry, Sergeant,' said a National Guard corporal. 'You can see the Indian Point nuclear plant from the bridge. No one's going across in either direction and—' he was interrupted by the roar of jets, a quartet of F-16s flying over head. 'Besides, the higher ups think the aliens are going to come up here and we're moving in all kinds of heavy stuff to defend the place. I don't think you want to be anywhere near here.'

'I'll try the Hamilton Fish Bridge.'

With no other choice they backtracked onto the Thruway and headed north. Traffic was heavy, but it moved. About twenty miles later there was a series of loud cracks in the sky behind them.

'Look!' Kristin said. 'Light! Long streaks of light!'

Grant risked turning his head and saw a half dozen yellow streaks making their way across the sky. Realizing that everyone else was doing the same and afraid that he'd get hit, Grant pulled over on the grass island in the middle.

'Must be the aliens.'

'What are they doing?'

'Think they're hitting the Bear Mountain Bridge, or maybe the power plant.'

The streaks of light continued tracking downwards. Missiles reached up from the ground, and half of the light streaks flashed and disappeared. Seconds later there was a rumbling sound. A pair of large, black dots appeared in the sky. They were too big to be fighter jets. These were alien ships.

Afraid the aliens would come after the Hamilton Fish Bridge next, Grant got back on the road. When they got there Grant found the bridge intact and the National Guard waving traffic across in both directions. Antiaircraft guns were deployed at either end of the bridge. There was a radar station on a hill on the east bank, and a bit south, a battery of six Patriot Missile launchers. Looking south, there were several smoke columns and the flaming wreck of an F-22 on the river bank.

From the New York Thruway Grant got on the Taconic Parkway. They drove slowly, cautiously, passing hundreds of pulled over cars and families camping on the road side. Grant kept going after the sun went down. Past midnight Grant took the exit for RT 23, which would take them into Massachusetts. There was an old diner at the end of the ramp. He half expected it to be closed, but there was a large banner hanging from the roof proclaiming in orange spray paint STILL OPEN. The lights were on, and the parking lot full.

The route was lined with little towns run by sheriffs who would bust you for going over twenty-five mph, and Grant was worried they'd stop him. He was surprised once again when he got to the first town, Hillsdale, and the sheriff waved him through. He stopped and asked a pair of shotgun wielding deputies why.

'By presidential executive order,' said one.

'Yeah,' said the other. 'Towns are to allow free movement. Anyone not cooperating will be replaced by military commanders.'

'Figure large concentrations of people are a target. Keep 'em moving so they can get to where they're going.'

'Cool. Any news?' asked Grant.

'Lot's of fighting over the Atlantic. We've used nukes.'

'They sank a couple of our carriers.'

Grant thought of his little brother, a Marine lieutenant in the security detail on the USS Harry Truman. He thanked the sheriffs and moved on. The road east was clogged with cars, a snaking line of headlights moving at about twenty mph. Westbound traffic was much lighter. The gas stations were busy; at one there was a man pumping gas with a rifle slung over his back, but there didn't seem to be any trouble. They were still even taking credit cards. Every few minutes there was the roar of a jet engine, sometimes a sonic boom. Over the border Grant saw flashing lights in his side view and pulled over. Rather than stop, the police car kept going at forty mph, followed by a convoy of military vehicles; Humvees, APCs, and M-1 tanks on HET trailers, Grant counted fourteen, a company.

The roaring military convoy finally woke Kristin. She'd been asleep since the last twenty miles of the Taconic, leaning against his back, arms wrapped around his waist.

'How much longer?' she asked as the last vehicle in the convoy, a police car running its light, passed by.

'Not far.'

They climbed further into the Berkshire Mountains, finally leveling off at Great Barrington. Grant thought of the town as his second home, and he was glad to see the alien invasion hadn't changed it, though there was a heavy law enforcement presence. The local bohemians were collecting supplies for disaster relief. Some of the hippies were already protesting the war. One sign claimed America's nuclear arsenal and missile defense network had provoked the aliens into attacking Earth. The town theater and schools had been converted to a makeshift hospital for refugees coming east from Boston. The meadows outside of town were choked with civilian helicopters. Several more were in the sky, some landing from the west, others heading back east.

Grant rode several miles further, climbing another mountain, before turning onto a gravel road that you couldn't see if you didn't know it was there. After a few hundred yards the road ended at the family's summer home. Grant was wondering why the lights were off when several shots rang out. His old combat reflexes kicking in, Grant skid the bike to the ground and threw Kristin behind it. There were no more shots. Instead he heard shouting, and recognized the voice.

'Brad!' Grant shouted.

There was silence, then, 'Grant?'

'Why the hell are you shooting at me?'

'I thought you were those bastards from the town!'

'What?' *What is he talking about?* 'I'm standing up!'

The house floodlights went up, illuminating the road and the yard. Brad came out from behind a tree.

'Jesus, it *is* you!'

Brad ran over to Grant and embraced him. Brad being six foot four and built like a linebacker, the smaller-framed Grant was enveloped in a massive bear hug.

'Took you long enough to get here, Grant.'

'Took me long enough! Do you have any idea what the roads are like? And what do you mean about those bastards from town?'

Brad had always hated the people who ran the town because summer residents, as the Canavan family and other people who didn't live there year round were called, paid taxes but were not allowed to vote. Ever since he took over the house Brad had fought the town tooth and nail on everything from dump permits to hardwired smoke detectors.

'Those bastards came down here not twelve hours after the fighting started and tried to kick us out.' His face twisted in hatred. 'Said since we were summer residents we had no right to be here and needed the house for family members of people who live here year round.'

'Where were they going to put you guys?'

'In the high school gym.'

'Jesus. So what happened?'

'I told 'em to go to hell.'

'And?'

'And when they tried to take the house anyway, I shot up a cop car. They said they'd be back, and I swear...'

As Brad was talking, Kristin got up from behind the Kawasaki and walked over to where Grant and Brad were standing.

'You okay?' Grant asked.

Kristin brushed dirt off her jeans and gravel out of her hair. 'Yeah.'

'Whose the harpie?'

'Harpie?' Kristin asked incredulously.

Grant balled his fist to punch Brad in the head, but before he could, Kristin kicked him right in the crotch. Grant laughed as his older brother fell in a heap to the ground...

'Madam President, we've taken a serious hit. They tried to land on the East Coast and we stopped them. We've taken their best punch, and we're still standing.'

'What do you say, Mr. Chairman?'

'Madam President, we still have an air force. We still have a navy. We can still fight.'

'Then we will fight, Mr. Chairman, Mr. Secretary. What do you recommend?'

'Rest and recoup, gather our strength.'

'I agree with the Chairman, Madam President.'

'And if I may suggest, the combination of F-15 launched ASATs and Mid Course Interceptors greatly disrupted Jai operations, but our stockpiles are low.'

'With your permission, I'll place emergency orders from both.'

'And Madam President, we will need more nukes.'

'Must we?'
'Yes.'

As the sun crept towards its zenith, the entire Canavan family sat at the outdoor picnic table eagerly awaiting the president's speech. Brad played with the dials on an old radio, becoming more and more frustrated with each burst of static. Next to him sat his teenage daughter, Callie, her arms around her little brothers, Michael and Patrick, so their father wouldn't yell at them for squirming. For their part, the boys took turns pulling at the long red hair Callie had inherited from their mother. Grant and Kristin sat on the other bench with Brad's wife, Deborah.

When he found the AM station out of Albany, Brad set the radio down and impatiently paced along the deck. After a report of a massive defeat inflicted by the aliens upon Chinese and South Korean forces over the Sea of Japan, an announcer spoke. 'Ladies and gentlemen, the President of the United States.' There was a brief pause before the president began.

'My fellow Americans. Just over seventy-two hours ago the aliens, whose arrival we have anticipated for almost a year began a war against the United States and the rest of Earth. Though we have been hit hard, America survives and fights back. As I speak to you, the full might of the United States Armed Forces is being brought to bear against the enemy.

'I would like to share with you what we have learned about the invaders. They call themselves Jai, and as we suspected, come from the Tau Ceti system, about eleven light years from Earth. They are, on average, smaller than humans, but bipedal, meaning they have two arms and legs. They tend to be skinny. The two large, Manhattan-sized ships we had been tracking settled over the North and South Poles. From these positions they are launching attacks against the entire planet.

'Let me reassure you that, though technologically more advanced, the Jai are not invulnerable. In battles over the North Atlantic and off the eastern seaboard we have shot down their fighter craft and large carrier ships. The military has used every weapon at hand, including nuclear missiles. Other nations have resorted to the nuclear option as well. Our armed forces are coordinating with those of NATO and other nations. On this morning humanity stands as one.

'There is little more than I can tell you right now. Know that your government is functioning and in charge.

'The Jai are learning the lesson given to tyrants of the past, that a world united behind the awesome might of the United States and the west cannot be defeated. As the evils of Hitler, Stalin, and Osama were eradicated, the Jai will be as well. Until then, guard yourselves and your families, and be prepared to help the brave men and women of our armed forces in any way they ask.

'May God bless you all, and God bless the United States of America.'

As an announcer came back on and began telling everyone what they'd just heard, Brad turned the radio off.

'So, what do you think?' He asked Grant.

'I don't know.' He leaned back on his bench and stretched. 'Sounds like we're fighting back.'

'I never liked her.'

Callie spoke, 'You're not going to break the radio the way you did the flat screen when she was elected, are you, Dad?'

Brad glared at his daughter, 'They teach you to talk to adults like that at school?'

'It's not my fault you broke the two-thousand-dollar TV.'

Deborah rolled her eyes not only at the mention of that notorious family incident but at Callie's joy at tweaking her father.

Sensing from long experience that a fight was brewing between Brad and his daughter, Grant stood up and reached out for Kristin's hand. 'C'mon,' he said. 'I'll show you around.'

'Ok.'

The Canavan family summer home was a small, two-story, cinder block cottage with an open deck and an attached garage. The lower level was dug into the ground and excavated so it opened up to the lake. On the lakeshore was a dock with a motorboat, rowboat, and several canoes. Grant started with the upstairs, a kitchen, a family room and two bedrooms decorated with local memorabilia, lake knickknacks like oars, mounted fish, and family photos. On the wall space between the two bedrooms was a picture of a Marine in full dress uniform. Kristin paused here and admired. The Marine pictured was a big man, with a large, oval face accentuated by his bristle haircut. His grey eyes were small, tilted inwards slightly, and hard looking.

'Is that your father?' she asked.

'Yup.'

'Brad looks just like him.'

'Yeah, looks more like our father than our father did.' Grant said. 'He's always been just like him, too.'

'What do you mean?'

'Nothing, c'mon,' Grant said, not wanting to dwell on it. 'I'll show you the downstairs.'

About half of the downstairs was taken up by a large, wood-paneled bedroom. At one end there was a queen-sized bed covered with fashion magazines and cosmetics. Opposite was a pair of bunk beds made up in Star Wars and Spiderman sheets. A line of duct tape, no doubt laid down by Callie, divided the room down the middle. She had been gracious enough to leave a gap in the tape so the boys could enter and exit their side. Two lines of parallel tape traced a corridor from which they were not allowed to stray.

The rest of the basement was taken up by a rec room. It was decorated with antique maps of Ireland, Guinness and Jameson's advertisements, and the pictures of Irish heroes like Brian Baru, Finn Mac Cool, and Michael Collins. In the far corner opposite the door was a pair of old black and white photos. A bronze placard under one read 'Grant Family, 1915' another read, 'Bradleys, 1932.'

'You guys sure like Ireland,' remarked Kristin.

'Yeah... my brother wanted to deck the room out with our father's Marine memorabilia, but Deborah and I talked him into giving the room an Irish theme instead.'

'Oh.'

'Better than hanging the old bastard's trophies form Vietnam and the Gulf War.'

'You shouldn't talk that way about your father.'

Grant looked at her. 'If you had lived with my father, you'd have some choice names for him too.'

As he had with many other girls, Grant ended the tour down by the dock. The lake stretched to the southeast for three quarters of a mile, its long shore lined with houses. Tall pines framed the entire lake. Half a mile past the lake's south end, overlooking a marshy field, was a thickly wooded ridge (known as Westridge, to the locals) that peaked at a few thousand feet before tapering off to the east.

'What d'ya think?'

'It's beautiful,' she said. Then, 'Is this how you end the tour with all the girls?'

Grant looked at his feet. *She's sharper than I give her credit for,* he thought as Kristin stared at him, expecting an answer.

Brad spared him from having to give one. 'Grant, get up here!' he shouted.

Grant ran back to the house where he found Brad by the front door, an M-16 in his hands. Another leaned up against the wall.

'What's happening?'

Brad nodded towards the road. 'Someone's coming.' Brad threw his M-16 to him. Out of habit Grant checked the barrel and cartridge. 'Let's go,' Brad said.

'Damn, shouldn't have let Callie go,' Brad said as they walked out to the road.

'Go where?' Grant asked.

'The Colbys made it up here.'

Grant laughed. The Colby boy, Tim, was Callie's age, and last summer had spent every free moment he had at their place. One morning Grant had taken his nephews on a hike and found Callie and Tim making out on a rock.

'What's funny?'

'Nothing.'

Two vehicles, a police car and a Humvee, rounded the last bend and stopped. The police car doors opened, and out stepped a sheriff and an army captain. Brad chambered a round. Grant looked at his brother.

'What the hell are you doing?'

The captain held up a hand. 'Easy, fellas, no need for that.'

'There was last time,' said Brad, his eyes boring in on the sheriff.

'We are aware of your situation, sir,' said the captain. 'The town leadership has been removed.'

'Removed? By whom?' Brad asked.

'By the military."

'Oh.'

'May I approach?' the captain asked.

'Why should I trust you?'

Grant elbowed his brother in the side. 'Knock it off, Brad.'

As the brothers slung their rifles, the captain approached. 'Captain John Nelson, Unites States Army, First Brigade Combat Team, Forty-Second Infantry Division,' he extended his hand to Brad, who took it.

'Bradley Canavan, Captain, USMC.'

'Grant, Sergeant, USMC.'

'Marines huh?'

'We're both out, but our little brother is a lance corporal on the *Truman*,' Brad said with pride.

'Oh.'

'Heard anything about her?'

'No,' Nelson replied. 'Navy's fighting like hell, though.' Nelson cleared his throat. 'Gentlemen, there's going to be an increased military presence in this area. The President has ordered us to make sure the aliens can't advance into the interior of the United States. Hudson River is the battle line. '

'Not sure I like you bringing the war to our home,' said Brad.

'Mr. Canavan, you don't have a choice.'

'Shut up, Brad,' Grant said to Brad. 'What can we do to help?'

'Stay out of the way.'

'We can do that.'

'Alright, gentlemen, I have a lot of stops to make, so if you don't mind...'

They shook hands again.

As they walked back to the house, Grant asked, 'What do you suppose is coming?'

'We'll see soon enough.'

They did the next morning when the sound of heavy vehicles along the main road woke the whole family. As Kristin dreamily rolled around the bed trying to wake up, Grant got dressed. He found Brad on the porch with a pair of binoculars to his eyes. He peered through the morning mist coming off the water to the far end of the lake and spoke without taking the binoculars off his eyes. 'A bunch of Blackhawk helicopters landed in that large field between the lake and Westridge a while ago. Not long after a bunch of Chinooks followed. I can't see anything, though.'

'Must be something big going on over there,' Grant opined.

'Yeah.'

'We need to know what else is going on around here,' said Brad.

'We do?'

'Yeah.'

Grant looked at his brother, 'What do you want to do?'

141

'A recon through the woods.'

'Are you nuts?'

Brad shrugged. 'What's the big deal?'

'The big deal is that we go snooping around where we're not wanted the army is liable to shoot us.'

'Hey,' Brad said, 'I used to be in Recon, they'll never know I'm there.'

Realizing that left to his own devises, Brad would poke around the wrong place getting himself and the whole family in a lot of trouble, Grant said, 'You know what, you're right. We should know what's going on. I'll go.'

'I should go with you.'

Grant smiled inwardly, knowing what he was about to say would end the debate. 'No, Brad. Stay here. Watch over the house and kids.'

Brad nodded. 'You're right.'

Leaving Kristin in the family room with Deborah, who began a long conversation about overbearing Canavan men, Grant set out down the road. Brad wanted him to take an M-16, which Grant thought was pointless. He managed to placate his older brother by taking along his Beretta.

He was just getting to the trail when Callie called after him. 'Grant, can I come too?'

Dressed in jeans, boots, a sweatshirt, and with a .22 slung over her back, Callie eagerly bounded towards him.

'Go back.'

'Aww come on,' Callie said as she caught up with him.

'Your father know you're here?'

'What do you think?'

'And what would he say if he knew you were carrying a twenty-two?'

'He'd hope I bring back a rabbit. I'm a good shot.'

Grant conceded with a shrug.

They walked into the woods and picked up the main trail. During the course of his childhood Grant had learned every path, every tree, every rock in countless games of army, cowboys and Indians, and ambush with his brothers. Later he'd shown his niece and nephews the same ins and outs he had learned. Callie led the way, and when the trail forked one yard inside the tree line right towards the main road, or left along the lakeshore past the Colby's, she tried to lead them left.

'Don't even think about it,' Grant said.

'But Grant...'

'Timmy can come by the house later.'

Callie turned around and came back to the fork, a sour expression on her face for Grant's benefit. They walked on in silence, Grant couldn't tell if Callie was truly angry, or trying to work up the nerve to say something.

Callie cleared things up when she said, 'Mom says that you used to spend a lot of time at the Colby's.'

'Yeah? Where did she hear that?'

'From my dad.'

'I suppose that's true. Timmy's dad taught me how to swim, fish, stuff like that.'

'She said you were hiding from my dad.'

'I guess. Our father, too.'

'Why?'

Grant laughed. 'Your dad was always pushing me around. I got sick of it, but I wasn't big enough to fight back.'

Callie sensed she didn't have all the facts. 'You said you were trying to get away from Grandpa.'

'I guess I just didn't want to be around him.'

'Why not?'

Grant felt a pang of guilt. Michael Canavan had always talked about dead relatives with reverence and respect, giving them an aura of infallibility. 'My dad was the kind of guy who got everything the first time you showed it to him. He never failed, near as I can tell, not once. He never understood things didn't come easy to me.'

'You learned guitar fast.'

'Yeah. But I was inspired,' he said without further elaboration. 'Once when I was about eight, my father took me fishing out on the lake, and he got real mad when I couldn't cast a line. When I couldn't get it after a few tries, he just gave up trying to show me.'

'My dad's kind of like that. Jerk.'

Grant stopped, turned around and said, 'Don't you ever talk that way about your father around me again.' He resumed walking. 'Your dad's not that bad a guy,' Grant said. 'It's just that he's like our father.'

'A jerk?'

Grant laughed. It took guts to call her father a jerk after that tongue-lashing. She was her father's daughter. 'No, headstrong. Knows he's right. Can't stand that other people think different.'

The path led down a gentle slope into a clearing to a broken up concrete bridge which had long ago fallen into the stream below. When Grant got to the foot of the bridge he stopped. On the right side was a shallow pond on the left was a large, sunken clearing more than a mile long and as wide as a couple of football fields. The clearing itself was bracketed on the left by a ridge, and on the right by the main road.

Today the clearing was filled with army trucks, Humvees, and soldiers. Grant counted six Patriot Missile launchers clustered around a radio tower and a large radar dish. Overlooking the clearing on the main road was an army trailer with a glass oval mounted like a cannon in its flatbed. Down the bed was a small shack and a radar array.

'Wow, what's all that?' Callie asked.

'Missile batteries, and I think that thing on the road is a laser.' said Grant. 'Let's go.'

They continued up the trail until it emptied onto the main road. As they walked down towards the house, several army trucks and trailers with heavy equipment passed them. The soldiers waved, more to Callie than Grant, he knew. By the time Grant and Callie got to the gravel road, Deborah overtook them in the family Explorer. They got in and saw it was filled with brown grocery bags.

'Jesus, they have all this in town?' Grant asked.

'Prices were a little higher, but it wasn't that bad. The manager at Price Chopper says the roads are still open and they got a shipment early this morning. All the local farmers have dumped their produce on the market, too.'

'While they still can,' said Grant.

'Town's filled with soldiers and military vehicles. I saw choppers landing on Monument Mountain.'

'Just like here,' Grant told her about the Patriot battery. 'We both saw it.'

Deborah looked at her daughter. 'You went with him?'

Callie nodded.

'And how is Timmy Colby?'

'Mom!' Callie blushed. 'Grant wouldn't let me go.'

Deborah smiled.

Military trucks and helicopters were an omnipresent sound as the Canavan family made the best of their situation. Since he didn't want to sit at the picnic table obsessively listening to the radio, Grant played guitar with Callie. After lunch, he took Michael and Patrick fishing, and showed the wide eyed boys the ins and outs of his motorcycle. Deborah and Kristin made dinner out of the trout Grant and the boys caught. Callie refused to help, insisting it was sexist for all the women to cook. Besides, Tim was coming by to take her for a walk, and the last thing she needed was to smell like fish. Finally, after a day that seemed remarkably normal, Brad and Grant retired to the rec-room to share a glass of Jameson's.

After pouring two glasses, Brad took one and held it up in toast, 'To Dad.'

They clinked glasses.

'What's it been, five years now?' asked Brad.

'Yeah…What'dya think he'd be doing right now?'

'Probably screaming at the radio, telling the president to fire off every nuke in the arsenal.'

Brad laughed. 'If he weren't running down to Camp Pendleton to re-enlist.' He finished off his glass and poured another.

'And Mom would be rolling her eyes.'

Brad held up his glass again. 'And Ricky.'

'Ricky.'

Grant nodded. As was so often the case, the brothers had trouble finding something to talk about. There was awkward silence between them, until: 'Kristin seems nice. Where's she from?'

'Lives in Hackettstown.' Momentarily forgetting that the town had been annihilated. 'I think she's from Philly.'

'She Catholic?'

Grant rolled his eyes as his brother began the screening process he had for all of his relatives' romantic interests. 'We're not getting married just yet, Brad.'

'Well, is she?'

'I don't know.'

'She Irish?'

Grant shrugged.

'What's her last name?'

Grant was about to answer, when he realized he didn't know. He shrugged again.

'Jesus Christ, Grant. When did you meet this girl?'

"Bout two hours before the Jai got here."

Brad became visibly angry. 'You took some girl you just met all the way up here? What the hell for?'

'I dunno, kind of felt responsible for her, I guess.'

'Responsible for her,' he incredulously repeated. 'You mean you...'

'What do I gotta do, draw a picture?'

Brad looked away, ground his teeth, and then looked back. 'You were violating some girl not an hour before the aliens arrived?' Brad shook his head. 'Real typical of you.'

'What do you mean, real typical?'

'Whole planet's getting ready for the biggest event in human history, maybe the biggest war too. All except you. You're off thinking with the wrong head. Imagine that.'

Grant slammed his glass down on the bar. 'Well what the hell do you want me to do? Run off and re-enlist?'

'Better than what you have been doing. Playing guitar for a bar tab. Working construction side jobs. What's the matter with you?'

Grant sat erect in his bar stool. 'Back off, Brad.'

'No. You were a good Marine; why didn't you stick with it?'

'You wouldn't understand.'

'What do you mean, I wouldn't understand?'

'You were a peacetime Marine.'

'So that gives you the right to bum around New Jersey. Good god, what would Dad think?'

'He'd think I had a right to be tired of shooting kids in suicide belts.'

'Oh don't give me that crap,' said Brad. 'Dad saw all kinds of horrors in Vietnam and still volunteered for a second tour.'

'That's because he loved being a Marine.'

'And you didn't?'

'I only enlisted because that's what Dad expected of me.'

'You don't mean that.'

'The hell I don't. You and dad practically shoved me into the recruiting office. I didn't want to go.'

For once Brad didn't have anything to say, he just stared at his brother, stunned at hearing his previously unimaginable words. *One of Michael Canavan's sons not wanting to be a Marine? Impossible.* 'I'm just happy Dad isn't around to hear you say that.'

Always ready to argue, Brad waited for Grant to reply. After getting several seconds of silence, he finished off his whisky and walked out of the rec-room, his face twisted in disgust.

Grant polished off his Jameson's and shook his head. 'Well, the secret's out,' he said to no one.

Unable to sleep, Grant spent the night in the family room, listening for war news over the radio while he quietly strummed his guitar. He had his Beretta on his hip and a beer on the end table. Every half hour he'd go outside and walk the property to get some air and make sure everything was okay. There was no sound except for the distant roar of jet engines. He saw some green dots arcing across the sky and knew they must be Jai ships.

Past midnight Grant heard the shuffle of feet on the floor, looked up, and saw a groggy Kristin walking into the room, looking good to him in a T-shirt and wool socks. She sat on the couch next to him, swigged his beer, took a cigarette from the pack out on the coffee table, and lit it.

'Any news on Philadelphia?' she asked.

'No,' he took his beer back from her and finished it. 'We and the Russians have launched an attack on that ship over the North Pole.'

'Oh,' she said, not really getting the importance. As she had several times a day, Kristin picked up the phone to try to call her father, but got no dial tone.

'Doesn't sound like it's going very well.'

Grant turned his attention back to his guitar. Kristin listened for a minute. 'What's that song? It's beautiful.'

'Zeppelin, 'That's the Way,'' he answered.

'Deborah told me you didn't start playing guitar until after you got out of the Marines.'

'Yeah.'

'How come?'

Grant shrugged.

'There must be some reason.'

Grant let out a short, ironic laugh. 'There was this kid, Matt, in my squad, played guitar. He was good. A guitar god. I mean Hendrix, Page, Angus, he was up there.'

'He was such a good musician, why did he join the Marines?'

'He enlisted for the GI Bill. Wanted to go to school, major in music.'

'Oh.'

'About three days after we had finished slugging it out with this head-hacking Sharia squad, we were in this village resting, cleaning our equipment, usual stuff before moving out. After chow, he was sitting on the hood of a Humvee playing 'That's the Way.' This cute little kid, six years old maybe, walks up to him and starts copying him, you know, playing air guitar. He finishes the song, and the kid reaches under his shirt and detonates a bomb, blows himself and Matt to Hell.'

Kristin put her hand to her mouth in horror. 'Oh my god...'

Grant's face twisted in bitterness. 'The kid waited till the song was over, then detonated.' He shook his head. 'Matt couldn't play guitar anymore, so I figured I would.'

Kristin kissed Grant on the cheek and put her arm around him. He reached up and took her hand.

'A couple of months after, they wanted me to go to officer's candidate school, said I had real leadership potential. I said no way.'

'Why?'

'I wasn't going to be responsible for sending a bunch of eighteen and nineteen-year-olds to get blown up by kids. I served the rest of my hitch and went home. Brad was furious.'

'What business was it of his?'

'Since our dad died, Brad thinks he's the family patriarch.' Grant finished his beer. 'What's your last name?'

'I was wondering when you'd ask. Alberti.'

'An Italian!' he proclaimed. 'My father would never have heard of it.'

Kristin laughed. 'I wouldn't tell my father about you drunken Irish.'

Grant laughed too.

'Why did you want to know?'

'My brother asked me, and I realized I didn't know.' He smirked, 'Why don't you go back and lie down.'

Kristin got closer to him, laying her head on his chest and tucking her arm beneath her cheek. 'Na, I'd rather be here with you.'

Grant put his arm around Kristin and kissed the top of her head. Within a few minutes she was asleep. Grant listened to her soft breathing while news filtered in of devastating Jai attacks against Russia and Alaska...

'Situation?'

'The Jai are coming en masse.'

'Mr. Chairmen, what is our response?'

'We've committed everything.'

'Reserves?'

'Committed, Mr. Secretary.'

'So we're all in.'

'That is correct, Mr. Secretary.'

'I must inform the president.'

Despite the November chill Grant was playing hide and seek in the backyard with his nephews when a Blackhawk helicopter flew overhead so low its skids clipped the top off a tree on the lakeshore. Another followed, and then another and another. He got up and watched the Blackhawks make their way across the lake to the big field below Westridge. Grant may have been an infantryman, but he knew helicopters flying low and fast was bad news.

'Michael! Patrick!' Get over here!'

'C'mon uncle Grant,' Michael replied.

Grant was in no mood for backtalk. 'Now!'

Hearing the yell of their normally calm uncle brought the boys out of their hiding spots. Grant took each of them by the hand and ran with them up to the porch. Deborah stood on the rail looking up to the sky. When she saw the trio, she started giving orders. 'Boys, get inside and see if Kristin needs help with dinner.'

Without hesitation the boys went inside.

'Something's going on,' said Grant.

'Uh-huh.'

He turned on the radio that had been sitting on the picnic table. The reception was weak and filled with static. 'This is the Emergency Broadcast System... citizens are ordered off the streets and strongly urged to take underground shelter...' After more static the message repeated itself. 'This is the Emergency Broadcast System. Massive military activity is taking place in North America in the form of air and ground combat...'

Deborah cast a worried glance to the road. Brad went to town an hour before and hadn't returned, and Callie had gone for a hike with Tim. She walked inside and started issuing orders. 'Boys, get your blankets and pillows and take them down to the rec room.' She came back out and started shouting for Callie.

Grant stared at the sky until he heard the rumble of tires on the gravel road. He ran out front in time to see a .50-caliber-armed Humvee pull up. The machinegun was manned, and the soldiers inside were in full battle gear. An officer got out of the shotgun seat.

'Hey!' he shouted at Grant. 'The CO says if you have any brains you'll get in your cellar and dig to China. The Jai are coming.' He got back in the Humvee. 'Big time!' he added, as the Humvee did a U-Turn.

A minute later Brad came barreling down the road in the Explorer. He parked the SUV besides the garage and hopped out.

'Something big is happening,' said Brad. 'What was that Humvee doing here?'

'Warning us to get inside. What's going on in town?'

'Place is crawling with troops all in battle gear, and a column of tanks came through town. A big one. Looked like a whole Brigade Combat Team.'

'Where was it headed?'

'North, towards Pittsfield.'

There was the roar of jet engines in the sky, a quartet of F-15s high in the sky, with a dozen F-16 following just above the tree tops.

'Deborah, get inside!' Brad shouted. 'I'll get Callie.'

Brad grabbed his wife by the arm and led her inside.

'You too, Brad!' Grant shouted as the roar of jet engines grew louder.

'Like hell!'

'Watch over your family!' He took the M-16 and bandolier from his brother. 'Go! I'll find her.'

So that his brother didn't have time to argue, Grant turned and ran down the road. He went onto the trail, down the path he and Callie had taken before. He heard missiles launching, lots of them, and knew they must have from the Patriot battery he and Callie had seen. The crew held nothing back, firing two dozen missiles inside of a minute.

'Callie!' he shouted.

The only reply he got was series of explosions in the sky, followed by the now familiar sound of several whistles piercing the air. There came a tremendous tree rocking blast which threw Grant to the ground.

'Callie!' he shouted again.

Then he saw flames tearing through the woods towards him. Grant scrambled to his feet and ran in the opposite direction. When he hit the lakeshore he didn't stop but dove into the water, plunging to the muddy bottom as the flames surged overhead. Grant stayed under as long as he could before coming up for air. The flames had receded, leaving a smoldering landscape covered in felled trees. But that's not what held Grant's attention.

High in the dimming northern sky he saw a jetliner. Grant wondered what it was doing in a battle zone when an orange beam reached out from the nose and tore into the eastern twilight. The beam pulsated for three seconds and ceased. The jetliner then fired another three-second burst, then another and another. To the east Grant saw several yellow dots. The beams reached out for them, making them flare and disappear. The jetliner's fire was joined by a laser from the base of Westridge, except now the targets were much, much closer. The ground laser fired again and again, causing a series of tremendous explosions no more than a few kilometers away. The Patriot battery on the ridge came to life, sending a barrage of missiles into the air. Grant heard the whistling sound then he saw a blinding flash, and then several more. He slammed his eyes shut against the glare. Reopening them, Grant saw an explosion atop the ridge, and another halfway down, but the laser and missile batteries kept firing.

Grant looked back to the trail, there was a crater filled with flaming wreckage. He picked out what had to be a wing, and he was sure he could see a fuselage, only it wasn't any he recognized. 'Jesus Christ!' he shouted to no one. 'That's a Jai ship!'

Seeing no sign of Callie and Tim he got up and ran over the smashed ground into the trees. Grant picked up the trail and ran down it, shouting after Tim and Callie over the roar of missile launches and explosions. Finally, he came to the trail split and shouted down both forks.

'Grant!' a young male voice replied.

Grant looked down the fork leading to the Patriot battery and saw Tim running towards him.

'Oh my god! Oh my god! Did you see it!' He shouted with the enthusiasm of a boy who has just seen a successful Hail Mary touchdown pass. 'The Patriot battery was firing missiles, then all of the sudden there was this whistle sound and the next thing I know the whole thing was smashed flat, and then there was this explosion, and this big parachute fell out of the sky, and we saw this Jai get out, and me and Callie rushed it....'

Grant grabbed Tim by the shoulders. 'What do you mean 'rushed it'?'

'The two of us just bum rushed it, like in football, and knocked it to the ground.'

'You captured a Jai?'

'Yeah! Callie's with it now!'

'Take me there.'

They ran down the trail to a small clump of boulders just inside the tree line. The Jai was splayed on the ground amongst the rocks. Its hands were raised above its head, and its white eyes looked oddly human as they stared down the barrel of Callie's .22. She stood astride the Jai, her eyes boring into the thing, as if staring hard enough could kill it. At her feet lay a grey helmet, too small for an adult human but big enough for the Jai. It had a large crack in the center where Callie had clubbed it with her rifle.

'Callie!' Grant shouted over the sound of rockets launching in the distance. 'What the hell are you doing?'

'I got one, Grant! I got one!'

'Hey, I got him too!' Tim protested.

'Enough!' Grant shouted.

'I'm going to kill him!'

'No you're not!' shouted Grant. 'We're taking this thing to the army and...'

'Grant!' Tim shouted. 'Look!'

Past the smoldering wreckage of the Patriot battery Grant saw a long, cylindrical ship coming down into the field. When it was barely off the ground a door opened and out came Jai soldiers. They spread out and formed a perimeter. Then the cylinder ship touched down.

'Oh crap!' shouted Grant. 'Callie, get clear of that thing!' She looked at Grant and hesitated. 'Now!' he bellowed.

He looked over at the Jai ship and saw a cargo door opening up, more troops were pouring out, lots of them.

'You two are going back to the house, right now.' he said.

'But Grant, what about the Jai?'

'I'll carry him. Now, if I don't make it, Callie, you tell your father what you saw here, and he'll know what to do.'

The kids nodded.

'Go! I'm right behind you.'

Callie and Tim took off down the trail. Grant walked over to the Jai and knelt down. The Jai turned its elongated head to him, just like a Jihadist would have, but he didn't move otherwise.

'Now I got no idea if you speak English, but you're coming with me. You fight back, I'll kill you.' Grant ran his finger across his neck for emphasis.

Grant slung the Jai over his shoulder and made his way back to the house. Brad was waiting for him in front of the garage, an M-16 in his hands. Grant dropped the Jai at his brother's feet, ran into the garage, and pushed his motorcycle out.

'Where the hell are you going?' Brad shouted over a series of sonic booms.

'Tell the army about the Jai!'

'What the hell am I supposed to do with this,' he gestured to the Jai with the barrel of his M-16.

Grant started his Kawasaki. 'Guard him.'

He took the motorcycle down the dirt road and hung a right towards Westridge. He didn't have far to go before he found a column of Humvees parked on the side of the road, their .50-caliber machineguns pointed towards the streaking, flashing sky above. A solider walked out from a Humvee and pointed his M-16 at him. Grant brought his Kawasaki to a screeching halt.

'Easy there, soldier. Who's in charge here?' Grant asked.

'None of your goddamn business,' was his reply. 'You just turn right back around and get out of here. Half our convoy got shot up a while ago. The Jai will come back, only this time we got Stingers for 'em.'

'You don't have to wait for them! A bunch landed right near my house! Ships, troops, everything!'

'No kidding?'

'You think I'm out here for a joy ride?'

The soldier waved Grant over to his Humvee. 'Wait here.' He ran down the road.

The Humvee had a large scorch mark down the front door and the window had been blasted out. Grant looked at the soldier manning the .50 caliber. His head was wrapped in a bandage, his left eye swollen shut and caked with blood. He looked warily upward. Grant followed his gaze just in time to see a pair of F-16s streak across the tree tops, nose cannons blazing.

The soldier came back with his CO.

'I'm Captain Jim Leguizmon. I'm told you have some intel.'

'Sergeant Grant Canavan, United States Marines.' Hearing Grant's old rank, Leguizmon took notice. 'The aliens landed about half a click from my house.'

'They landed?'

'Infantry, Captain. Lot's of em.'

Leguizmon looked back down the road which led right to the big anti air battery on Westridge.

'The battery's been kicking hell of the Jai, Captain,' said the sergeant. 'We have to protect it.'

'Alright,' said Leguizmon. 'Show me on the map.'

As a great flash in the sky briefly illuminated the whole landscape, the captain spread a map on the Humvee's hood and shined a light down upon it.

'Right here,' Grant pointed. 'After you get to the top of the hill here, the road we're on will lead right past it. But, there's a trail that leads to it too.' Grant outlined the rough course of the trail on the map.

'Can you lead us to them?'

'Absolutely.'

Leguizmon looked at the map for another second. 'Okay, get the men ready to move out.'

'Yes, sir.'

'And get me all the Javelin missiles we have left.'

'Yes, sir.' The sergeant walked back down the column. 'All right, boys and girls! Get ready to dismount and march...'

With Grant on the passenger side running board of the lead Humvee, the convoy rolled until they got to the dirt road. Leguizmon ordered them to halt, then got out and gathered his XO and noncoms.

'I'm taking this platoon and goddamn outflanking the bastards. Lt. Swift, take the Humvees and Bradleys up the road here. Stop when you get to the top of the hill, don't advance until I give the order. When you do advance, blast any Jai you see, and make sure you bring the landing field under fire. Go!' He patted the hood, 'Now, Sgt. Canavan, lead the way.'

At a trot Grant led the soldiers to the house where they found Brad standing guard over the captured Jai. Captain Leguizmon detailed two men to take the Jai back to the missile battery and left two more to help Brad stand watch over the house. Grant then led the platoon into the woods. No one noticed when a teenage girl attached herself to the back of the column.

'No talking from here on in.' Captain Leguizmon ordered.

As Grant and the platoon moved down the trail, they heard the whooshing sound of missiles, and the eerie whistle of Jai bombs. There were flashes and explosions, and off in the distance, through the trees, Grant saw an F-16 explode. They topped the last rise before the field just in time to see a pair of Hellfire missiles get knocked out of the sky by a Jai laser. The explosion illuminated the Jai landing ship, which had opened up all its bays and was unloading armored cars.

They consulted the map, Grant showed Leguizmon exactly where they were, and pointed up the trail. 'We cross the busted up bridge right here, and the trail leads up the hill to the main road.'

'Right,' Leguizmon said. Then in a loud whisper, 'First squad deploy here, second right on the other side of the bridge. Third stay back fifty yards.'

With his platoon spread out along the trail, Leguizmon deployed an M-60 crew behind the bridge, put a .30 caliber at the end of the line, and his two Javelins in the center. Then he radioed headquarters. When he was done reporting, Leguizmon turned to Grant and said, 'I got artillery ready, and the old man is sending a platoon of M-Is ...' he held up his hand and called in the strike coordinates to the howitzer battery. While Leguizmon was talking, another Hellfire missile came in and was shot down by a Jai laser, lighting up the field. Grant looked over at the Javelins.

'Lieutenant, the Jai will knock down those Javelins before they get close.'

'Can we get closer?'

Grant pointed back the way they came. 'The trail back there forks and parallels the field. It will lead right to them. I can take some men over.'

'No, way, Sergeant, I need you here in case we have to pull back.'

Grant was about to protest, but never had the chance.

'I can take them, Uncle Grant,' said a young female voice.

Grant prayed that Callie wasn't standing behind him. Grant turned around, grabbed Callie, and dragged her to the ground. 'What the hell are you doing here?' he demanded.

Callie shrugged.

'Does she know these trails?' Leguizmon asked.

'Don't even think about. She's not old enough for this.'

'I am too!'

Leguizmon grabbed him by the arm. 'There's no time, Canavan. You know what's at stake.'

'See, the captain thinks I should go!' Callie added.

'Ahhh, damn it!' Grant conceded, punching the ground.

Leguizmon spoke to Callie, 'Take the Javelins and third squad as close as you can. Understand?'

He low crawled over to third platoon and gave their sergeant his instructions. When he was finished Callie stepped forward and said, 'Follow me, guys.'

First platoon and the two Javelin crews followed the fourteen-year-old girl back into the woods.

As the rest of the platoon waited, the Jai armored cars started their engines, no more than a low hum, and slowly made their way up the embankment towards the road. At the same time, a large group of infantry moved down the field in two lines, each Jai about two meters apart.

'Do they see us?' Grant asked.

Leguizmon shook his head. 'I don't know.'

They stayed quiet—the only sounds were distant explosions in the sky—and kept their heads down, each man waiting in agony for the order to fire.

'How long should it take your niece to get my squad over there?' Leguizmon whispered.

'The trail goes up into the woods and snakes back down to the field, it's a big U...'

'Captain!' a sergeant whispered, 'They see us.'

The Jai were scattering and hitting the ground.

'Open fire!' shouted Leguizmon.

The entire trail came alive with small arms fire as Leguizmon radioed Lieutenant Swift. 'Red One, roll, over. Get up here, quick. How battery! Drop on target. Over!'

As the Jai sent rounds slamming into the Earth and broken bridge, 105mm howitzer shells screamed overhead. Grant expected to see a quartet of explosions in the field, but instead saw the green Jai laser fire once, then again and again, knocking down all but one shell, it landed fifty yards past the ship.

'How battery! They have some sort of laser defense. Your shells aren't getting through....No! No! Do not let up! Drop fifty and keep firing!'

The shells kept coming and bursting in the sky. Only scattered rounds got through, and these did little damage. Then, some sort of high powered rocket came out from the Jai line and slammed into the broken bridge. Grant ducked as Earth landed all around him. He looked up and saw the captain peak over the lip of the trail, only to be covered in his brains a second later as a Jai slug exploded his head.

'Holy Jesus!' Grant shouted.

Grant heard screaming as more men got shot. Ominously, the .30 caliber fell silent.

'What the hell do we do now?' Shouted a soldier down the line as he crouched to the ground for dear life.

'How the hell should I know?' Grant demanded.

'Well, the captain and sergeant are dead! That leaves you!'

'Me?'

'You!'

'Throw me your helmet?' Grant said.

'Why?'

'You said I was in charge! So throw me your helmet!'

The soldier tossed his helmet to Grant, who held it above the lip of the trail. In a second it was shot out of his hand.

'They must have some sort of guided bullets! Stick your head out it gets blown off, and I—'

Grant was interrupted by the sound of renewed firing. This time it was coming from the main road overlooking the field. Humvee mounted .50-calibers were cutting loose as were the 20mm cannons mounted atop a trio of Bradley fighting vehicles. The fire lasted for about ten seconds before it was replaced by more explosions. If Grant had learned anything in the previous war, it was the sound of an exploding Humvee. This was followed by another, and then another.

'Grenades!' Grant shouted. 'Throw your grenades into the field!'

Grant leaped on Leguizmon's body and pulled two grenades off his belt. He lobbed these with the rest of the soldiers; there were more explosions.

Then someone shouted. 'My head's still on. We must have taken out whatever was shooting those guided bullets!'

Grant poked his head over the lip of the trail, feeling his bowels tighten with the fear that it would get shot off as he did so. The Jai were pulling back down to the other end of the field, leaving several of their dead comrades where they lay. There was a trio of fires on the road, but Swift kept fighting. At the far end of the field, the armored cars were bringing their cannon to bear on the road. One Bradley exploded, then another. A rocket streaked from Swifts's column but was shot out of the sky. Suddenly, the Jai's left flank came alive with small arms fire. Two rockets streaked out from the woods, exploding with a flash of light. A great secondary explosion welled up, and suddenly, the How battery's arty rounds started hitting their mark.

'We got it! We got it!' Grant shouted as the small arms fire continued.

With the Jai laser gone, Swift's men concentrated rocket fire on the lead armored car and exploded it. This was followed by a quartet of explosions amongst the Jai armored column. Grant looked to the road and saw a platoon of M-1s making its way into the fight, commanders riding in the cupola, oblivious to the danger as they manually fired their coaxial machineguns.

The Jai were taking hell from every weapon the Americans could throw at them. Grant was so entranced he didn't notice the army Apaches swoop in over head, their 30mm cannons cutting through the night, and unleash a barrage of

Hellfire missiles. Grant saw the flames sprouting up around the Jai landing field, and remembered Callie was out there. He climbed onto the trail and looked down at the platoon hat had become his.

'Get down, sir!' someone shouted.

'My fourteen-year-old niece is out there!' he replied. 'You all do what you want, but I'm going to get her. Anyone who's coming, follow me!'

With that, Grant jumped down to the field and ran into the waist high grass. The platoon followed....

The rest of the night the Canavans watched a spectacular light show as the United States battled the enemy for control of the Earth. The sky was crossed with missile contrails, blue and red lasers, and tracer rounds, and pierced by whistling bombs and sonic booms. Blue dots streaked across the upper reaches of the atmosphere, pursued by smaller blue dots until they winked out one by one. An hour before sunrise, a flight of B-1 bombers flew east at a speed of mach two and unleashed a volley of nuclear tipped cruise missiles. Ten minutes later a big Jai carrier flashed high across the sky engulfed in nuclear flame. Land and sea based nukes had been used elsewhere, they learned, in battles up and down the east coast.

By dawn there were no more flashes in the sky, no more strange whistling sounds, and no more sky splitting explosions, only a blue sky shrouded in haze and the occasional column of black smoke. The crisp morning smelled of cordite, gasoline, and fire. Dazed and tired soldiers sprawled over the lawn, some asleep, the rest eating eggs and toast as fast as Deborah and Kristin could crank them out.

Grant sat on the picnic bench, absentmindedly playing his guitar. After going through a set of *Black Sabbath* songs, he set his guitar down and placed a cold bottle of beer over his throbbing eye. Once he heard how Grant had sent Callie into a firefight, Brad punched him out. As he helped his younger brother off the ground, his face lit up and he asked, 'So, she do okay?'

'Yeah'

'These army guys seem to think you're their CO.'

Grant shrugged. 'Well, after their captain and NCOs got killed someone had to take charge.'

'Dad would be proud.'

Kristin popped her head out of the kitchen. 'The radio says the president about to speak.'

'Bring it out here!' Brad yelled.

Kristin put the radio on the picnic table. Everyone, Canavans and soldiers, gathered and waited. Finally, the president spoke.

'My fellow Americans. I take to the airwaves this morning to announce that I have demanded and received the surrender of all Jai forces on Earth.'

The rest of the President's words were drowned out by the sound of cheers.

When the president finished her announcement the news anchor returned, and threw the broadcast to a reporter sailing with an American carrier battle group in the south Atlantic.

'I'm here with Admiral Jim Pixley aboard the *USS. Harry Truman*. Admiral Pixley says the president has personally authorized him to describe the details of the battle. Admiral, what happened exactly?'

'Well, while our boys and the Russians were taking hell up on the North Pole, our battle group maneuvered into position off Cape Horn. The bad weather there helped mask our movement. As the battle up north got more intense, the Jai sent more and more of their carrier ships to join the fight. By last night there was only one left over the South Pole. That's when we struck.'

'The two carriers in our battle group, *Truman*, and *Bush* launched everything we had, over a hundred aircraft. These were joined by British Tornados out of the Falklands. We lost two thirds of our aircraft, but we got the last carrier ship, and knocked down all their bombers. Now the Pole Ship had only its own defenses and land based batteries on Antarctica. This was considered thin enough to risk a nuclear launch. We had two ballistic subs in position, one of our own *Ohios*, and one Russian *Oscar*. They fired every ICBM they had, destroyed the Jai land defenses and scored several hits on the Pole Ship, crashing it onto the Ross Ice Shelf.'

'You have confirmation of this?' The reporter asked.

'Sure do. A Marine recon team risked their lives to take photos.'

'I'm looking at the photos now,' said the reporter. 'They show the long, cylindrical Jai polar ship lying on its side. There are several scorch marks left by missile warheads, and a pair of huge chunks taken out of its front. These pictures are simply incredible. Your Marines took an extraordinary risk getting them.'

'They sure did. It was a tough task, that's why I put the best officer I had in charge of the operation. His name's Lieutenant Ricky Canavan.'

'Is he available to talk?'

'No, I'm afraid he's leading a mission to collect Jai prisoners.'

Brad exclaimed, 'How about that! Ricky's a hero!'

Grant smiled as the reporter kicked the segment back to the studio, where the anchor was joined by a White House spokesmen. 'Do we know where the other ship is?' the anchor asked.

'It has left Earth's atmosphere and is currently orbiting the moon. Several of their ships have made landings there.'

'It hasn't surrendered?'

'Not at this time, no.'

'So we are still in a state of war.'

'That is correct.'

I did not plan to be a war time president. I did not plan for my name to mentioned alongside great men like Lincoln and Roosevelt. I do not think myself to be the equal of those saviors of the republic and I do not seek to be remembered in that way. I defended my nation as any commander-in-chief would, nothing more. Whether or not I succeeded is not for me to say. That judgment will be made long after I am gone and will begin when my term in office ends in a just a few years.

My fellow Americans, I speak to you tonight, from the Oval Office to tell you that I will not seek a second term as President of the United States. If nominated I will not accept. I do so because it is my belief that I have done all I can, and that the nation will be better served by a new leader. . .

As her time in office dwindles it is hard to escape the conclusion that the president seems deeply moved by the events of the late war, perhaps even transformed. Insiders say she has, for several months, been in some kind of funk, a personal malaise as she contemplates her central role in the enormous events of the last few years. There are rumors of sleepless nights, tremendous mental anguish, and even anti-depressants. We cannot blame the president, a committed environmentalist, for being troubled by America's use of dozens of nuclear weapons. But we urge her to consider the alternative.

Anonymous sources claim the president plans a simple retirement spent in seclusion in her Midwestern home. If so we wish her well, but urge her to consider using her talents in some other way. Perhaps the incoming president (supported by this magazine) will appoint her to head a rebuilding commission, or maybe to head a relief agency, ala Herbert Hoover after the First World War, to help nations devastated in the past conflict; Japan, South Africa and Russia come to mind.

Informed readers know that this magazine vigorously opposed the president during the last election. Even so, her management of the war, though not always perfect (is any commander-in-chief's?) was good enough to defeat the invasion.. This magazine, and we hope, this nation will remember her fondly.

The Weekly Standard.

Chapter 10: Third Temple

Arrival + Generations

I call upon Allah, Peace Be Upon Him, to destroy the Zionists, the descendents of Pigs and Monkeys, to direct the weapons of the blessed aliens to destroy the Zionist entity. I call on Muslims the world over to come to the aid of the blessed aliens...

Sermon broadcast on al Jazeera

Ha Ha Ha! Why wouldn't they blame the Jews?

Before, During, and After: Blogging the Aliens

Tonight we sit to commemorate the great event, the great Arrival, the time when those from the stars came and made war on our people and the enemies of our people, the event when began our salvation.

[Here a glass of wine is poured.]

It was then that the Israeli people, like the Hebrews of old, were surrounded by enemies.

In the south the Hamas plotted our destruction. In the east, in the land of Judea and Samaria, the Fatah plotted our destruction. In the north, in the land of Cedars, the Hezbollah plotted our destruction.

Our enemies were aided by the Assad in the land of Damascus, and by the most dangerous of all, by the Amandinajead in the land of the Persian kings, the land of the great Cyrus who returned our people to the land of Israel, the land of David, the land of our fathers and our father's fathers.

[Here a glass of wine is drunk to commemorate the founding of the state of Israel.]

Our enemies welcomed the Arrivers, welcomed the visitors as angels from heaven, as soldiers sent by their prophet to destroy us. This they did on the first night.

On the second night they attacked our people. By the dozen, and then dozens of dozens, the deadly gulls flew from the north. Like scorpion tails they struck our land, killed our people.

[Here a second glass is poured, and the reader dips his finger in his glass of wine and recites the name of each city that was struck]:

Jerusalem
Tel Aviv
Haifa
Eilat
Beersheba
Dimona

And from the land of Judea and Samaria the forces of the Fatah struck the valley of the Jordan and made war upon Jerusalem and then did destroy the wall of the Second Temple.

[Here all in attendance take and eat a piece of bitter herbs to commemorate the destruction of the Wailing Wall.]

From the south the Hamas added their gulls to the onslaught and breached the great wall that kept the peace between them and our people and sent the evil, the sadistic bombers against the land of Israel. And so did the Egyptians, the descendents of Pharaoh, send their chariots to destroy the people of Israel, the people of Hashem.

[A concoction of bitter herbs is mixed in salt water and passed throughout the table, readers dip parsley in the mixture and eat.]

Oh Hashem, our lord, king of the universe we eat these bitter herbs to commemorate the suffering of our people during the Arrival, the war waged upon us by our enemies.

It is the duty of all of Hashem's people, our lord, king of the universe, to commemorate the destruction of the Wailing Wall, just as we commemorate the passage of our people from Egypt.

Oh Hashem, our lord, king of the universe we ask that you destroy these nations that do not heed your word, these scorpions, the evil ones. Call out your wrath and bring destruction to them. Let the land be sowed with salt, and let no two stones be left together. Wipe their memory from your land, our lord Hashem, king of the universe. Bring to the evil doers your justice, cruel and swift.

[Here the bitter herbs are placed on the center plate to commemorate god's wrath on behalf of his people and mixed with honey to show that justice in the name of Hashem is sweet.]

When the curious son asks, What have we done to this land? Tell him:

We brought water to this land where there was no water.

We raised crops where there were no crops.

We invented things where no things had been invented.

We built great cities where no great cities had been built.

[The head of the table dabs a bit of moror on matza and passes the matza around the table. All those present eat the moror and matza.]

We eat this moror and matza to commemorate the founding of the nation of Israel, to celebrate the great works of the people of Hashem, our lord, our god.

When the ignorant son asks, why did we return to the land of Israel? Tell him:

Because of the great holocaust perpetrated by those whose name we shall not speak.

When the wise son asks, why do they hate us? Tell him:

We cannot know what is in the heart of the corpulent, the corrupt, the poor and the ignorant.

When the ignorant son asks, why did we fight? Tell him:

We fight because when we offered them peace, they refused.

We fight because when we offered them land, they refused.

We fight because when we offered them the temple, they refused.

When the ignorant son asks, 'but I was not there, why do we say *we?*' Tell him:

It is the duty of all of the chosen people of Hashem, our lord, king of the universe to say we. For we were there, we, the progeny of our fathers and our father's fathers. We means the chosen people of Hashem, our lord, king of the universe, we means the citizens of the state of Israel, we means the descendents of Abraham, of Moses, of Joshua, David, and Solomon.

And so the leaders of the land of Israel unleashed the fury of the Jewish people. Falcons, Eagles, Lions and Phantoms took to the sky and brought fire to the ground. By the hundreds the Merkevas rolled into the land of the Cedars. Men came from the sky as if dropped by Hashem. Men came up from the water and onto the land. A great battle was brought to the land of the Cedars. There was much fire, and the cedars burned.

Assad of the Syrians took umbrage and sent his army to the land of the Cedars. There in the Valley of Bekaa the iron chariots clashed in great battles that shook the very Earth. Assad fired his arrows as well and brought much sorrow to the Galilee until they were destroyed by the beasts of the sky and the ground. And then the Merkevas went across the Bekaa to the plain of Damascus and fought another titanic struggle against Assad, in the very shadow of Mount Hermon.

And then the enemies of the chosen people of Hashem, our lord king of the universe, called out to their false prophets, and called out for help. But the Arrivers did not help, could not help as they were locked in battle with the great nations.

When the wise son asks:

Why did the Arrivers not help the enemies of the chosen people of Hashem? Tell him:

Because we are the chosen people of Hashem, our lord, king of the universe, and he protected us because we worship Hashem, because we keep the Sabbath holy in praise of Hashem, because we follow the commandments that Hashem, our lord, king of the universe, handed down to Moses atop Mt. Sinai.

And then the enemies of Hashem, our lord, king of the universe asked the great nations to come to their rescue. And when the great nations said they could not help, the enemies of the chosen people of Hashem, our lord, king of the universe, had only themselves. And they cowered as the great war birds brought thunder from the sky, and the missiles rained down.

And then the heroes of the chosen people of Hashem, our lord, king of the universe, did do battle with descendents of Pharaoh. The Golanis and the Givatis, and the Sa'ar's did bring their great Merkevas south to Sinai, to the land of Moses, and fought a great battle there and did leave the chariots of the descendents of Pharaoh burning at the pass the great Arik once won, and on the shores of Sea of Reeds, and on the banks of the great Suez.

Across the Jordan the Abdullah, the great, the wise Abdullah defended his people and his throne with his very life. His family a target, the radiant Rania killed, Abdullah the Great struck back against the Fatah and brought much suffering to their people and caught the Fatah between his pincer and the pincer of the chosen people of Hashem, our lord, king of the universe.

[Here a third cup of wine is poured and drunk in celebration of victory.]

And great men of the Merkevas did level their spears upon the cities and farms of Pharaoh's descendents, naked now that their armies lay vanquished.

But what about the Peace? They cried, what about the Accord of David?!

And the soldiers of Hashem, Our lord our god, king of the universe replied:

You broke the Peace. You ignored the Accord of David. Now our spears point toward your deceitful hearts.

And then they asked:

What of your god?! What of your Hashem? What of your commandments? Is this not murder?

And there was great anguish amongst the soldiers of Hashem, our lord, king of the universe.

The good soldiers asked:

Do we wash our spears in blood?!

Yes, said some. No, said others.

The wise ones asked:

Is this the way of Moses?

No they replied.

The wise ones asked:

Is this the way of Joshua?

No they replied.

The wise ones asked:

Is this the way of David?

No they replied.

The wise ones asked:

Is this the way of the gentile saint, the Wingate, who taught our fathers and our father's fathers the way of the sword?

No they replied.

The wise ones asked:

Is this the way of Dayan?

No they replied.

So the soldiers of Hashem, our lord, king of the universe gathered with their leaders and decided that Pharaoh's descendents would be allowed to leave their cities and their farms.

And after Pharaoh's decedents left their cities and their farms and the banks of the Suez and the Sea of Reeds their great city, greatest in all the near world, was destroyed, and their farms were razed and their crops burned, and a great swath of destruction was wrought along the banks of the Suez. And this they could do as the great nations were fighting the Arrivers. And then the soldiers of Hashem, of our lord, king of the universe returned to the land of Israel.

It was then that the leaders of the chosen people of Hashem, our lord, king of the universe did agree with the great Abdullah the Hashemite, the king of Jordan that the enemies of Hashem should be sent away from the land of Israel and the kingdom of Jordan.

And they did send away the enemies of Hashem's chosen people.

They were sent from the land of Judea and Samaria.

And they cried:

But we will live with you in peace!

And the people of Israel replied:

We, the chosen people of Hashem, our lord, king of the universe, tried to give you peace, and in return you gave us war.

And these enemies of the chosen people of Hashem were sent to the land between the rivers and then to the land of the Amadinajead, the land of Cyrus the great Persian king, who returned the Hebrews to the land of Israel.

They were sent from the land of the Cedars. And many of the people of the Cedars forced them to leave.

And they cried:

But we will make war upon you no more!

And the people of Israel replied:

You have already killed our children, killed our wives, killed our young men, and we will listen to your promises no more.

And they were sent to the land of the Amadinejead.

And for many generations war raged in the land of the great Persian kings until the usurpers of the Cedars and the squatters of Judea and Samaria were absorbed into the land of the Persian kings and disappeared as did the lost tribes of Israel in the land of the Assyrians.

[It is customary here for the head of the table to pause and serve dinner.]

As the armies of the Hezbollah, and the Hamas, and the Fatah and the Assad of Damascus were defeated, and their soldiers lay dead in and around the land of Hashem our lord, king of the universe the war between the Arrivers and the great nations raged. And as the great nations won precious victories and secured themselves, the Arrivers then did wonder if they could find allies among them.

Then they did look to the children of Israel, the children of Hashem, our lord, king of the universe. And the Arrivers did know our suffering, lo these many years at the hands of the emperors of Rome and the emperors of Greeks, the depredations inflicted by knights of the cross, the humiliations suffered in the land of Dreyfuss, followers of Marx and holocaust by they whose names shall not be spoken.

The ignorant son asked:

Why should we not visit revenge upon those who oppressed us?

The curious son asked:

Indeed what do we owe these people who have inflicted so much suffering upon we, the Children of Israel?

And then did the Ignorant son and the curious son speak of our great suffering, the deprivations that we the chosen people of Hashem, our lord, king of the universe, suffer at the hands of those who do not heed his word.

And the wise son replied:

Indeed you are right, we have suffered greatly at the hands of those who do not worship Hashem, those who have taken his words and twisted and mistranslated them, those who take the rants of an illiterate thief of camels and call them the word of Hashem. Yet we shall not strike our fellow man, for this is not what our fathers taught us and is not what our father's fathers taught. Were we to do so, were we to take up arms with the Arrivers, we, the children of Israel, would be ignoring the word of Hashem, our lord, king of the universe.

At this the curious son and the ignorant son agreed and the leaders of Israel told the Arrivers that the children of Hashem, our lord, king of the universe were not their friends.

And the Arrivers asked:

Are the children of Israel our enemy?

The children of Israel replied:

The enemy of man is our enemy. The enemy of the great nation that has helped the children of Israel is our enemy.

[Here a glass of wine is drunk, and a new one is poured to celebrate the wisdom of the Hebrews.]

And the Arrivers sent two of their great ships, and a great battle was fought at sea and in the air, and the battle was not won until the leaders of Israel threw their sun weapons at the Arrivers and destroyed one of the ships and forced the other to flee to the stars.

When the danger to the land of Israel had passed the children of Israel sent their Eagles, Falcons, Lions of the sky to help the great nation who had so often helped the children of Israel and later helped that nation build the great ships which smote the Arrivers from our sky.

[Here a cup of wine is poured and sweet snacks are passed around the table to commemorate the founding of the third temple in Jerusalem...]

Chapter 11: **The Battle of Luna**

Arrival + 10 years

The recent Jai raid on Norfolk shows that they are not leaving the solar system, and they are not going to leave us alone. We know that their remaining Pole Ship is on the dark side of the moon. The Jai are also building large structures on both poles of the moon as well as several small structures at the equator. Our astronomers have also seen activity on Mars, and suspect the carrier ship that left Mars last year has taken up station in the asteroid belt. We believe they will build some sort of base in the belt for ore mining.

Prisoners seem to the think that Zetroc Nanreh will not be inclined to make peace or return home and will be determined to continue the fight. . .

Defense Intelligence Agency Report on Jai Activity since the Late War

The first winter was the hardest. There was never enough food, not enough electricity and too many people who didn't know how to do without. Folks went hungry; we all lost weight. An old guy I know said that winter reminded him of when he was a kid during the Great Depression. No one actually starved to death, though. The army and National Guard went all over the country distributing food. There were some riots, but the army took care of those too.

There was a shortage of doctors and hospitals. You don't detonate a couple hundred megatons worth of nukes in your own atmosphere without a lot folks of getting radiation poisoning. Lots of cancer, lots of birth defects too. We'll be dealing with that for generations. A lot of people died of things we wouldn't have worried about before Arrival, certain kinds of cancers for example. Diabetics died because there was no place to get insulin. It felt like a decade or so got lopped off your life expectancy.

The war was not the end of civilization. The aftermath was not The Day After *or* Threads. *We lost some things, but not everything. That spring the sun came out again. People went into their back yards and plowed them over. Soon everyone was a farmer. Neighborhood garden clubs became farming clubs. The gardeners helped people out, helped them get started. The*

Feds recommended planting a lot of starchy stuff, but people did their own thing, and by the summer, in my town at least, there was a healthy trade in fruits and vegetables. By then the roads were on their way to getting fixed, power was turning back on, we even got TV back, regular old-fashioned TV, though, not cable and satellite. People had to rig their houses with makeshift antennas again. You ever see a coat hanger sticking out of a flat screen TV?

In the end the Feds determined that nineteen million Americans had been killed. The casualties were spread all over. That said, nearly half came from the West Coast. After the first lull in the fighting the Jai had tried to scare us into submission and unleashed a ruthless attack on the West Coast after they had broken through the Aleutian defense. They smacked LA, San Diego, San Francisco, Portland, Seattle. They followed up the assault by broadcasting a message demanding our surrender and offering a piece of the spoils if we helped them defeat the Chinese, who fought on regardless of losses. The president responded by ordering one of the Ohio subs to launch at the Jai armada off the coast of California, took a few of their big ships out with that volley.

Anyway, things slowly got back to normal, in a retro-1960s low-tech kind of way. Even with the losses we suffered, there were jobs. Something always had be cleaned up, knocked down, or rebuilt. Besides, there were less people than their used to be. We began making our own steel again, appliances, cars, and electronics too. Detroit never had it so good.

Of course, every once in a while the whole country would panic because of a report of a Jai ship coming over from the moon. Sometimes the reports were real. They'd raid a naval base, or knock down some piece of infrastructure just for the heck of it. The Jai didn't just hit us. Russia, China, everyone came in for it from time to time. After most of the decade had passed, people began wondering how long were we going to take this. Couldn't we do something to retake the moon from them? Turns out we had been planning to do just that all along. . .

Before, During, and After: Blogging the Aliens

In another war she was named *USS Eisenhower*. Any naval enthusiast would have recognized her profile, but there were oddities. The command island had been stripped away. Amidships were four massive sixteen-inch guns, the kind which gave the old Iowa-Class battleships their teeth. On the port and starboard bow were two slits apiece. Further back was a quartet of weapons blisters, each sporting four missile launchers. Great steel plates had been riveted onto the hull and welded together; up-armoring the ship far beyond the thin hull of a Jai carrier. The armor dramatically increased the ship's tonnage as did a gigantic dome shaped push-plate attached to the stern. Only internal ballast tanks and exterior air-filled bladders kept *United States Space Ship Wasp* afloat. Stripped of her propeller screws, a fleet of tugs had been needed to tow *Wasp* to the center of the South Pacific lagoon in which she now floated. At the midnight hour water was pumped into the push plate. As more and more water filled the plate, *Wasp's* bow lifted into the air, first forty-five degrees, and then ninety degrees, at which point the push plate sunk into the sand and muck and settled onto the bottom of the lagoon. *Wasp* stuck out of the water like a skyscraper.

A large oval bridge had been built inside the ship. Here computers and monitors were arrayed in U shaped banks throughout the deck—weapons, sensors, communications, damage control. In the center was a single chair, itself surrounded by a bank of monitors where the occupant could view data from any of *Wasp's* operating systems. A black receiver was on the right arm, from which the captain could talk to any section chief with the push of a button as well as a second launch facility at Green Bay. On the left arm was a red phone, also with several buttons. These led to Cheyenne Mountain, Space Command's Salt Flat Station, and the White House.

Captain Steven J. Masters sat in the command chair. He wore the same blue jump suit as the rest of the crew and eschewed the many campaign ribbons he had earned for Operation Desert Storm, the War on Terror, the Jai invasion, and a pair of subsequent skirmishes fought during the previous decade. His face was thin with sharp, prominent angles. Above his left eye he bore a scar from the several stitches he needed after starting a fight with a fellow Annapolis classmate who accused him of being an affirmative action candidate. Masters had always silently given thanks to god for Midshipman Carter, whose rank bigotry had pushed him to get near perfect grades at Annapolis, sharpening his mind for the later pursuit of a graduate degree in naval history.

Masters' keen, exacting eye surveyed the bridge and the ship he knew every inch of. For more than a year he had taken his daily five-mile run through *Wasp*. Starting at the bridge, he worked his way back to the weapons deck, passing row after row of missile racks, the entryways to the great sixteen guns, past conduction tubes running nearly a hundred yards back to the fusion thrusters. He had anonymously worked on much of the equipment himself, secretly, before formally taking command, riveting and welding armor plates to the hull, installing guidance systems and pulse regulators to *Wasp's* T-SLAMs (Tomahawk Space-Land Attack Missiles), testing the sixteen-inch guns' feeder chains. Later he had participated in training exercises and gunnery mock ups. Masters even swabbed the deck, anything to gain a perfect understanding of *Wasp* and how she operated.

Though not really a vain man, Masters couldn't help but feel a sense of personal satisfaction as the ship readied to launch. He had been made captain of *USSS Wasp* via executive order by virtue of the fact that he had commanded an attack submarine which sunk a Jai carrier that had landed in Chesapeake Bay. Once in charge, Masters had taken a bayonet to the bureaucracy, eliminating whole programs and putting the construction of the various sections under the men who would command them in battle. Rather than the high-tech interplanetary vessel of NASA's dreams, under Masters' authority *Wasp* became a simple Earth-Moon orbiter packed with brutal, low-tech weapons.

Masters pushed a button on his armrest and brought a live feed of the sensor display to his monitor. *Wasp's* sensors were kept passive for fear that would reveal her position to the Jai so the onscreen data was relayed from Earth-based radar arrays. Two carrier ships were nearly halfway between the Earth and the moon and travelling at just over half a G. The ship's designated targets ALPHA and BRAVO (on Masters' orders always *targets*, never *contacts*), were more than one thousand miles apart. At their current speed they would achieve Earth orbit in less than three hours. The DIA suspected the Jai's timing, launching an attack as *Wasp* was getting ready to take orbit, was a coincidence, as their trajectory suggested a destination over Asia.

The two ships had launched from small single-ship facilities built by the Jai on either of the moon's poles. The DIA knew that on the dark side of the moon, where it couldn't be seen from Earth, was the original surviving Jai Pole Ship. They could only speculate about what other facilities had been constructed there. At least fourteen carrier ships were docked or in orbit around the moon. Two more ships were known to be on Mars protecting the extensive facilities the Jai had built there. Another pair was in the asteroid belt protecting a large space station which harvested and refined ore. The bombers they carried were designed for atmospheric fighting only, and therefore irrelevant to the fight ahead. There was also a Jai base on Ceres where it was believed that Zetroc Nanreh made his headquarters. Several landing ships were docked there as well. Everyone, except the president perhaps, understood that the upcoming battle would be the first of many.

While he waited for the Black Phone to beep, Masters mentally conducted an engagement with ALPHA and BRAVO. By the time Masters had imagined and fought two different scenarios the Black Phone beeped once. Masters picked it up.

The launch commander ashore spoke, 'Captain, geology says you've reached the bottom.'

'Very well.' Masters hung up the Black Phone. 'Mr. Glazer.'

'Captain,' replied the ship's executive officer.

'Begin the countdown.'

'Aye, aye, Captain.'

Masters' monitor flashed black for a moment and then showed a digital clock counting down from ten minutes. He kept his eyes on the Red Phone, fearing that the president would get cold feet and call off the attack. Since his election the year before, the new president had made it clear he had little faith in *Wasp*. Only the hundreds of billions spent on the ship so far had prevented him from killing the program his first day in office. In an Oval Office meeting Masters had assured the president that a show of force could lead to some kind of negotiated settlement.

'A fleet in being, Mr. President. Often the *threat* of force is enough...'

'Well you convinced him, for now...' said Glazer as they left the White House. 'And you only had to lie a little to the president.'

'Whatever it takes to get us into space,' Masters had replied.

Masters was actually surprised when the countdown broke the one-minute mark. When Glazer finished the countdown Masters gave a one word order, 'Fire.'

The entire bridge crew was slammed into their crash chairs by the massive force of a nuclear explosion. There was second explosion, and a third, and then a fourth, a whole string, in one second intervals; each a fifteen-kiloton nuclear blast which propelled *Wasp* further and further into the atmosphere until Masters felt himself being pulled against the straps on his crash chair. He pressed a button on his armrest and brought the live feed from an exterior camera to his monitor. The camera pointed forward, down the armadillo shell that had once been *Wasp's* flight deck. He panned the camera right, bringing Earth into view.

'We have achieved orbit,' announced the helmsman.

The bridge crew stirred in their crash chairs, there was slight murmuring and a few audible sighs of relief, but no cheering. Too much work lay ahead.

Masters picked up the Black Phone and punched a button patching him into the ship's intercom.

'This is Captain Masters. *USSS Wasp* has achieved orbit and is seeking out the enemy. We've all come a long way. Every man and woman aboard this ship should be proud of what we have accomplished. Well done.'

Finally, there was a cheer throughout the ship.

'The battle we have waited for is now before us. You all know your jobs. The United States expects each one of you to do your duty. I know you will. I want you all to remember one thing. This ship is a blunt instrument. We are a buzz saw, we are the dealers. We will seek out the enemy, engage him with every weapon at hand, and destroy him without mercy.'

He paused for effect.

'Before we begin this battle in earnest, I just want you all to know that you have my complete confidence.' A moment, and then, 'Let us now bow our heads... Mr. Glazer?'

When Master's learned Glazer was Jewish, a person of the book, according to his Baptist background, he insisted that important meetings be begun with a Hebrew prayer. On this day Glazer said a short Hebrew prayer for victory.

'Thank you, Commander. Mr. Huggins?'

The weapons officer bowed his head and said a quick Christian prayer for deliverance and victory.

'Amen. Commander Glazer, report to the Blue Bridge.'

'Aye, aye, Captain.'

Glazer unstrapped himself and floated out of the main 'Gold' bridge for the reserve 'Blue' bridge from which he would command the ship if the Gold Bridge was destroyed.

'Detach push plate,' Masters ordered.

A tech pressed several buttons, firing off dozens of tiny explosives which severed the push plate from the ship. The push plate drifted behind *Wasp*.

'Alright, Ms. Rogers,' Masters said to the sensor array commander, 'let's throw on the sensors. We'll let the enemy know we're here.'

'Aye, aye, Captain.' Rogers issued orders to the sensor tech who flipped a few switches bringing the ship's radar and infrared sensors on line. 'We have acquired targets ALPHA and BRAVO.'

The sensor readout appeared on Masters' monitor. ALPHA and BRAVO were accelerating at the Jai standard .6 Gs. They had not yet altered course to engage *Wasp*.

Masters keyed the engineering button on the Black Phone and said, 'Engineering, accelerate us to one G.'

'Aye aye, Captain.'

Wasp's fusion engine was based on the Jai design recovered from their numerous lost carrier ships and built with the help of Israeli engineers. Technicians in the engine room injected deuterium and tritium pellets into a magnetic core. An engineer fired an ion laser which exploded the pellet's outer layer. The force of the shock wave fused the pellets together, creating nuclear fusion and generating a tremendous amount of energy, which was then directed out the aft of the ship. The engineers kept injecting deuterium and tritium pellets into the core, repeating the process until one gravity had been attained.

Lt. Rogers reported, 'Two new targets. Designate CHARLIE and DELTA. Coming around from the dark side of the moon. Speed point nine Gs and accelerating. ALPHA and BRAVO are accelerating and coming around to an intercept course.'

'Very well.'

'Shall we open fire, Captain?' Huggins asked.

'Negative, Mr. Huggins. Let's not reveal what we can do, yet.'

'Aye, aye, Captain.'

Masters brought a live video feed onto his monitor. The camera was trained on a pair of dim points of light in the distance, targets ALPHA and BRAVO. There was a flicker of white light from each. A second later Masters' computer display flashed and informed him that *Wasp* had been hit by a pair of lasers.

Damage Control reported, 'Burst three seconds...' after 3.36 seconds the laser fire ceased.

ALPHA and BRAVO fired again and then again.

'One plate slightly buckled, forward compartment,' said the damage control officer.

Masters waited for more laser bursts, but none were forth coming. *Probably just wanted to see what we can take,* he thought.

Rogers spoke again, 'Captain, CHARLIE and DELTA are accelerating, 1.6 Gs and rising now...' A moment later. 'Missile Contact, dead ahead. Four...no eight, now twel-...now sixteen bogeys closing fast, thirty plus Gs...'

Masters spoke to the countermeasures officer, 'Lieutenant Velarde, countermeasures free.'

Lieutenant Velarde sat before three computer banks, one for each of *Wasp's* countermeasures systems, each manned by a separate technician. Velarde ordered a technician to bring *Wasp's* forward Gatling guns on line. Sensors fed data on the incoming bogeys into the fire control computer, which targeted the six forward Gatlings accordingly. Less than five seconds after Masters gave the order the six forward Gatlings fired quick bursts of steel pellets into space at hundreds of Gs per second. Masters watched his screen as the blips representing the incoming bogeys winked out in groups of three. In seconds all the missiles were destroyed…

'Contact! Sixteen bogeys…thirty two bogeys…now forty eight.'

ALPHA and BRAVO fired their forward lasers, hitting *Wasp's* hull with bursts of energy.

'Captain, CHARLIE is decelerating and turning toward us,' said Rogers.

'What about DELTA?'

'DELTA's course has changed as well, twelve degrees, trying to work around our flank.'

'Final missile destroyed.' Velarde reported.

'Bogeys,' said Rogers. 'Sixteen…thirty two….forty eight…'

'Lieutenant Velarde,' Masters said, 'Fire a string of EMP bombs.'

'Yes, sir.'

'EMP bombs, one string, forward rack.'

'Bomb string ready,' replied the EMP technician.

'Fire.'

'Bombs away.'

The forward bomb rack flung a quartet of EMP bombs at the oncoming missiles. When they were within one hundred kilometers, the bombs exploded in succession bombarding the incoming missiles with electromagnetic pulses. More than half of the missiles streaked off into space on their last trajectory.

'Mr. Huggins.'

'Captain.'

'You may commence firing the sixteen-inch guns. Your targets are ALPHA and BRAVO.'

Huggins sat before a small bank of computer stations, one for each weapons system, guns, atom bomb caster, forward laser batteries, T-SLAM missiles. Each weapons system was manned by a spacemen. He punched a few buttons and said, 'Spacemen Paradee, synchronize guns and target ALPHA.'

'Aye, aye, Commander.'

Paradee withdrew a joystick from its holster below his station. The joystick had a handle with four triggers and a thumb operated mouse for aiming the guns. A computer screen before him showed real time images of the Jai ships. He zoomed in on ALPHA and brought a red crosshairs down upon it. When all four guns (deck, keel, starboard, and port) were lined up on the target, the crosshairs turned green.

'Guns ready, Commander.'

'Spacemen Paradee, shoot.'

'Shooting all sixteens,' Paradee replied.

He pressed the triggers on his joystick hurling twelve sixteen-inch Depleted Uranium shells at ALPHA. The shells sped toward the target at a constant 820 meters per second, over eighty Gs. Paradee reached under the joystick and slammed the red button on the bottom, beginning the automated loading process. He reported as the shells closed, 'Fifty seconds till impact...forty-five seconds till impact.'

'New contacts,' said Rogers. 'Looks like Jai counter measures targeting the DU shells.'

Seconds later the forward cameras reported several flashes of light.

'One shell knocked off course. The rest, no effect.'

'ALPHA must have fired hit-to-kill kinetic energy warheads, Captain,' said Huggins. 'But I don't think they were made with solid DU shells in mind.'

Masters said nothing. Instead he watched the visual scanner as it reported a second, larger flash of light which caused static to roll across the screen.

'Nuclear blast,' said Rodgers

'Six shells gone, three still on course time to target, ten...'

Though Masters did not show it of course, his gut tightened as he followed the trajectory of the shells. Cameras showed several pinpricks of light from ALPHA followed by several yellow bursts as the ship's point defenses engaged the shells.

'Impact!' reported Huggins. 'Two shells impacted forward of the engine compartment.'

'The third?' asked Masters.

'Missed, Captain.'

'ALPHA altering course four degrees...eight degrees.'

'Helm, alter course, keep us on an intercept vector with ALPHA.'

'Aye, aye, Captain.'

Wasp's aft starboard thrusters came to life, expelling xenon gas into space and turning the great ship several degrees toward ALPHA.

'Ms. Rogers, what is BRAVO doing?'

'Same course. ALPHA is accelerating.'

'CHARLIE and DELTA?'

'Same course and speed.'

Masters looked at the sensor readout. The four Jai carrier ships were deploying in an arc on *Wasp's* port. At its current speed DELTA would be behind *Wasp* in minutes. *Wasp's* push plate drifted several hundred kilometers to the rear at a little more than half a G.

'Very well. Mr. Huggins, continue engaging ALPHA, sixteens only.'

'Aye, aye.'

'Helm, accelerate to two Gs.'

'Aye, aye, Captain.'

'Sixteens reloaded,' reported Paradee.

Huggins responded with one word, 'Shoot.'

Paradee sent another DU barrage into space. This time ALPHA didn't bother with missiles. Instead its gunners flung a trio of atom bombs at the incoming shells. They had the range and vaporized the volley hundreds of miles before impact.

'Captain, request permission to load burst shells,' Huggins asked.

'Granted.'

Huggins nodded to Paradee, who hit a selector switch on the joystick reload button, sending specially modified DUB burst shells up the spout.

'Shoot.'

'On the way.'

Paradee depressed all four triggers, firing another sixteen shells into space. Again ALPHA fired a trio of atom bombs. This time when the DU shells were at the halfway mark, Paradee pressed a button that fired a small rocket engine affixed to the back of each shell. The engine's three second burst added hundreds of Gs to the shell's speed, accelerating them well past the A-bomb's detonation point. The Jai followed with a flurry of point defense fire, destroying a pair of shells and knocking three more off course. Emergency acceleration took ALPHA out of the path of another DU shell. But the other six impacted in a staccato line across the ship. Bulkheads cracked and decks collapsed as the shells tore into ALPHA's hull. Seeing ALPHA's distress, the other carrier ships brought their lasers to bear on *Wasp*, subjecting her to several three second laser bursts.

'Plates hot, but holding,' reported Damage Control.

Sensors brought the visual scanner onto ALPHA and magnified until the ship filled the screen.

'Mr. Huggins, what do you make of that?'

Huggins hunched over and looked at its screen. 'It's trailing atmosphere from at least two hits. Looks as if one of the main engines is down.'

'Engines hit?'

'Could be Captain, we're only getting one heat plume now. Its acceleration is halved to 1.1 Gs.'

'Sixteens reloaded.'

'Shoot.'

Paradee shot another volley into space. This time ALPHA fired six A-bombs staggered in 112-mile intervals, each with random detonation points; all twelve DU shells were destroyed. ALPHA fired its forward and aft lasers and put a volley of missiles in space as well.

'Captain, request permission to fire our forward battery.'

Masters was reluctant to reveal the existence of the forward lasers so early in the battle, still there was a chance to destroy a target.

'Captain, new targets,' said Rogers.

Masters looked at his screen and saw a pair of Jai ships indicated just above the moon's North Pole. 'I see them.'

'Two carrier ships, one point two Gs and accelerating hard. One point three Gs...Designate Targets ECHO and FOXTROT.'

'Just launched, Ms. Rogers?'

'Judging by their speed, probably, Captain.'

'Alright, Mr. Huggins, you may employ the forward batteries.'

'Aye, aye, sir.' Huggins turned to his laser tech. 'Spaceman Martinez, bring the forward batteries online and fire on my order.'

'Sir.'

Martinez took hold of a joystick, pressed a button synchronizing the two forward batteries and brought them to bear on ALPHA. When the crosshairs on his view screen turned green he reported, 'ALPHA targeted, Lieutenant.'

'Fire.'

Martinez squeezed the trigger, producing a three-second laser burst from each forward battery. 'Direct hit, Lieutenant,' Martinez said.

Masters punched a button, magnifying ALPHA's image on his view screen. There was a large scorch mark on the hull and a gash several feet long and a few feet high.

'We've hulled it,' Huggins said. 'Continue firing, fire for effect.'

Martinez fired the forward batteries, running the crosshairs down the length of ALPHA's hull as he did so. At the same time the other Jai ships fired their own lasers and launched a volley of missiles.

'Incoming,' reported Rogers. 'Bogeys from BRAVO, CHARLIE, and DELTA.'

Master's screen came alive with dozens of little red points, each representing an incoming bogey. He picked up his Black Phone. 'Engineering, bring our acceleration up to two Gs. I want distance between *Wasp* and those other contacts.'

'Aye, aye, Captain.'

'That's not going to work, Martinez,' Huggins said, as the scattered laser bursts failed to penetrate the hull. 'Pick one spot and concentrate on it until you bore through.'

Martinez chose a spot close to the fore of the ship and fired again. Two points turned black and then red until, 'Target hulled, Captain...its leaking atmosphere.' The hull plates between the two laser points peeled back under the stress and broke free. The forward batteries had torn open a great hole in ALPHA. Martinez picked another spot amidships and went to work.

'More Bogeys!' Rogers reported.

'They can tell ALPHA's in big trouble,' said Huggins.

'ALPHA is no longer accelerating. Maintaining constant course and speed.'

By then Martinez had opened up another gash in ALPHA's mid section. Rather than move on, he fired into the gap again and again until there was an orange fireball within.

'Oh my god,' someone said.

The force of an internal explosion ripped down ALPHA's hull, collapsed the main deck and shattered all of the armor plates amidships. The blast blew the aft quarter away from the rest of ship which spun wildly on its own trajectory. What remained of ALPHA drifted under the momentum of two Gs. Spinning like a Ferris wheel.

'ALPHA destroyed,' Huggins reported.

There was no time to celebrate as dozens of missiles were closing in on *Wasp*. Velarde calmly coordinated the ship's countermeasures. He ordered the forward Gatlings decoupled, which allowed each to engage individual targets. Every few seconds a red point on the sensor readout disappeared. But there was nothing to be done about the Jai's laser fire. Images from the exterior cameras flashed white and a second later there was an explosion near *Wasp's* fore and then another. *Wasp* rattled with the force of the blast.

Damage Control gave the hull a quick look over. 'A few plates bent, Captain, but we took the hit OK.'

Masters looked at the sensor display. CHARLIE was clearly taking up a position behind *Wasp's* push plate, just as Masters had hoped, while DELTA continued working around to the aft. BRAVO had stopped accelerating but had not reversed. ECHO and FOXTROT were nearing two Gs, but were still more than a hundred thousand miles away.

'Helm, bring us to an intercept course with ECHO and FOXTROT.'

'Aye, aye, sir.'

Wasp's starboard thrusters fired, slowly turning the ship. When *Wasp* had come about and faced ECHO and FOXTROT Masters said, 'Lt. Huggins, engage ECHO and FOXTROT, forward batteries and guns only. Fire at your discretion.'

Huggins ordered a full volley from all four of the sixteens targeted at ECHO and FOXTROT. The targets responded with barrages of their own, alternating volleys of twelve missiles apiece. BRAVO added its fire as well.

'Captain DELTA has now taken up position eleven point two miles behind our push plate.'

'Captain, shall we fire-,'

'Not yet, Mr. Huggins.'

ECHO and FOXTROT continued to close. BRAVO accelerated past two Gs and launched a volley of missiles. As DELTA closed in behind *Wasp's* push plate CHARLIE crossed *Wasp's* T and came around to an intercept course. The Jai's plan looked clear to Masters. They had two ships blocking the moon, while three more prevented *Wasp* from retreating back toward Earth. All targets were pointed at *Wasp* and accelerating. They were committed.

With a hornet's nest of ordnance closing in, Velarde calmly directed *Wasp's* defenses, coordinating the Gatling guns against the incoming missiles and taking out a cluster of twelve with a pair of atom bombs.

'Captain, we're going to take some hits,' Velarde reported.

The force of the multiple blasts sent shockwaves reverberating throughout *Wasp*, armor plates gave, steam valves snapped. Numerous damage control sensors tripped. Red lights blinked on Masters' monitor showing where the damage was inflicted. Damage Control dispatched several Packrats, small, compact robots, to the stricken areas.

'Captain, all targets accelerating,' reported Rogers.

They think they have us, Masters thought.

Another volley closed in. Only the last minute firing of a string of atom bombs prevented a catastrophic hit. Even so several missiles and kinetic energy warheads got through. Once again *Wasp* rattled with the force of several explosions.

'Captain we're trailing atmosphere,' reported Damage Control. 'Dispatching a damage control party.'

Masters picked up the Black Phone and pressed a button patching him into the XO. 'Mr. Glazer, your thoughts on the situation. If you were Jai, what would you do?'

The XO rubbed his chin for a moment and said. 'Judging by their accelerations and weapons expenditure they're coming in for the kill.'

Wasp shook with the force of another blast.

'Yes.'

'They think we're the only ship, but they also fear us.'

'Mmm.'

Wasp was hit by another missile volley, which rattled her so hard that Masters was knocked back against his seat. He rubbed the back of his head in annoyance.

'They wouldn't be unleashing hell on us right now if they didn't fear us, Captain. And if I may, Captain, tactically, the Jai may have us hemmed in, but they're extremely vulnerable to an external threat.'

Wasp rattled again as a volley of missiles impacted.

'I agree.'

Masters pressed another button patching him into Great Lakes Launch facility.

'Commander Ganesan.'

'Sir.'

'Fire.'

'Aye, aye, sir!'

A second later the ghost town of Green Bay was annihilated by a nuclear explosion. A series of violent nuclear detonations propelled *USSS Hornet* into orbit above the Great Lakes, about five thousand miles from *Wasp* and behind target DELTA. '*Wasp*, this is *Hornet*. We have achieved orbit, awaiting orders,' Ganesan reported.

'Accelerate and engage target DELTA. Weapons free, Commander Ganesan, hit them with everything you have.'

'Aye aye, Captain.'

Masters hung up the Black Phone. 'Mr. Huggins.'

'Captain.'

'Arm and detonate the push plate mine.'

'Aye, aye, Captain.'

'Spaceman Lawson, arm push plate mine.'

The A-bomb gunner pressed a few buttons. A large metal panel at the top of the push plate's concave side slid open, revealing a small platform 'Mine armed.'

'Fire.'

'Aye, aye.'

The gunner pressed another button, and a second later a one-megaton warhead catapulted from the push plate. The mine detonated within a mile of DELTA, and the massive force of the blast collapsed DELTA's nose and shattered several bulkheads. The ship's power plant was shorted out as was the electrical system. DELTA drifted dead in space. As DELTA foundered Masters took control of a starboard camera, trained it on *Hornet*, and zoomed in until she filled the screen. The forward laser battery fired again and again while *Hornet's* missile racks disgorged rows of T-SLAM missiles.

'ECHO and FOXTROT are turning and decelerating,' Rogers reported.

Both targets were turning their aft 180 degrees and using the engine to slow down and reverse momentum, a move Masters didn't quite understand until sensors reported, 'Two new targets, designate GOLF and HOTEL. One point twelve Gs and accelerating.'

Master's sensor readout showed the two new targets coming out from behind the dark side of the moon. BRAVO was trying to turn back toward the moon.

'Mr. Huggins, BRAVO is not to escape.'

'Aye, aye, Captain.' Huggins turned to the weapons pit. 'Spacemen Lawson, give me a spread of A-bombs. Paradee, keep those sixteens firing.'

'No T-SLAMs, Mr. Huggins?' Masters asked.

'Not at this time, Captain.'

The bridge crew waited for Masters to override, but he only said, 'Carry on.'

Huggins ordered Martinez to run a succession of laser bursts down BRAVO's hull. This was followed up by DU shells fired in echelon, a quartet of which made it through BRAVO's point defenses and slammed into the hull. More plates buckled and BRAVO trailed atmosphere.

'Spacemen Lawson, fire a burst of A-bombs at that breach,' ordered Huggins.

'Aye, aye, sir.'

The caster spat out a trio of atom bombs. Lawson waited five seconds and fired another trio. BRAVO's point defenses took out the first four, but two got through, each detonating less than a quarter mile from the hull. The force of the blast opened the breach further and collapsed several bulkheads.

'We have secondary explosions...' reported Rogers, 'BRAVO's engines are dead.'

'Fire one atom bomb, Spaceman Lawson. Set the fuse to impact.'

'Aye, aye, sir.'

The lone atom bomb sailed through space untouched, embedded in the hull breach and blew the ship in two.

'Target BRAVO destroyed,' Huggins reported.

While *Wasp* destroyed BRAVO, Commander Ganesan concentrated on CHARLIE, which simply had no answer for the awesome firepower of *Hornet's* combined weapons systems. Ganesan watched with restrained glee as the ship's forward batteries melted CHARLIE's armor and the sixteen's DU shells tore through the hull. *Hornet's* weapons officer flooded CHARLIE's point defense with a barrage of T-SLAMs followed by a string of A-bombs from the caster. The T-SLAMs did not breach the hull but still managed to take out several point lasers and kinetic guns and drew enough attention from the remaining defenses for the last A-bomb to get through and detonate. The explosion breached CHARLIE's hull in two places, just ahead of the engine compartment and amidships. *Hornet's* weapons officer ordered the forward laser battery be brought to bear. The laser tech pumped several laser blasts into the breach. CHARLIE's skipper tried to turn the ship away from the oppressive fire, but a pair of A-bombs detonated above the breach and sheered the ship in half. A cloud of oxygen, debris, and bodies formed in the growing space between the two halves of the ship.

'Well done, Commander Ganesan.'

'Thank you, Captain. What about these other contacts, Captain? Let's go get 'em. You take GOLF and HOTEL, I'll go after ECHO and FOXTROT.'

'Now hold on, Commander...' Masters said.

Glazer chimed in next, 'Makes sense, Captain.'

Masters rubbed his chin. *We've destroyed four ships and they're eager to go get the rest. Can't say I blame them.*

'We're an aggressive, blunt instrument, aren't we Captain?' There was no hiding the challenge in Ganesan's voice.

'This is no time to go wobly, Captain,' Glazer said.

Masters nodded to himself. 'Captain Ganesan, accelerate at one point five G.s' 'Helm, bring us about and decelerate to one point five Gs.

'Aye, aye, Captain.'

As *Hornet* raced forward *Wasp's* helmsman turned the ship 180 degrees so that its engines slowly reversed the momentum. The sensor readout showed *Hornet* plowing ahead. He picked up the Black Phone and punched up Ganesan.

'Commander, you're getting too far ahead, slow down.'

'But that will allow the targets to reorganize.'

'Then they do. We go forward together.'

'Aye, aye, Captain.'

She sounds like a 16 year old who just got her car taken away, Masters thought.

He watched as the four targets came together and formed a box 112 x 112 miles, and then accelerated forward at less than half a G. From top to bottom HOTEL and FOXTROT were on the right, GOLF and ECHO were on the left. *Why not accelerate faster?* Masters wondered. *Why wait?* He punched up Glazer. 'What do you make of their slow acceleration?'

'Probably buying time, Captain.'

Masters nodded. 'Probably. Alright helm, decelerate to one G and take us forward.' He picked up the Black Phone and punched up *Hornet*. 'Captain Ganeson, maintain acceleration and engage the enemy. We'll catch them between us.'

'Aye, aye, sir.'

As *Hornet* accelerated towards the Jai's starboard, *Wasp turned 180 degrees again* moved against their port. The distance between the two battle groups closed to forty thousand and then thirty thousand miles. As they pushed in further Masters saw his gunners eyeing their weapons system, itching to fire. When they pushed past twenty-five thousand miles Masters picked up the Black Phone and said, 'Commander Ganesan, engage ECHO. Just like we practiced, I'll fire my guns at the nose, you'll fire ahead.'

'Aye, aye, Captain.'

'And I'm launching my strike force.'

Hornet and *Wasp* fired spreads of DU shells at ECHO's current trajectory and across her anticipated trajectory should she accelerate.

'Mr. Huggins, weapons free. But keep the sixteens on ECHO.'

'Aye, aye, Captain.'

Masters punched up the strike bay on the Black Phone. 'Flight control, this is the captain.'

'Sir,' said the flight control officer.

'Launch strike force. Your target is GOLF,' Masters ordered.

'Aye, aye, sir.'

The Black Phone beeped. 'What about my strike group, Captain?' Ganesan asked.

'Keep it in reserve.'

'Aye, aye.'

Within the bowels of the ship an alarm sounded and a dispassionate voice said *'All personnel evacuate strike bay.'* Fifteen seconds later the strike bay was filled by vacuum. What had once been the flight deck of an aircraft carrier peeled back, opening the bay to space. The four capsules in the bay were released. Their pilots used simple xenon gas jets to put distance between themselves and spread out line abreast ahead of *Wasp*. Inside was a crew of four, captain, helm, sensors, and of course a weapons officer who had at his disposal a forward laser turret, an atom bomb caster, and a rack of ten modified AMRAAM missiles, each with a small nuclear warhead.

'Wasp-One on station.'
'Wasp-Two on station.'
'Wasp-Three on station.'
'Wasp-Four on station.'
'Very good, strike group. Accelerate and engage.'
'Aye, aye, Captain.'
'Good hunting, Strike Force, and god bless. We salute you.'
'Much obliged, Captain,' said the strike group leader. 'We'll get him for you.'

Masters watched the sensor read out as Lieutenant Jeff Gallop led his attack boats toward GOLF. He'd gotten the command after leading a successful ASAT raid on a carrier ship years earlier during a skirmish over Hudson Bay. During their time together, Masters had come to admire Gallop very much. He'd taken a hand in the determining the attack boat's weapons load out, getting the small forward laser installed instead of a DU gun, and when it was suggested that the commander fight the squadron from an AWACs type ship from the rear, he nixed the idea.

Strike Force's lasers fired in unison and hit the target's hull with three seconds bursts. GOLF lashed back with laser fire of its own but each capsule pilot used attitude thruster jets to dodge them. When GOLF threw an atom bomb at each capsule, helmsman fired a 1 kiloton atom bomb which accelerated them past the incoming detonation point. When Strike Force closed to within 10,000 miles Gallop ordered his gunners to fire half their modified AMRAAM Missile. As the AMRAAMs closed in the pilots turned the attack boats 180 degrees and fired off a trio of A-bombs in quick succession accelerating them away from GOLF. They then swung back around, allowing the gunners to fire their lasers. Under cover of the supporting laser blasts, a dozen AMRAAMs got through GOLF's missile barrage. Seven made it through the point defenses and exploded in an arc around target. The ship rattled with the force of several atomic blasts. In several places GOLF leaked atmosphere. The fusion fire from its engines had ceased as well. Her weapons were still operable though, and a trio of lasers lashed out from GOLF and focused on Gallop's attack boat. The concentrated attack overwhelmed the attack boat's heat shield and melted the command deck. Wasp-One exploded into a million pieces. Wasp-Two took command of Strike Force and ordered the three attack boats to renew their laser barrage.

Meanwhile *Hornet* poured fire into FOXTROT, alternating between A-bomb barrages, missile volleys, and gun salvos, all while maintaining forward battery laser fire. *Wasp* inflicted the same pain upon on ECHO. HOTEL feebly divided its fire against *Wasp* and *Hornet*. The sustained Jai attack was beginning to make itself felt, with more and more missiles penetrating *Wasp*'s point defenses. *Wasp* shook furiously from a pair of direct missiles hits. Moments later the bridge lights dimmed as an atom bomb detonated less than a mile away.

Huggins decided it was time to bring the T-SLAMS into the fight, 'Alright Spaceman Park, arm missile racks and fire.'

'Aye, aye, Lieutenant,' said Park. He punched some buttons and targeted Echo. 'Missile rack one away...rack two away...rack three away...' Park reported as he fired each quartet into space.

Atom bombs preceded the volley, detonating well ahead of the incoming missiles and clearing out the Jai countermeasures. A pair of A-bombs got through ECHO's point defense and detonated on the hull. A second volley of A-bombs followed, one detonated on the fore. Martinez fired several short bursts into the widening breach in ECHO's hull, a gash nearly twenty meters long and three meters wide just aft of the nose cone. A volley of DU rounds came next, tearing a new gash down the hull and starting a crack running all the way to the back of the engine compartment.

'A little more of the 16s, Mr. Huggins,' Masters ordered.

'Aye, aye, Captain.' Huggins turned to the gunner and said, 'Spacemen Paradee, shoot.'

The gunner depressed the trigger, sending twelve DU rounds hurling toward ECHO, 'On the way. Reloading.'

The follow-on volley of DU rounds widened the gash.

Masters was so focused on ECHO's impending doom that he didn't notice when a pair of atom bombs fired by *Hornet* exploded just above FOXTROT's engines, shattering them and sending the ship into a slow cartwheel. A second string of atom bombs finished it off, detonating directly beneath the ship and exploding it in a blue ball of fire.

Masters called *Hornet* on the Black Phone, 'Well done, Commander.'

'Thank you, Captain,' Ganesan said. 'Accelerating and engaging HOTEL.'

Masters wanted to reign in Ganesan but decided there was probably no stopping her. As FOXTROT began to break up, Masters gave orders to Strike Force, 'Wasp-Two, keep the pressure on GOLF.'

'Aye, aye, Captain.'

While Strike Force began the process of decelerating, *Hornet* unleashed its fury on HOTEL, hitting the carrier ship with a string of A-bombs followed up by several racks of T-SLAM missiles. Master's readout showed HOTEL accelerating past 2.6 Gs.

He's trying to get out from the trap, thought Masters.

Huggins needed no orders from the captain. On Huggins command Spaceman Paradee led HOTEL with volley after volley of DU shells expertly spacing them along the ship's projected trajectory. The DU shells never had a chance to impact. Caught between the twin daggers of *Hornet* and *Wasp*, the embattled carrier ship was engulfed by over lapping A-bomb strings and shaken apart by the might of their shockwaves. The sensor readout showed no targets, just an expanding cloud of the dead hulk of HOTEL floating along its last trajectory.

Masters picked up the Black Phone. 'Commander Ganesan, decelerate and bring *Hornet* in line with *Wasp*, five hundred miles to my port.'

'Aye, aye, Captain.'

'I want a full damage report on *Hornet*.'

'Sir.'

'And well done.'

'Aye, aye, Captain!'

Data streamed into Masters' consul. Blue lines showed expended ammunition—288 DU shells, 23 missile racks, and 30 A-bomb strings. A second screen showed damage to various sections of the ship and their repair status. There were two hull breaches aft of the bridge, both about three meters in diameter, and a third forward of the fusion drive. Two members of the engine team had been killed. Several members of the damage control parties had suffered minor burns. Wasp-Four had been destroyed as well. Masters uttered a quick prayer for the dead.

Decelerating *Hornet* and bringing her in line with *Wasp* took time, time Masters would rather have used to accelerate toward the moon. But no one knew what was on the dark side, and it had been agreed before the launch that the ships would attack in unison. The plan was for *Hornet* to strike the Jai base at the moon's North Pole while *Wasp* struck the base at the south. Once the pole targets had been dealt with each ship would continue around to the dark side of the moon and attack whatever awaited there. As *Hornet* slowly got into place and *Wasp's* Strike Force reformed around the ship, Masters saw no reason to diverge from the plan.

Masters' Black Phone beeped, the Damage Control Officer was calling him. Masters picked up the phone and said, 'Report.'

'No major systems damage, Captain. Bulkheads and decks are secure. Radiation shielding is holding too. The armor has taken a hell of a beating, but is fine for now.'

'What do you mean *'for now'?*'

'I wouldn't put the ship through another pounding like that, Captain. We do, we're going to take a lot of damage.'

'Very well, thank you, Lieutenant.'

'Aye, aye, sir.'

Wasp was not equipped with a formal kitchen, but she did have a mess hall and a storage locker filled with finger foods and bottled drinks. Masters ordered rations to be passed out amongst the bridge crew and even allowed himself a bottle of vitamin water. After drinking half of it Masters leaned back, closed his eyes and visualized the battle ahead. Most of the bridge crew took turns at the head in a small compartment in the back.

He plotted the course *Hornet* and *Wasp* would take to the moon and imagined the Jai's reactions to his actions.

The Red Phone gave off a quiet but insistent beep. A few seconds later it beeped again.

What the Hell do they want? Are they serious? Masters thought.

The Red Phone beeped again. He took a moment to compose himself, then took a deep breath and picked it up.

'Masters.'

'Captain Masters, this is the secretary defense.'

Oh Jesus give me strength, he thought. 'Mr. Secretary.'

'The president has instructed me to tell you that we have received a message from the Jai.'

'I'm sorry, Mr. Secretary. The Jai have contacted the president?'

'Yes, and they want to negotiate.'

'Negotiate?'

'Yes, Captain.'

'Negotiate what?'

'A ceasefire.'

'He's not considering it?'

'In fact I'm recommending he agree to their terms.'

'*What* terms?'

'In exchange for calling you off, the Jai agree to stop bombarding Earth.'

Masters could feel the anger rising within him, but he kept it in check. 'One moment Mr. Secretary.' Masters replaced the Red Phone.

'Helm, accelerate to two Gs now.' He punched up *Hornet.* 'Commander Ganesan, accelerate to two G's. I'll explain later.'

'Aye, aye, Captain.'

He picked up the Red Phone again. 'Mr. Secretary, I must say I strongly recommend that the president reject this.'

'Why?'

'We have the Jai on the run, Mr. Secretary. They wouldn't be trying to negotiate if they weren't in big, big trouble.'

'I understand, Captain, but you should know that we are picking up activity around the Jai base in the asteroid belt, and above Venus, and we don't know what it means.'

'Mr. Secretary, am I being ordered to break off the attack?'

'The president has not yet given that order.'

Not yet, 'Does the president want my opinion?'

'He does.'

'My answer is keep fighting.'

'Thank you, Captain, I will pass that along.'

The Secretary of Defense hung up the phone.

'Sensors. Any enemy activity?'

'Nothing in place, Captain, but there is movement on the moon's surface.'

Masters thought for a moment and punched up Glazer on his Black Phone, 'Mr. Glazer, the enemy seems to be quiet, what do you make of this?'

'Not sure, Captain. But since there is a lull in the fighting I suggest we begin bombarding suspected Jai sites on the moon's surface.'

'Yes.'

Masters ordered *Wasp* and *Hornet* to come parallel with the moon's equator.

In the months before the launch, Masters and his officers had poured over satellite and telescope photos of the moon and identified definite and suspected Jai installations on the surface. Masters punched a few buttons and brought up a map of the moon. It was dotted with red markers for confirmed targets and blue markers for suspected targets. In the years since their occupation of the moon the Jai had constructed an extensive light rail system running between the poles and had built several installations along the line. Tracks crisscrossed the surface now, some ran to the various facilities, others just stopped. The DIA strongly suspected these were leading to underground installations. There were also several dozen laser and missile batteries placed at the equator and around the poles.

'OK.' He said. 'Mr. Huggins, begin bombardment of Jai targets on the moon's surface. I want to save our nukes, so DU shells only.'

'Any specific targets, Captain?'

'Use your discretion.'

'Aye, aye, Captain.

Huggins first target was the rail line running from the North Pole down to the Archimedes Crater. A spread of DU shells cratered it in several places. He then took out a pair of ore mines just to the south in the Appenninus Mountains. From there he fired volleys against the dozens of suspected targets throughout the moon's northern hemisphere. In one case, the crew was rewarded by a spectacular secondary explosion in the Eratosthenes Crater, probably some kind of fuel dump for Jai mining equipmet.

Masters punched up Glazer, 'Mr Glazer, why do you suppose the enemy has not tried to defend their installations?'

'Either they can't or they don't want to reveal their defenses. They don't feel what we're hitting is valuable enough.'

'I want those defenses revealed.' He spoke to Huggins. 'All right Mr. Huggins, enough fooling around. Concentrate fire on the North Pole base.'

'Aye, aye, Captain.'

'Weapons free.'

While Huggins lined up the target Masters picked up the Black Phone and ordered *Hornet* to strike the South Pole base. Huggins began with a string of atom bombs and followed up with a DU volley. This time the Jai defense went live. Missiles fired from the pole bases and from several locations on the moon's surface. Huggins targeted these with several racks of T-SLAMs and follow on volleys of DU shells. The first salvos were shot down, but Huggins kept firing. As the pressure increased more Jai defenses revealed their locations. Huggins brought the forward laser batteries to bear upon them, pock marking the surface with quick bursts of laser fire.

'Captain, might I suggest that *Hornet* concentrate fire on the northern hemisphere as well?' Huggins said, 'We're close to overwhelming them here.'

'Excellent idea, Mr. Huggins.'

Masters picked up the Black Phone and ordered *Hornet* to shift fire to the northern hemisphere. Under the combined fire the Jai laser and missile batteries were systematically overwhelmed. One by one they were destroyed, usually by a volley of DU shells followed by a T-SLAM strike. With no batteries to support it the North Pole orbiting station was quickly shredded by volleys of DU shells and finished off by a rack of T-SLAMs. The surface base remained and Masters was about to order all fire be directed upon it when the Red Phone buzzed.

Masters picked it up. 'Captain Masters, this is the Secretary of Defense.'

'Mr. Secretary, how can I help you?'

'The president orders you to cease offensive operations while we negotiate a final ceasefire.'

'Mr. Secretary, I don't think that's practical.'

'What you think is not important. We are close to cementing a deal, but the Jai insist you stop firing on them before the negotiations continue. That is an order. Do you understand?'

'Completely, Mr. Secretary.'

'Good.'

The Secretary of Defense hung up.

Damn idiots. Masters picked up his Black Phone and punched up the ship's intercom.

'This is the captain. I would like first to congratulate all of you on the job done so far. We have hurt the enemy and hurt him badly. The Secretary of Defense has informed me that the Jai have contacted the president and are seeking to negotiate terms. In response to the enemy's offer to negotiate the president has ordered me to press home the attack. That is all.'

Masters called *Hornet*.

'Commander Ganesan.'

'Sir.'

'What follows is for your ears only.'

'Understood.'

'The president is negotiating ceasefire terms with Jai.'

'Good god, Captain, no!'

'Calm down, Commander.'

'Sorry, sir.'

'I have one order for you.'

'Sir?'

'Pick up your Red Phone.'

'Done.'

'Now rip the wires out.'

'Aye, aye, Captain.'

Masters heard plastic breaking apart.

'We will carry on as planned. Masters out.'

'Aye, aye, Sir!'

Masters did the same to his Red Phone. 'Alright Commander Ganesan. We're going to hit the North Pole base and continue on to the dark side of the moon.'

'What about the South Pole base, Captain?' Ganesen asked.

'We can deal with it as soon as we destroy whatever is on the dark side.'

'Aye, aye, Captain.'

'We'll go in echelon, with *Wasp* in the lead and *Hornet* following five hundred miles behind.' Masters knew Ganesen wanted to object but also knew she would never dare speak up. 'I'm going to accelerate at three Gs, you're coming ahead at two. When I'm over the dark side, I'll relay what I find to you.'

'So I can hit it.'

'Yes.'

'While you engage, we'll decelerate and come back around to support.'

'Aye, aye, Captain.'

Wasp and *Hornet* had only advanced a few thousand miles when Rogers reported new contacts.

'Captain I have a new target. It's a carrier ship. Designate target INDIA.'

Masters brought one of the external cameras to bear on the target. There it was, a Jai carrier ship coming around from the moon's dark side a few hundred miles above the equator.

'Speed two point two eight Gs and accelerating.'

Masters followed the ship on the radar readout and its plotted trajectory, which would take the vessel between the North Pole and *Hornet*.

There is no way they're sending one ship after us, what would be the point?

'New target, speed two point two eight Gs and accelerating. Designate target JULLIETTE.' After another minute passed, 'New target speed two point two eight Gs and accelerating. Designate KILO.' After seeing the third carrier ship Masters knew a fourth would emerge, and it did a minute later, 'New target. Designate target LIMA.'

Masters watched the red targets on his monitor as they accelerated and closed the gap between themselves and *Wasp*. The carriers were not in a box formation, rather, they were line-abreast, each separated by 112 miles. When three minutes passed and a fifth carrier did not reveal itself Masters considered the options available to him. In a few moments he reached the decision. Masters punched *Hornet* up on the Black Phone. Ganesan spoke first.

'Captain, I suggest we make three Gs and race those incoming carrier ships to the pole. We can beat them.'

'Negative, Commander.'

'Aye, aye, sir.'

'I'm ordering you to continue to make for the pole, blast that base to bits, and swing around to the dark side. Launch your own Strike Force and take *Wasp's* Strike Force too.'

'What about the incoming carrier ships?'

'I'm going to meet them head on.'

'Captain—'

'Shut up, Ganesan, the order is given.'

'Aye, aye, Captain.'

'When you cross over the pole, hit everything Jai. I will see you on the other side.'

'Aye, aye, Captain.'

Masters turned his attention back to the bridge.

'Helm, maneuver so that the incoming targets are between *Wasp* and the moon.'

'Aye, aye, Captain.'

'We'll make sure any moon batteries have to fire through their own ships to get to us.'

'Shall we go up to three Gs?'

'No, I want to maintain some maneuvering ability. Besides, I don't want to pass the targets too quickly. Those four ships are going to die.'

Wasp broke to port and accelerated toward the new threat. Because the targets were coming line- abreast, *Wasp* would have to pass and engage all four. But until they did, the odds might as well have been one to one as only their lead ship could target all of its weapons on *Wasp*. Whoever was commanding the attack group had the same thought. All four ships fired missile salvos. A-bomb spurts from *Wasp* vaporized the first three volleys.

'Mr. Huggins, hit target INDIA with everything you have.'

'Aye, aye, Captain.'

'I want that carrier ship to be junk by the time we draw past.'

Huggins began the assault with the sixteen-inch guns. Even though the starboard battery could not be brought to bear, there would never be a better time to use the sixteens as the distance and angle of the incoming carrier ships gave them close to a head on shot.

As the forward batteries began lasing the carrier ship's nose cone, Glazer called.

'Captain, I suggest we accelerate and close as quickly as possible.'

'Why?'

'They're deployed line-abreast, not in echelon where they could all fire. Given the plastering the lead carrier is taking, someone is going to figure out they should redeploy in echelon. We should move up at them now before whoever in command there figures out what the hell he is doing.'

Masters could hear the irritation in Glazer's voice, not as an American, but as a naval officer angered that a commander didn't know how to handle his ships.

Masters pursed his lips in thought and said, 'Ok, Commander, you've talked me into it. Helm accelerate to three Gs.'

'Aye, aye, Captain.'

As the range rapidly decreased, *Wasp's* DU shells scored more and more hits on INDIA. Several quick bursts by the forward battery opened up a large gash in the ship's nose cone. Huggins kept pouring the fire on INDIA as he targeted T-SLAM missiles against ships further down the line. A string of A-bombs fired at a range of less than ten thousand miles finished it off. Huggins brought the sixteens and the forward battery to bear on JULLIETTE.

Wasp took another missile hit and then another and yet another, its force knocked Masters forward so hard he broke one of the seat straps and slammed against his consul. He reached up to his throbbing forehead and felt blood. Masters tried to open his eyes, and then realized they were open, he couldn't see anything because the bridge was full of smoke. Masters reached out and felt a flat screen monitor, then an armrest. He pulled himself into the chair. He may not have been able to see through the smoke, but Master's could still hear as Huggins calmly fought the ship.

'Forward battery locked on!'

'Fire.'

'Hit!'

'Fire.'

'Hit!'

'Fire at will...'

'DU shells up.'

'Shoot.'

'On the way!'

'Reload....'

'Rounds up.'

'Shoot.'

'On the way!'

'Missile tech, give me a volley of T-SLAMs, target KILO...

'Rack fifty-one away...Rack fifty-two away....Rack fifty-three away...'

'Hit 'em again.'

'Rack fifty-four away...Rack fifty-five away...Rack fifty-six away...'

'Forward battery, target KILO.'

'Aye, aye...locked on.'

'Fire.'

'Hit!'

'Fire.'

'Hit!'

'Fire at will.'

The carrier ships hit back with alternating volleys of missiles and lasers. As *Wasp* shook again and again, Damage Control kept tabs on the accumulating carnage and routed teams to deal with the multiple crisis aboard ship. Masters could only listen as reports flooded in.

'This is Damage-two. I'm in the Blue Bridge, everyone's dead.'

'This is Damage-one the port bulkhead has been vaporized! We're sucking vacuum down here!'

Eventually all Masters could hear was Huggins and his bevy of gunners as they used their elegantly simple and brut weapons upon the enemy without remorse or relent.

'Rack fifty-eight away.'

'Missiles, fire T-SLAMs up and down the line until the targets are destroyed or you run dry, whichever comes first.'

'Aye, aye.'

'Rack sixty away...

'Bring the forward battery to bear on LIMA.'

'Aye, aye.'

'Locked on.'

'Fire.'

'Hit.'

'Rack sixty-two away...'

'Rounds up!'

'Shoot.'

'On the way!'

'A-bomb spurt impacted. Look at that gash open up in KILO's hull!'

'Rack sixty-four away...'

'Rounds up!'

'Shoot.'

'On the way!'

Rack sixty-six away...'

'Forward battery, target that breach in KILO.'

'Locked on!'

'Fire.'

'Hit!'

'Rack sixty-eight away...'

'Laser hit forward, two plates have buckled, we're leaking atmosphere in one compartment....make that two...'

'Caster, target LIMA.'

'Fired.'

'Give 'em another one.'

'Fired.'

'LIMA targeted. Rack seventy away...rack seventy-one away...rack seventy-two away...'

'Hit! Two A-bomb hits right on top of each other, that bastard's leaking atmosphere.'

'Pour it on. Make them suffer.'

'Aye, aye, Lt. Huggins, bomb fired!'

'Rack seventy-four away...'

'Shoot.'

'On the way!'

'Forward Battery, fire.'

'Hit!'

'Shoot.'

'On the way!'

'Fire.'

'Hit!'

'Rack seventy-eight away...rack seventy-nine away...'

Wasp shook with horrible violence as a Jai laser sliced through the armor and then through several bulkheads

'JULLIETTE is adrift, KILO is running. Guns, caster, missiles, forward battery, everything, target LIMA. Fire your guns. Fire your guns!'

Masters heard a cacophony of "Hit!" and 'On the way...hit,' then Huggins shouting, 'Into that breach. Everything. Fire...Fire!'

Wasp shook again and then again and then suddenly all seemed still. After a few moments of quiet Damage Control got the air filters back online and the smoke cleared enough for Masters to see his monitor. The sensor readout showed only one Jai carrier, KILO drifting away from *Wasp*. The weapons inventory revealed a quartet of red bars well below the 50 percent mark. He next saw the damage redoubt, dozens of pixels blinked red, indicating hits up and down the ship. Next to the list a tab read: thirteen confirmed killed, nine confirmed wounded. He touched the wounded tab and saw several burn victims listed.

'Helm,' he said. 'Helm....'

'Helm's dead, Captain.' It was Velarde.

Masters looked forward and saw the helmsmen lying back in his chair, bubbles of blood popped out from a gash in his neck.

'I've got it, Captain,' said Velarde.

'We've taken a hell of a beating, Captain,' said Damage Control.

'Should we think about calling for the Space Shuttles, have them pick us up?' asked Velarde.

'Negative. Take us around to the dark side of the moon.'

'Aye, aye, sir. Fire the forward xenon thrusters. Take us down to one G by halves.'

As he waited, Masters trained an exterior camera on *Wasp's* hull. There were countless pockmarks on the hull and a pair of long gashes across the port side. Light reflected out of the gashes as damage repair Packrats worked within the breaches. The port sixteen had been shorn off the hull by a nuclear blast. On what had once been the ship's flight deck, most of the armored plates had been dented, many twisted, and some punctured. Laser scars were everywhere.

Masters brought the camera to bear on the moon's North Pole and zoomed in. He nodded in satisfaction. There were several craters where the moon base had been. The orbital dock lay shattered on the surface, having crashed after taking several DU shell hits. The South Pole base was untouched, and there were several installations still undamaged, but these were holding their fire. He'd deal with them later.

Wasp's acceleration dipped below two Gs. By the time it dropped under 1.5Gs medical orderlies came to the bridge and tended to the surviving crew's injuries, mostly minor cuts and burns. The morgue sent people up to care for the five crewmen cut down at their posts. The mess orderly came too and handed out drinks and sandwiches to the crew. Masters gratefully took a vitamin water. Though he wanted to down it in one swift gulp, he made himself drink slowly and deliberately, if for no other reason than to set an example for the crew.

Less than an hour later, the dark side of the moon came into *Wasp's* view. *Hornet* orbited above the northern hemisphere, nose pointed menacingly toward the surface. There were several fresh craters on the moon, the result of nuclear bursts, but in the middle of the craters lay the Jai Pole Ship that had escaped the final battle a decade before. It was undamaged.

Master's Black Phone beeped.

'Captain Masters, it is good to see you,' Captain Ganesan said.

'And you, Commander. Please report.'

'We destroyed both the North polar base and the station above. I sent both strike groups over the pole, but the Jai had set an ambush. I'm sorry captain but all ships were destroyed. I thought...'

'It's war, Commander. Continue.'

Ganesan cleared her throat and continued. 'I brought *Hornet* over the pole and engaged enemy batteries as they came online. Once we got past the first line, their fire was uncoordinated and sporadic. My gunners dispatched them without too much trouble.'

'Damage?'

'Several hits to our underbelly, but no casualties, and only a small breach.'

'From there we reduced the installations around the base. Mostly point defense, lasers, missile launchers. I'm sorry to say a carrier ship escaped. It's heading for Venus now.'

'Escaped?'

'Yes, Captain, it was the ship damaged last year during the Australian raid.'

'Fine, Commander, but explain to me please why the rest of the base has not been destroyed?'

'There's a problem, Captain. There are people there.'

'People? Humans?'

'Yes several hundred, I have been contacted by one, their leader I guess.'

'Is he still on?'

'Yes.'

'Transfer him to me.'

'Aye, aye, Captain. It's a digital image link.'

Master's screen blinked and then was filled by a thin, gray-haired face.

He spoke with a slow, easy drawl.

'Captain? This is reverend Thomas Blight, late of the Episcopal Diocese of Los Angeles, now pastor to several hundred congregants here on the moon, including dozens of Jai.' Bewildered, Masters stared at the man for a few seconds.

'Am I to understand that while your nation has been locked in a death struggle for its survival you have been trying to negotiate a separate peace with the Jai?'

'Yes I have, Captain, and I think I have come up with a plan that—'

'You realize that you've committed a crime?'

'A crime?'

'Yes, you're in violation of the Logan Act.'

'The Logan Act?'

'I studied history at Annapolis, sir. The Logan Act forbids private citizens from negotiating with an enemy power.'

'I hardly think that at a time like this—'

Masters was running out of patience, 'That alone makes you a felon.'

'They've offered to help us put aside our differences.'

Masters 'What in hell do you think you're doing? We're fighting for our lives up here, and you're negotiating with the Jai?'

'We are all part of the human family, Captain.' He paused and emphasized the word family. His voice was self satisfied and smug.

'The Jai aren't human.'

'But we are all God's creatures, Captain.'

'If you prefer to think so, pastor, but that is not really what is at issue here.'

'At issue?'

'I am here to destroy the Jai presence on the moon.'

The pastor's face went white, he stammered for a few seconds before speaking, 'But Captain, you can't, there are seven hundred and twenty one people here, including children!'

'And they will be spared if the Jai commander surrenders.'

The screen got fuzzy and went blank. A few seconds later it came on again. This time Masters was staring at the face of a Jai. It was wrinkled and sagged, showing his age.

'Leader Kan-Kes, I am,' he said in inverted English.

'Captain Steven J. Masters. I will waste no time with you. Surrender or be destroyed.'

'Leave we will. Let our ship go, and I will give you your moon.'

'Our moon is not yours to give.'

The Jai said nothing.

'Do you surrender or not?'

'Serious?'

'Yes.'

'I won't.'

He won't surrender because it will be an intelligence windfall, Masters thought. *I wouldn't either, not with those remaining ships and bases in the system.*

'Put the pastor back on.'

The pastor reappeared on the screen.

'Pastor, I am about to nuke the Jai base.'

'But Captain, we are all civilians! The children!'

'I will pray for them, pastor, and even you.'

Masters leveled his gaze at the tired bridge crew; no one spoke. Then he looked at Lawson. 'Spaceman Lawson, well done. Stand at attention.'

'Captain?'

'I said Ten-hut!'

Lawson unbuckled himself and stood up, ramrod straight.

'Captain, you don't have to do this,' Lawson said.

'Shut up.'

Masters unbuckled himself, and in the low gravity hopped over to Lawson's chair. He sat down and buckled himself in. The screen showed a pair of A-bombs ready to fire. He pressed the abort button and looked at Lawson. 'You will bear absolutely no responsibility for this.'

'Aye, aye, Captain.'

'Anyone who is uncomfortable with this action is invited to leave the bridge.'

Masters looked around, no one got up from their crash chairs.

Masters retargeted the caster for the Jai base and without ceremony pressed the away button.

In the minutes after contact was lost with Wasp *we tried desperately to reestablish a link. When it became clear that the Red Phone had been destroyed the secretary ordered Space Command to establish a video uplink, but by then both* Wasp *and* Hornet *were on the other side of the moon and incommunicado. The president was understandably livid as was the secretary. When*

Wasp and Hornet emerged from the Dark side the president and secretary held a private meeting before speaking again with Captain Masters. I was not privy to either the meeting or their subsequent conversation. Neither was anyone else, and no notes were taken.

It is obvious to me and many others then present in the White House Situation Room that the president and secretary of defense took the politically expedient path and chose to cover up the mutiny. This outrage, this usurpation of the national command authority...

Mutiny! The secret history of the Battle of Luna: The story the government doesn't want you to know.

Even if Captain Masters mutinied, so what?

Lead editorial, The Weekly Standard

It is the opinion of this congressional commission that there is no compelling evidence to prove that the Battle of Luna ended in a mutiny. No surviving crewmembers from either Wasp or Hornet are aware that orders were disobeyed. In his own memoirs Captain Master's maintains that the president ordered him to press home the attack and testified as such before Congress, and since Admiral Ganesen was killed commanding Mars Task Force...

A Line through the Desert: The Battle of 73 Easting

Jake Bloom doesn't like high school very much and he's always felt out of place in his synagogue. He's not thrilled with his parents either. But he loves Led Zeppelin and his girlfriend, Patricia. Seeking to emulate the Israeli soldiers he's always admired, much to the horror of his overprotective parents, Jake joins the army the day after graduating high school. When his summer romance with Patricia ends in heartbreak, as it must, Jake leaves for the army jaded and embittered. In the elite 2nd Armored Cavalry Regiment Jake finds the purpose and brotherhood he's always yearned for. When the regiment is deployed to the Persian Gulf as part of Operation Desert Storm, Jake meets the challenges of tedium, duty, and the horrors of war with honor and good humor—who knew you could blast heavy metal music at the Iraqis? Now if he could only put Patricia out of his mind…

"Pitch perfect." *Omri Ceren, Mere Rhetoric*

"Stroock has done a good job of capturing the life of a soldier in a combat unit throughout his service in Germany and the Middle East." *General Phil Bolte, Cavalry Journal*

"Stroock not only tells us about military life, he makes us feel it." *William Katz, Urgent Agenda*

"Jewish 'Jarhead'….with the GenX *attitude* Stroock brings to this unsentimental, fast-paced book, should make it a favorite with history and military buffs." *Kathy Shaidle, Eaxminer.com*

10200123R00121

Made in the USA
Charleston, SC
15 November 2011